HOW TO CATCH A
BOGLE

HOW TO CATCH A

BOGLE

CATHERINE JINKS

ILLUSTRATED BY

SARAH WATTS

HOUGHTON MIFFLIN HARCOURT

Boston   New York

www.hmhco.com

The text of this book is set in 12/19 Carre Noir Std Light.
Fortunaschwein typeface by Anke Art
Design by Christine Kettner

The Library of Congress has cataloged the hardcover edition as follows:
Jinks, Catherine.
How to catch a bogle / Catherine Jinks.
p. cm.
Summary: In 1870s London, a young orphan girl becomes the apprentice to a man who traps
monsters for a living.
[1. Monsters—Fiction. 2. Supernatural—Fiction. 3. Apprentices—Fiction. 4. Orphans—Fiction.
5. London (England)—History—19th century—Fiction. 6. Great Britain—History—Victoria,
1837–1901—Fiction.] I. Title.
PZ7.J5754Ho 2013
2012045936

ISBN: 978-0-544-08708-8 hardcover
ISBN: 978-0-544-33627-8 paperback

Manufactured in the U.S.A.
DOC 10 9 8 7 6 5 4 3
4500643879

LONDON, ENGLAND, C. 1870

Two Missing Boys

The front door was painted black, with a shiny brass knocker that made a satisfying noise when Alfred used it. *Rat-tat-tat.*

Birdie spied a lace curtain twitching in the drawing room window.

"Someone's at home," she remarked. Alfred said nothing. He looked tired after their long walk—but then again he always looked tired. His gray mustache drooped. His shoulders were bent. His brown eyes sagged at the corners under his wide, floppy hat brim.

Suddenly the door was flung open. A housemaid in a

white cap peered at them suspiciously, her gaze lingering on Alfred's frayed canvas trousers and baggy green coat. "Yes?" she asked. "What's yer business?"

Alfred removed his hat. "The name is Bunce," he replied in his gravelly voice. "I came here on account of I were sent for."

"Sent for?" the housemaid echoed.

"A Miss Ellen Meggs sent for me, by passing word through Tom Cobbings."

"Oh!" The housemaid put a hand to her mouth. "Are you the Go-Devil Man?"

"The bogler. Aye."

"And I'm Birdie. I'm the 'prentice." Because Birdie was very small and thin and pale, she was often ignored. So she liked to wear the most colorful clothes she could find. This summer her dress was a dull cotton drab, but she had added a little cape made of yellow satin, very soiled and creased, and there were red feathers on her battered straw hat.

Stepping out of her master's shadow, she beamed up at the housemaid, eager to make friends. The housemaid, however, was too flustered to notice Birdie.

"Oh, why did you knock on *this* door?" she lamented. "The hawker's door is down by the coal hole! Come in quick, afore the neighbors see you both." Hustling Alfred and Birdie across the threshold, she slammed the door and said, "*I'm* Ellen Meggs. I'm the one as sent for you. My mistress knows nothing o' this, nor won't neither, if I have my way."

"Ain't she in?" Birdie asked shrewdly, glancing through the door to her left. It opened off a handsome entrance hall that Birdie thought finer than anything she had ever seen in her life—a lofty space with carpet on the stairs and paper on the walls and a bronze statue in one corner. The cedar joinery gleamed, and the air smelled of lemon.

But there was a broom propped against the hat stand. And through the door that she'd spotted, Birdie could make out furniture swathed in dust sheets.

"Mrs. Plumeridge is at the seaside for her health," Ellen replied. "Oh, but there's other old cats across the way that *never* leave their parlor windows, and they'll have seen you come in, sure as eggs!" She stamped her foot in frustration, her round, pink face growing even pinker under its frizz of sandy hair.

Alfred sighed. His shoulders were slumped beneath the weight of his sack, which he never let his apprentice carry, no matter how desperately she pleaded. "What's yer particulars, Miss Meggs?" he inquired. "Tom Cobbings had none to give, save for yer name and where I'd find you. Is there a bogle in this house?"

Ellen opened her mouth, then hesitated. Her gaze had fallen on Birdie, whose blue eyes, freckled nose, and flyaway curls looked as delicate as fine china. Birdie knew exactly what the housemaid was thinking, because everyone always thought the same thing.

Only Alfred understood that Birdie was a heroine, brave and quick and valiant.

"I ain't afeared o' bogles, Miss Meggs," Birdie announced. "Though I'm only ten years old, I've helped bring down many a one. Ain't that so, Mr. Bunce?"

"Aye, but we've heard enough from you, lass." Alfred was growing impatient. Birdie could tell by the way he shifted from one ill-shod foot to the other. "What's yer particulars, Miss Meggs?" he repeated. "Who gave you me name?"

"A friend," Ellen answered. "She's Scotch but lives here in London. She said you got rid of a worricow, or some such thing, as lived in a coal hole in Hackney and took a little shoe binder's child." She threw him a questioning glance. When Alfred nodded, she continued hastily. "Hearing that made me wonder about the chimney sweep's boys. For we've lost two in the past month, and I cannot believe they *both* ran away." By now she was anxiously fiddling with her apron, crushing it between her restless hands, then smoothing it out again. "In the Dane Hills, where my ma were raised, a creature they called Black Annis used to eat children. And would tan their skins for its adornment, or so I've heard—"

"Tell me about the sweep's boys," Alfred interrupted. "They went missing, you say?"

"From this house," Ellen assured him solemnly. "They disappeared up the dining room chimney, and no one's seen 'em since."

"Perhaps they're stuck," Birdie proposed. She knew that sweeps' boys often became wedged in chimneys, where they sometimes died.

"No." Ellen shook her head. "That chimney draws as well as it ever did, and there's been no stink." Lowering her voice, she added, "The sweep told me them boys must have climbed to the rooftops and run away. They do that sometimes, he said. But he won't come back, which is strange. And I'll not send for another sweep, no matter what the mistress wants. Not if there's a bad'un up there."

"We'll find out soon enough," Alfred assured her. Then he raised the subject of his fee. "It'll be fivepence for the visit and six shillings a bogle, with the cost o' the salt on top. Did Tom mention that?"

The housemaid gave a grunt. She seemed resigned to the expense, which wasn't unreasonable. "Ma's paying," she admitted. "She won't have me in any house that's bedeviled, but this is a good situation. If I'm to stay, I must stump up, for Mrs. Plumeridge never will. Mrs. Plumeridge don't believe in bogles or the like. No, not even white ladies."

She stopped for a moment to draw breath, giving Birdie a chance to inform her that the first fivepence had to be paid in advance. It was Birdie's job to ask, because Alfred often forgot. Once Ellen had agreed to these terms, they all trooped into the dining room, which opened off the hall. It was a very dark room, with maroon walls and a thick Axminster carpet. But the white dust sheets on the tables, chairs, and sideboard lightened the atmosphere a little — as did the muslin roses in the fireplace.

Ellen pointed at these roses, saying, "Mrs. Plumeridge dines in here only at Christmas, or when her nephew comes, for she likes to eat off trays. So we rarely light a fire in this room."

"Then why clean the chimney?" It seemed like a foolish extravagance to Birdie, who was finding it hard enough to understand why one person would want so many rooms, let alone so many fireplaces.

Ellen explained that her mistress, who was "very particular," had a morbid fear of rats' nests in her unused chimneys. Meanwhile, Alfred was examining the marble mantelpiece and shiny steel grate. "Have you lit a fire in here since the boys vanished?" he asked Ellen gruffly.

"Only once, to see if it would draw."

"Did it smoke?"

"No."

"You've smelled nothing? Seen no strange marks, nor heard any peculiar noises?"

Ellen thought hard for a moment. Finally she said, "No."

It was Alfred's turn to grunt. Then he surveyed the room, frowning, and told her in an undertone, "We must move that table. And the chairs."

"Oh, but—"

"Else I'll catch nothing, and you'll have wasted yer fivepence."

So Ellen helped Alfred to shift the table, while Birdie moved the chairs. All the furniture was extremely heavy. After a generous space had been cleared in front of the fireplace, Ellen went downstairs to fetch Alfred's fee, leaving him to make his preparations.

First he rolled up the carpet until a wide expanse of parquet floor was showing. Then he took a bag of salt from his sack and traced a large circle on the ground. But the circle wasn't perfect; he left a small break in its smooth line just opposite the hearthstone.

When Ellen returned, he was carefully unwrapping a short staff, which had a sharp end like a spearhead. On catching sight of it, the housemaid blanched.

"Oh, you'll not be making a mess in here?" she exclaimed. "I'll lose my place if you do!"

Alfred put a finger to his lips. Birdie, who was by the door, took Ellen's arm and nudged her into the hall, saying,

"There's a puddle or two on occasion, but nothing to fret about."

"Oh dear . . ."

"And you must air the room after. And if you stay to watch, you must keep to the hall, quiet as a mouse." Though Birdie spoke with confidence, in a calm and steady voice, her stomach was starting to knot and her heart to pound. These familiar symptoms overtook her before every job. But she had learned to ignore them. "And the door must stand open," she finished. "Open and clear. Whatever you do, don't shut the door — else how shall I escape when the time comes?"

By this time Ellen was wringing her hands. "Must I stay?" she whimpered.

"No. Some like to, on account of they don't trust us and think we're running a caper." Birdie grinned suddenly, recalling one man who'd paid for his suspicions with a bump on the head. He'd fallen over in a dead faint and had afterward sicked up all his tea. "Once they see the bogle, they soon change their tune," she remarked, "though they're in no great danger."

"I'll stand clear," said Ellen. "Beside the front door."

Birdie inclined her head.

"With a poker," Ellen added.

Birdie didn't tell her that a poker would have little effect on a monster, because she knew that Ellen wouldn't need to defend herself. No customer ever had, and none ever would. Not while Alfred was in charge.

Not while Birdie was his apprentice.

"There's nothing to fear," she insisted, patting the older girl's apron bow. "Why, it's no more'n catching a rat. For there's rats as big as bogles where I come from, and they ain't never eaten us yet!"

Then Birdie laughed gaily, and took Ellen's fivepence, and went to help Alfred bait his trap.

2

Six Shillings' Worth

Alfred stood to the left of the fireplace, his salt in one hand, his staff in the other. He didn't speak to Birdie, who took up her usual position inside his magic circle. Though she'd turned her back on him, the little mirror she was holding gave her a clear view of everything that lay behind her: Alfred, the fireplace, the gap in the ring of salt.

She had to take only one step—a single step across the white line on the floor—and she would be safe. But she couldn't do it yet. Not until they'd lured their quarry out of its hiding place. Not until they'd baited their trap.

Suddenly Alfred gave a nod. It was her cue, and it made

her heart leap. The blood was thundering in her ears. When she began to sing, however, her voice was clear and calm.

> *"O come list awhile, and you shall hear*
> *By the rolling sea lived a maiden fair.*
> *Her father had followed the smuggling trade,*
> *Like a warlike hero,*
> *Like a warlike hero as never were afraid."*

Birdie didn't take her eyes off the mirror for a second. She could see that Alfred's own eyes were fixed on the fireplace as he waited, poised like a cat, for the bogle to emerge. The waiting was always the worst part. Sometimes they waited for hours, and Birdie would sing herself hoarse. Sometimes they waited for no more than five minutes. Whether short or long, though, the wait always seemed endless to Birdie.

She had trained herself to stay alert. She had learned to ignore her growling stomach, bulging bladder, and stiff joints. Nothing could distract her, not cooking smells, nor stray dogs, nor the thought of what might happen if she faltered for even an instant. And since she couldn't afford to let her mind wander, time would slow to a crawl.

Singing made no difference, because she knew her songs too well. She didn't have to think about the words or the tunes any more than she had to think about breathing. Since the songs emerged from her mouth without conscious effort, they didn't help her in the least.

"With her pistols loaded she went abroad.
And by her side hung a glittering sword,
In her belt two daggers; well armed for war
Was this female smuggler,
Was this female smuggler, who never feared a scar."

By now Birdie could actually *feel* the bogle's presence. Often she could sense when bogles were about, despite their stealthy behavior. It was the air, she decided. The air seemed dull and lifeless. And the shadows were thicker than normal, no matter how bright the day.

If ever a chill entered her soul, or the hope suddenly drained from her heart, she knew that a bogle was to blame. If ever a room was as glum as a crypt, casting a black pall over the future, then it was harboring a bogle.

So even though nothing stirred in the fireplace, Birdie kept singing. Because she was sure that in a nest of darkness somewhere close by, she had a very attentive listener.

"Now they had not sailed far from land
When a strange sail brought them to a stand.
'These are sea robbers,' this maid did cry,

'But the female smuggler,
But the female smuggler will conquer or die.' ''

There was a puff of soot. Birdie spied it, though it was gone in a flash. She knew what it meant. The bogle was coming. It was heading down the chimney like a sweep's boy. For an instant she thought of those poor missing children, caught in the darkness, confused and frightened. Then she banished the picture from her mind, before it had a chance to lodge there.

She had more important things to worry about.

When Alfred adjusted his grip on the staff, her own hand tensed in sympathy. The mirror began to shake. Her palms began to sweat. But still her voice remained rock steady.

"Alongside, then, this strange vessel came.
'Cheer up,' cried Jane, 'we will board the same;
We'll run our chances to rise or fall,'
Cried this female smuggler,
Cried this female smuggler, who never feared a pistol ball."

Slowly, silently, something dim and dense surged out of the chimney and onto the hearth. It came in a cloud of soot that blurred its hulking silhouette. It had eyes as red as rubies, and curling horns, and flaring nostrils. Its black scales were like chips of slate. Birdie even caught a glimpse of arms unfolding, but her hand was shaking so violently that the image in the mirror wasn't crystal clear.

Luckily, her voice wasn't shaky. It soared like an arrow, straight and true.

> *"Now they killed those pirates and took their store*
> *And soon returned to old England's shore.*
> *With a keg of brandy she walked along,*
> *Did this female smuggler,*
> *Did this female smuggler, and sweetly sang a song."*

Then Alfred sprang his trap.

He lunged forward. Birdie did the same. Their timing was perfect; they moved like dancers. He closed the magic circle as she jumped out of it. He threw down his salt as she ran for cover.

When the bogle hissed, she knew it was caught. She knew she was safe. And she turned just in time to see Alfred strike his blow.

He speared the monster from behind, while it was still intent on reaching Birdie. But it couldn't. The salt was stopping it. And before it could even *try* to retreat, Alfred thrust his staff into its flank.

One jab was all it took. Though the monster was quick,

it wasn't quick enough. It spun around, screeching, as Alfred yanked out his staff and then—*WHOMP!*

The foul thing exploded.

Sometimes bogles would deflate, very slowly, like unsuccessful Yorkshire puddings, until they were little more than piles of dust on the ground. Sometimes they would pop and shrivel, then evaporate into thin air. But *this* bogle split open like a giant grape. It erupted. It sent up a geyser of yellow slime that splattered over the walls, the ceiling, the dust sheets, the fireplace . . . and Alfred, too.

Birdie escaped the deluge by ducking into the hall.

"What *was* that?" squealed Ellen. She stood by the front door, an iron poker in her trembling hand. "Was that the bogle?"

Birdie didn't reply. She had already darted back into the dining room, which now smelled rancid—like a tannery full of rotten fish. Slime was dripping from Alfred's staff, and from his beaky nose, and from his bristling chin. Slime streaked his grubby green coat and dribbled off his thick, graying hair.

At his feet, entrapped by a circle of salt, lay something that looked like a huge, burst pimple. Birdie saw that its edges were beginning to shrink and dry.

"That was quick," she said at last.

"Aye," Alfred agreed. "It didn't keep us waiting."

"It must have been hungry."

"Like enough."

"Or very stupid."

"That too."

"It made a sad mess ..." Birdie muttered, as Alfred sprinkled the contents of a small glass bottle onto the putrid remains. He was just returning the bottle to his sack when Ellen stuck her head around the door and screamed.

"Oh! Oh *no!*"

Birdie hastened to assure her that the stains would fade quickly — that they were *already* fading — and that the stench wouldn't linger. Then, seeing that Ellen was weak at the knees and in no condition to open the nearest window, Birdie did it herself.

Alfred, meanwhile, was wiping his staff with a red flannel rag. Only after his weapon had been thoroughly cleaned, and bundled back into his sack, did he ask the drooping housemaid, "Would a drop o' brandy restore you?"

"Not from this house," Ellen croaked. "Mrs. Plumeridge marks the bottle."

In response, Alfred pulled a small flask from his sack. But the housemaid shook her head.

"Ma don't hold with the grog," she told him, "for it were the ruin of her own father."

Alfred shrugged and drank a few mouthfuls. Birdie, by this time, had fetched Ellen's broom from the hall. She began to sweep up the scattered salt, some of which was now brown and yellow. The bad smell was already fading, and the bogle's remains had become brittle and crusty.

As Birdie plied her broom, the puffs of air that she stirred up caused some of these dry flakes to crumble, until they were just yellow flecks like grains of sand.

"Ain't never much to a bogle," she announced cheerfully. "You could bury a round dozen in a bread tin."

"You've a pretty voice," Ellen mumbled from her post by the door. "The prettiest I ever heard."

Birdie grinned. "Which is how I got me name," she said. "For I'm Bridie McAdam, or would be, save that Mr. Bunce thought Bridie a foolish name for a girl as wouldn't be wed for many a year." Leaning on her broom, Birdie added, "When he first heard me singing, down by the canal at Limehouse, he thought I sounded like a little bird in a gutter. So he called me Birdie just as soon as he took me in. Ain't that so, Mr. Bunce?"

Alfred ignored her. "Bogles is solitary creatures," he gruffly informed the housemaid. "Weren't never but one to a lair. So I'll trouble you for them six shillings, Miss Meggs, and a penny for the salt."

"But is it dead?" she asked him. "Dead and gone?"

"It'll not trouble you further," Alfred replied.

"But where did it come from? And why was it here?" Ellen demanded.

Alfred shrugged. He had no real, abiding interest in

bogles, even though they were his livelihood. To him they were just vermin, plain and simple. He didn't worry about the whys and the wherefores.

"It'll not trouble you further," he repeated.

And he put out his hand for Ellen's six shillings, plus a penny for the salt.

3

An Unexpected Visitor

Alfred and Birdie lived in Bethnal Green. Their room was small and dark, with no view to speak of. But it was close to the Black Dog, where Alfred often drank, and to the Anchor Street Ragged School, which Birdie attended whenever she could. There was also a pump well around the corner and a water closet next door.

Birdie knew that she was very fortunate. She slept alone, on a straw paillasse, instead of sharing a bed with five others. She had her own stool, plate, cup, and knife. She didn't have to fetch coals and rarely had to carry water. Sometimes, after a successful day, Alfred would give her twopence to spend as she wished. In return, she had to cook and clean, mend the clothes, lay the fire, buy the food, and help kill as many bogles as they could find.

She was never beaten or ill used. Alfred had once or twice boxed her ears when she was very young, because she had let her thoughts wander. But she had quickly learned not to daydream at work, since a moment's inattention could be fatal. And Alfred was not vicious. He was a morose man who liked to brood on his troubles, instead of lashing out with his fists or his tongue. So while his moods could darken their little room for hours on end, Birdie never had to dodge a blow.

Luckily, he was in excellent spirits the day after his visit to Mrs. Plumeridge's house. Thanks to Ellen's six shillings, he and Birdie had supped like kings on pease pudding and salt beef. He had also filled his brandy flask and tobacco pouch. Smoking a fresh pipe after dinner, he had even offered Birdie twopence for "a good job o' work," adding that he had another job coming up that would help pay for their lamp oil.

Birdie was about to remind him that she needed new shoes when there was a knock at the door. As Birdie jumped to her feet, Alfred frowned.

"Who's there?" he barked.

The answer came in a high, cracked, wheedling voice. "Is that Fred Bunce?"

"It is," growled Alfred. "And who might you be?"

"Only yer old pal Sally Pickles, come to pay a call." Before Birdie could do more than gasp, the woman continued, "Here on business, Fred. Mayn't I please sit down for a spell?"

Birdie gazed at Alfred, a question in her eyes. She wanted to know if she should open the door to Sarah Pickles, whose reputation was poor even by the standards of Bethnal Green. Widely known as "the Matron," Sarah ran her own gang of pickpockets, most of them under twelve years old. She had twice offered to hire Birdie for begging and lookout work, at a rate of five shillings a day—or so Alfred claimed. Birdie had never spoken to Sarah herself. Though they had passed in the street often enough, they hadn't been formally introduced.

Alfred had made sure of that.

"What's yer business, Sally?" he asked. "If it's a child you're wanting, I've none to spare."

"The child I'm a-wanting ain't yer own, Fred. I've had three go missing in as many weeks. Summat's wrong." A pause. "It ain't natural."

Alfred puffed on his pipe for a moment, his brow creased, his expression glum. Then he stood up and went to the door.

Sarah Pickles was a fat woman with a face like a withered apple. She wore an old-fashioned coal-scuttle bonnet on her wispy gray hair, and had wrapped her shapeless bulk in layers of grubby, tattered shawls. With her was her son Charlie, a thin, pale, ferret-faced youth who didn't take off his hat when he crossed the threshold.

"Well, now, and ain't this a fine crib!" Sarah exclaimed, her little dark eyes darting from corner to corner. "Dry as a nut, and not a chink in the boards! I never knowed you was so comfortable, Fred. A toffken like this'un — why, it must be let for five shillings a week!"

"Three," Birdie corrected, then fell silent as Alfred glared at her.

"And here's little Birdie," Sarah remarked, with an indulgent smile that made Birdie's blood run cold. "She's growing up, Fred. She'll be a fine young woman soon, and then what's to be done with her?"

"None o' yer business," Alfred replied shortly. "And speaking o' business . . ."

The woman heaved a sigh. "I'll sit down if I may. Me knees ain't what they used to be." Shuffling over to Birdie's vacant stool, she lowered herself onto it and said, "Fact o' the matter is, I've had three boys vanish. And afore you say they've legged it, let me tell you it ain't so. For they took nothing with 'em that they had no right to, and was happy in their work."

Sarah went on to explain that one of the boys had been seen in the custody of a policeman before his disappearance. The other two had gone missing in the same part of town, near the Whitecross Street market. But though inquiries had been made at all the local station houses and police courts, no trace of the boys had been found.

"Mebbe you should look farther afield," Alfred suggested. "In Clerkenwell or Shoreditch—"

"We tried every lockup." Sarah spoke flatly. "Hatton Garden. Old Street. Lambeth. No one's seen 'em."

"I bin trawling for days," her son volunteered, sounding as if he wasn't pleased about it. Birdie noted his resentful air and wondered how Sarah had persuaded him to take part in the search at all.

Then she glanced back at Sarah and stopped wondering. The woman's eyes were like chips of slate.

"It's my belief they was snatched, not collared," Sarah went on. "Some cove in a trap's uniform marched 'em off afore they knew it were a caper. But my question to you is: Who done it and why?" Before Alfred could answer, she peered up at him with a smile of almost sinister goodwill and continued, "There's many a lay requires children. We all know that. And I bin a-making inquiries among those as may need a young'un for their business, now and then— for which no one condemns 'em—"

"I ain't got yer boys, Sal." Alfred cut her off brusquely. His tone was grim, his gaze even grimmer. "I don't feed children to bogles."

"I know that, Fred," Sarah assured him. "You're straight

as they come, and sharp besides. You'd *never* stoop so low. Me and Charlie was wondering, however, if you might know some other feller in the same line o' work as ain't got yer morals."

Another bogler? Birdie stared at Sarah in amazement. Though bogling was an ancient trade—and an honorable one—it was also very rare. Boglers weren't like knife grinders or dogcatchers.

"I'm the only bogler hereabouts," Alfred insisted.

"You're sure o' that?" Sarah didn't seem convinced. "He might be new in town."

But Alfred shook his head. "You're looking in the wrong place," he assured her, then went on to make a suggestion. "There's many a cadger likes to have a crippled child hanging off 'im, when they want to wring hearts," he pointed out. "And many a cracksman would like a little'un to squirm through iron bars into locked houses. You'll find no shortage o' rascals as would snatch a boy—or a girl—when they can't find no child willing to work for 'em."

"I know that," Sarah acknowledged. "I also know most o' the rascals you're thinking of—and put the word out among 'em. But *nothing's* come back, Fred."

Birdie was about to ask for the names of the missing boys when she heard a carriage rattling to a halt in the street outside. This was such an unusual noise that everyone immediately fell silent. Even Sarah Pickles looked startled.

Birdie turned to Alfred. "Shall I go and see who's come?" she queried.

Alfred hesitated for a moment. "Aye, do that," he said at last, reluctantly. As Birdie rushed out the door, he called after her, "Mind you don't linger!"

Birdie didn't bother replying, since she was already halfway down the passage that led to the street. Emerging into broad daylight, she discovered that many of her neighbors were doing the same, spilling like cockroaches from their own dingy courts and basement lairs. A large audience had already gathered to stare at the woman who was alighting from the hansom cab that had drawn up in front of Birdie's house. Some people were even hanging out of windows. But it was the cab that intrigued them, not the woman who climbed out of it. *She* was nothing special (as the old cane washer across the street loudly observed). In fact, she didn't look as if she were at all accustomed to using hired vehicles. There was a flustered air about her, and she wasn't wearing gloves.

Birdie judged her to be a servant, or a shop girl, or perhaps some kind of dressmaker. Her frizzy reddish hair was spilling out from beneath a battered straw hat tipped low over her forehead. She had wrapped herself in a trailing shawl, and her round, freckled face was damp with sweat.

"I'm looking for Mr. Alfred Bunce," she said, addressing

Birdie in a voice that proved, once and for all, that she wasn't a lady. "Does he live in this house?"

Birdie was delighted. "He does!" she exclaimed. "And I'm 'prenticed to him!"

"Then could you ask if he'd spare a moment? I've a message to deliver."

One of the men in the street shouted that she would do a lot better with *him* than with a scraggy old mutton bone like Alfred Bunce. Some of the other men laughed. Birdie told them to stow it or she would set a bogle upon 'em, and then they'd be sorry.

"Come and meet Mr. Bunce," she urged their visitor, who was looking more and more anxious.

"Oh, no." The woman shook her head. "I'll not go in."

"He won't hurt you," Birdie said shrewdly.

But the woman on the doorstep wasn't reassured. "I'm to take him back in the cab if he'll come, or give him Miss Edith's address if he cannot," she replied. "I'm not to stay on any account. Miss Edith said so."

Birdie frowned. "Who's Miss Edith?"

"The lady as sent me. Miss Edith Eames."

"Has she a bogle?" asked Birdie, who could think of no other reason why a lady should want to consult Alfred Bunce. But the question seemed to shock her redheaded companion.

"Oh, *no!*" the woman exclaimed, turning white.

"Then—"

"I don't know what she wants him for. But she'll make it worth his while." Backing away from Birdie, her gaze flicking fearfully up and down the busy street, the woman added, "I'll wait here. You tell him. And if he won't come now, I'll give you the address."

Birdie shrugged. Though mystified, she was happy to be the bearer of such remarkable and unexpected news. A summons! From a lady! Already she could feel many an awe-struck gaze upon her. For the hundredth time she secretly congratulated herself on being a bogler's girl; there was so much *excitement* and *variety* in a bogler's life.

As she turned to fetch Alfred, she was struck by a sudden thought.

"What's yer name?" she asked their visitor, who was already retreating toward the safety of the cab.

"I'm Mary Meggs," came the breathless response. "I ain't Miss Edith's maid. I work for her aunt, Mrs. Heppin-stall. But they live in the same house, and never exchange a harsh word. So I must do as Miss Edith bids me—whatever I might think of it."

4

Meeting Miss Eames

The hansom cab wasn't really designed for three passengers. Mary said as much when Alfred told her that his apprentice would be coming along too. But Birdie was so small that she managed to squeeze into the cab without much trouble. And Mary was so desperate to get away that she didn't have the patience to argue with Alfred.

Birdie couldn't believe her luck. She had never been in a cab before — and certainly never as far as Bloomsbury. According to Mary, Miss Edith Eames lived just off Great Russell Street. It was a long journey, all the way from the east to the west of London, and Birdie gloried in every inch of it. Sitting up there, behind a clip-clopping black horse, she felt like the Queen of England.

She knew that she had Sarah Pickles to thank for her good fortune. Alfred had been of two minds about taking Birdie with him, since Mary kept insisting that there were no bogles in the house where she worked. But Sarah Pickles had heard everything. She had even accompanied Alfred out to the cab, where Mary was waiting for him. Left behind, Birdie would have found herself alone with Sarah and Charlie Pickles.

Alfred hadn't wanted that. He didn't trust Sarah. So he'd taken a cautious approach, loading up the cab with his equipment as well as his apprentice. "Sal might steal our bedding while we're gone," he'd muttered, as Sarah waved them goodbye, "but she'll not take you with it, lass."

"Because I'd never go with her," Birdie had scoffed. "Not if she forced me at gunpoint!"

"Which it might yet come to if Sarah has her way." Alfred's grim tone had sent a chill running down Birdie's spine. But she'd done her best to ignore it, stoutly declaring that she'd faced too many monsters to be scared by an old crone like Sarah Pickles.

Later, parading through London on real leather seats, she asked herself, in pure exultation: *How could Sarah ever top this? I have the best job in the world!* Not that the first leg of their journey filled Birdie with wonder; she knew Bethnal Green and Shoreditch too well to marvel at the sights that greeted her as they bowled along. She saw the usual collection of dirty streets lined with pie shops and pawnbrokers, costers' stalls and public houses. Down the side alleys she glimpsed even dingier yards full of donkeys and dust heaps, where people were engaged in smelly occupations like boiling tripe or melting tallow. She saw match girls and watercress girls, men carrying rolls of cloth and men pushing barrows laden with furniture. She even recognized a few faces, and was pleased when a clothes-peg maker named Sam Wilson gaped like a fish upon beholding her.

She waved to him regally as she passed by.

Gradually, however, the city changed. Houses and shops became neater and more respectable, though here and there a patch of slum intruded. Imposing churches thrust their steeples above the crowds. A bustling market took Birdie's breath away; she was dazzled by all the bright fruit and fluttering ribbons. In a green park she spotted a white baby carriage that looked like a little cloud on wheels. In Holborn they went straight past the Royal Music Hall, and nearly knocked down a gentleman in a high hat as he tried to avoid a pile of horse manure.

"There's some would rather die than dirty their shoes,"

Alfred quietly observed, after they'd left this furious pedestrian far behind. It was only the second or third remark that Alfred had made since leaving Bethnal Green. Mary hadn't been very talkative either; she seemed nervous to be sharing a coach with Alfred, and would speak only when spoken to. Luckily, Birdie wasn't afraid to ask questions. And by the time they reached Bloomsbury Square, Mary had admitted that she was, indeed, related to Ellen Meggs, who had told her all about the bogle in Mrs. Plumeridge's chimney.

"Ellen had her evening free last night. She came all the way from Westbourne Park to tell me, and though we stayed in the kitchen, Miss Eames must have heard us talking." Suddenly Mary reached up to tap at the hatch in the roof. "Turn here!" she told the cabman, before fixing her attention on Birdie once more. "Ellen said *you* was there. In that room, with the bogle."

"Of course," Birdie replied.

Mary shuddered, drawing her shawl tightly around her. But she didn't say anything else until they reached their destination, which was a neat and narrow brick house in a line of almost identical houses tucked away near Saint George's church. While Alfred and Birdie alighted, Mary paid the fare. Then she headed for the steps that led down to the kitchen, stopping only when she heard her name spoken.

"Ah! I thought so." The lady who had appeared at the

front door of the house was dressed in several shades of mustard, with a modest bustle, no flounces, and the plainest of hairstyles. Her pale face was shaped like a cat's, wide at the cheekbones but tapering off to a pointed chin. She had clear hazel eyes under straight black brows, and there were lines around her eyes.

"You must be Mr. Bunce," she said briskly, extending a hand to Alfred, who was still standing in the street. Then she caught sight of Birdie. "And who is this?" she asked.

"He wouldn't come without her, miss," Mary complained. And since Alfred seemed to be momentarily speechless, Birdie answered for him.

"I'm the 'prentice," she announced.

"I see." After a moment's startled silence, the lady murmured, "And what is your name, dear?"

"Birdie."

"So nice to meet you, Birdie. *My* name is Edith Eames, and if you'd both step inside, I'll give you a full account of why I sent for you. Rest assured, I shan't keep you long." To her housemaid, who was already bound for the kitchen, Miss Eames said, "Could you bring us some tea, Mary? In the drawing room, I think."

"In the drawing room?" Mary looked askance at Alfred and Birdie. "But—"

"In the *drawing room,* Mary," Miss Eames repeated, her voice stern. "And bring a little cake, if you please."

Birdie grinned. Tea was a rare luxury. Though she didn't like it much, she would enjoy boasting about it to her friends. But it was the prospect of cake that made her heart pound.

Birdie loved cake.

She scurried after Miss Eames and soon found herself in a hall that wasn't quite as grand as Mrs. Plumeridge's, though still very handsome. The drawing room that opened off it was so pretty that Birdie didn't know where to look first. It had flowered wallpaper and tasseled curtains and embroidered fire screens. There were stuffed birds and gilt-framed pictures, books and cushions, a workbox, a piano, a red marble clock, and a white marble statue. The grate was full of fresh roses, and the carpet was so beautiful that Birdie was afraid to tread on it.

"Please sit down," Miss Eames said to Alfred, who was peering nervously at all the chairs on offer. They were spindly things, covered in damask.

"Mebbe I oughter stand," he replied, "else I dirty 'em."

But Miss Eames wouldn't let him stand. Instead, she draped the sturdiest chair in crocheted antimacassars, which she gathered from some of the other chairs in the room. Once he'd settled himself into a nest of white frills, with his sack on his knee and his hat on his sack, Miss Eames put Birdie on a footstool, arranged herself on an elegant fainting couch, and began to speak.

"Mr. Bunce, I have made a long and scientific study of English folklore. My main interest is in the faerie realm—those inhabitants of the spirit world that some call Elementals. It was always my understanding that belief in elfin peoples had been driven from our cities, and that it existed only among country dwellers steeped in the ancient traditions of our race. But when my housemaid told me about *your* occupation, I realized that I was wrong!"

Alfred stared at her blankly. So she cleared her throat and tried again.

"I'm told that you were recently hired to banish a child-eating beast from a house in Paddington. Is that correct?" she asked.

Alfred nodded mutely. It was Birdie who said, "A chimney bogle."

"A chimney bogle!" Miss Eames repeated, rolling the words around on her tongue with obvious delight. "How extraordinary. And did you actually *see* this creature?"

"Of course!" Birdie exclaimed. "You can't kill a bogle if you can't see it!"

"Ah! So you killed it, did you?" Before Birdie could answer, Miss Eames reached over to retrieve a book and pencil from a little table nearby. "What did it look like, this 'chimney bogle'?"

"Oh, it were big. And black."

As Miss Eames began to scribble in her book, Birdie

added, "We ain't never caught more'n a glimpse of any bogle, on account of how fast they move and how quick they die."

Then Alfred found his voice, at long last. "Have you a job for us, miss?" he asked gruffly.

Miss Eames shook her head. "I have not, as it happens, though I wish I had. So far I've not been fortunate enough to encounter a spirit of the elements in any guise, whether gnome or troll, sylph or brownie. But I am *very eager* to meet people who have." Leaning forward, her pencil poised, Miss Eames inquired, "Were you born in London, Mr. Bunce?"

"No." Alfred shifted uneasily. "I were brought here from the country as a little lad, nobbut five years old."

"I see." Miss Eames made a note in her book. "And did your father practice the same trade?"

"No. I were 'prenticed. Like Birdie."

"Afore me he had a boy called Jack, as went to sea, being too growed up for bogling work," Birdie revealed. She liked talking to Miss Eames, who listened with such flattering attention. But before Birdie could relate the story of her own first meeting with Alfred, on the banks of the Limehouse canal, Mary suddenly appeared with a tea tray—and everyone was briefly distracted by tea, plum cake, and slices of bread and butter.

Birdie tried to restrain herself. She took only one piece

of cake and two slices of bread, though she did put four heaped spoonfuls of sugar in her tea. The tea was served in beautiful cups with pictures painted on them. The sugar came in a crystal bowl.

Alfred ate nothing, and barely touched his tea. He looked deeply uncomfortable.

"Begging yer pardon, miss," he said as soon as Miss Eames had refreshed herself with a sip of tea and a bite of cake, "but what's it to you where I come from, or what me father did?"

Miss Eames carefully set down her teacup. "As I said, Mr. Bunce, I am a folklorist, with a *profound* interest in your profession." Smiling a little nervously, she clasped her hands together, cleared her throat, and confessed, "What I should like to do is write a paper on the topic. I'm sure it would be eagerly read, and very widely discussed. But before attempting such a thing, I should like to accompany you on your next encounter with a nature spirit. Of course I would be there as a witness and will undertake not to interfere in any way."

Birdie's jaw dropped, exposing a mouthful of chewed bread. Alfred frowned and said cautiously, "You want to come on a job, miss?"

"I do, yes."

"With me and Birdie?"

"Wherever chance may take you." As a final encouragement, Miss Eames fixed Alfred with a bright, penetrating look and in a businesslike manner declared, "Naturally I would pay you for the privilege. Let us say . . . half a crown? With a shilling in advance for your trouble."

5

LESSONS LEARNED

Alfred was silent for a moment. Then he said, "Three shillings."

"Done." Miss Eames sprang up and went over to a highly polished writing desk. "Perhaps you can use the extra sixpence to catch an omnibus home."

"Do you work for a newspaper, miss?" Birdie inquired. But her mouth was so full that the question emerged as a thick mumble.

She had to swallow before repeating herself.

Miss Eames paused in the act of unlocking a desk drawer. "I fear not," she answered. "Why do you ask?"

"Because you talked o' writing in a paper."

Miss Eames smiled. She had removed a purse from the drawer and was counting coins into her hand. "I may have the privilege of publishing my piece in some learned journal, or reading it before the Victoria Institute," she said. "But none of the *popular* periodicals would be interested in my work."

"I would be." Birdie had caught the wistful note in Miss Eames's voice and was keen to encourage her. "If you write about me and Mr. Bunce, mebbe you can read it to us. Once you finish, like."

"Could you not read it yourself, dear?" When Birdie shook her head, Miss Eames regarded her with narrowed eyes. "That's a shame. You look like a clever girl to me. Have you no paupers' schools in your neighborhood?"

"Aye, but . . ." Birdie trailed off and glanced at Alfred, who was scowling. "The master there can be heavy handed," she finally confessed. "He cut me across the face once. Besides, I ain't no scholar. I'm a bogler's girl."

Miss Eames didn't look convinced. But she abandoned the subject, crossing the room to give Alfred his shilling in advance. "Tell me where we should meet again, Mr. Bunce," she requested. "Or have you not settled the time and place of your next job of work?"

"Oh, aye," said Alfred. "I know where *that*'ll be." Pocketing his money, he went on to explain that two young mudlarks, or "grubbers," had gone missing while foraging for coal and wood on the riverbank. Though one of the boys had been an excellent swimmer, police had ruled that both of them must have drowned.

"It's a dangerous stretch o' river, with tides and boats and bogs," Alfred related. "But there's a tosher I know, name o' Crabbe, and *he* says—"

"I'm sorry, a what?" Miss Eames had returned to the couch, where she had retrieved her book and pencil. "What is a 'tosher,' pray?"

"Don't you know, miss?" Birdie couldn't hide her amazement. "A tosher is someone as trawls the sewers for a living, in search o' things to sell."

"And this tosher were down near the outfall at Shadwell," Alfred continued, "when he saw a grindylow take a boy, or so he says. By which he means—"

"A Yorkshire water monster!" Miss Eames exclaimed. "Yes, I've heard of grindylows. They are a species of nixie or water sprite, associated with bogs, lakes, and meres. They're said to eat children, like Peg Powler or Jinny Greenteeth."

Alfred frowned. "I know nothing o' Peg Powler, nor Jinny Greenteeth," he rumbled. "As for this grindylow, it's just a bogle by another name."

"Oh, but there are many *kinds* of bogle, Mr. Bunce." Again Miss Eames jumped up, this time heading for a book cupboard, from which she extracted a large, heavy volume bound in calfskin. "If you consult the antiquarian texts, you'll see that there are any number of water monsters scattered throughout England. The question we must ask ourselves is: Are they all local versions of the same beast, or are they different monsters entirely, with different habits and characteristics?"

She thrust the book under Alfred's nose, so sharply that he recoiled. When Birdie rushed to join him, she saw that the pages had fallen open at a picture of a creature—half hag, half troll—with long, tangled hair and a ragged cloak on its back.

"That don't look like no bogle *I* ever saw," Birdie commented, cocking her head to one side.

"It is perhaps drawn from a verbal description," Miss Eames said delicately, "and not from life."

"A bogle's a bogle." Alfred's tone was gruff. "I don't care what it looks like, long as I can kill it."

"Them sewer pipes is thick with bogles," Birdie added. "Ain't that right, Mr. Bunce?" To Miss Eames she remarked, "It's very likely me own ma died on account of a bogle. She were a tosher, see, but left me in a drain one day, and no one's seen her since."

"But how dreadful!" Miss Eames looked quite shocked. She set down her book, her brow creased in dismay. "Is that why you became a bogler's apprentice? To revenge yourself on your mother's killer?"

"Oh, no!" Birdie assured her cheerfully. "I were a tosher

too, until Mr. Bunce heard me sing. You need a sweet voice in this trade."

"You do?"

"A voice like honey," Birdie confirmed. Then she burst into song. *"I'd hang the highway robber — hang, boys, hang! I'd hang the burglar jobber — hang, boys, hang!"*

All at once the drawing room door opened again. But this time, instead of admitting Mary the housemaid, it yielded to the pressure of an elderly lady in a white lace cap. This lady was very small and thin, with gray hair arranged in ringlets over her ears. She wore a black gown and fingerless gloves. Her eyes were large and blue, her teeth stained and broken. She carried a walking stick.

"Why, and who is this little nightingale?" she demanded. "Edith, you never mentioned that we were expecting visitors."

"I'm sorry, did we disturb you? I thought you'd gone to Mr. Fotherington's house for tea. Isn't that what you usually do on a Friday?" Miss Eames sounded slightly flustered. Without waiting for a reply, she went on to explain, "This is Mr. Alfred Bunce and his apprentice."

"Come about the broken chairs?" her aunt queried.

"For my research." Miss Eames cleared her throat and said, "Mr. Bunce has been describing his life as a bogler."

"Really? How interesting." The old lady offered up a vague smile as she eyed Alfred's dusty boots. Then she addressed his apprentice. "You have such a pretty voice, dear. What were you singing?"

"'Hanging Johnny,'" Birdie supplied.

"Ah."

"This is my aunt, Mrs. Heppinstall," Miss Eames informed Alfred, who had risen from his seat. "She likes to hear about my research."

"But I much prefer to hear music," Mrs. Heppinstall admitted, her pale eyes still fixed on Birdie. "What is your name, child?"

"Birdie McAdam."

"Indeed? Well, with a pretty voice like yours, Birdie, you should be singing nicer songs. Do you *know* any nice songs?"

Birdie thought for a moment. She didn't understand what the old lady meant by "nice." "I know 'Down by the Greenwood Side,'" she volunteered. *"There was a duke's daughter dwelt at York—all alone and alone-a-a. She fell in love with her father's clerk, down by the greenwood side."*

The old lady nodded. "Yes, that *is* pretty."

"She took a knife both sharp and short—all alone and alone-a-a—and stabb'd her babes unto the heart, down by the greenwood side."

"Oh my goodness." Mrs. Heppinstall winced. "No, I don't think we need hear any more of *that*."

"Would you like some tea, Aunt Louisa?" Miss Eames

suddenly broke in, almost as if she was trying to change the subject. "I could ask Mary to make a fresh pot."

"No, thank you, Edith. I don't wish to disturb you, dear."

"You're not disturbing us at all. Mr. Bunce was just leaving. Is that not so, Mr. Bunce?"

"Aye." Alfred seemed anxious to go. Clutching his sack in one hand and his hat in the other, he began to sidle toward the door. "Goodbye, ma'am. Thank'ee, miss."

"Let me show you out, Mr. Bunce," Miss Eames said firmly. She ushered him over the threshold as Birdie lagged behind, throwing a wistful look at the remnants of the plum cake.

"I'll cut you a piece to take home," the old lady suggested. "So you can share it with your family."

"Oh, I ain't got no family," Birdie was forced to admit. "But there's plenty I know as would be happy to share a bite with me."

"You're an orphan, dear?" When Birdie nodded, Mrs. Heppinstall remarked, "How sad."

Birdie shrugged, her gaze still on the plum cake. "You don't miss what you never knowed," she advised Mrs. Heppinstall, who immediately picked up the entire cake—or what was left of it—and thrust it into Birdie's hands.

"Take it all," the old lady insisted.

Birdie blinked. She was about to mumble her thanks

when a horrible thought struck her. "I never said I were orphaned just to get more cake!" she protested. "I ain't no cadger, ma'am!"

"No, of course not. That is to say, while I've no idea what a cadger might be, if it is in any way wicked or dishonest, I'm quite convinced that you're nothing of the sort."

"Aye, but—"

"Take it, dear." Mrs. Heppinstall smiled and bobbed her head, so that her ringlets bounced like coils of wire. Then she leaned toward Birdie and with a twinkle in her eye murmured, "I'm not fond of plum cake, but Edith *will* have it. Our cook's next cake will be an almond one."

"Birdie!" It was Alfred, calling from the front doorstep. Birdie flashed a grin at Mrs. Heppinstall and ran to join him, clutching her slab of plum cake beneath the folds of her little yellow cape.

"So I shall meet you tomorrow at three o'clock," Miss Eames was saying to Alfred as Birdie dodged past her. "Near the sewage outfall at the bottom of New Gravel Lane, in Shadwell."

"Aye, but . . ." Alfred hesitated for a moment before feebly protesting, "It ain't no place for a lady, miss."

"I shall wear clothes appropriate to the task," Miss Eames promised. "There will be a lot of mud, I know."

Alfred glanced at Birdie, who saw the appeal in his eyes. So she piped up. "Them docks is as rough as fustian, miss.

If you dress like a lady, there'll be hell to pay." Seeing Miss Eames wince at the word *hell*, Birdie flushed and said, "Begging yer pardon."

"They don't like toffs in Shadwell," Alfred confirmed.

"You should buy yerself some slops," Birdie went on, thinking of all the bedraggled petticoats and moth-eaten jackets for sale in the slop-seller's stall near her own house. "Or borrow one o' Mary's dresses. And *don't* take a cab. Not to Shadwell."

"I'll—I'll take an omnibus," Miss Eames stammered.

"As far as Commercial Road," Birdie agreed. "But on no account ask the way, or you'll make a mark o' yerself. Stay mum till you find us."

"*If* you find us," Alfred muttered as a parting shot.

Birdie followed him down the front steps. When she turned back to wave at Miss Eames, however, she suffered a pang of remorse. Poor Miss Eames looked so anxious!

"Don't worry, miss. We'll keep you safe," Birdie promised. "There ain't a soul on the docks would cross a bogler, for fear o' what he fights. Once you're with us, you can do all the talking you want."

Then she offered Miss Eames a wink and a grin before racing to catch up with Alfred.

6

THE COLLAR

Birdie! Hi! Come 'ere!"

Birdie stopped and glanced around. She was picking her way along a narrow, busy street, carrying a covered basket full of cooked tripe. To her left was a jellied-eel shop. To her right was a slop seller's. Peering through a stream of pedestrians, Birdie caught sight of the slop seller, Emma Bridewell, waving at her.

"Birdie! Come see what *I* got!" Emma cried. "It's the prettiest article I ever laid eyes on!"

Birdie hesitated for a moment, but the lure of the old clothes was too strong. Emma's shop was so thickly hung with garments, or "slops," that its walls were barely visible.

Coats, capes, and gowns dangled above her head. Battered boots were lined up near the door. Piles of handkerchiefs spilled from a wooden tub.

Emma herself wore a skirt and blouse much drabber than most of the items she sold. She was a stout young woman with a slight limp and eyes permanently inflamed by her dusty, musty stock. "Look at this here collar!" she was saying. "Real point lace, fine as fine! Did you ever see such piecework?" She darted forward to arrange the collar around Birdie's neck, then thrust Birdie toward a spotted mirror hanging by the shop door. "There, now! Ain't you a picture? That'll dress up any frock, no matter how plain."

It was true. Though slightly torn and yellow, the collar made Birdie's soiled cotton dress look almost like a ball gown.

"How much?" Birdie asked, gently fingering a knotted leaf.

"For you, dear, only a shilling."

"*A shilling?* Why, I could buy a pair o' wool trousers for ninepence!"

"But this is point lace, Birdie — real point lace, same as royalty wears." Emma whipped the collar off Birdie's shoulders and held it up to the light. "That's silk, that is. Hand-made. Feel it. There's ladies in the West End would be glad to pay a florin for quality stuff like this."

Birdie thought briefly about Mrs. Heppinstall's white

lace cap. Then she shook her head. "I ain't got the chink," she said ruefully.

"Ninepence ha'penny. That's me last offer."

"No." Birdie turned away. Her visit to Bloomsbury the previous afternoon had exposed her to a whole new world of daintiness; for the first time she found herself pining after lace and fresh flowers and gold-rimmed teacups. But she knew that such things were beyond her reach. "Lace is for ladies," she told Emma, averting her eyes from all the silk and satin on display. As she moved off down the street, she reminded herself that Miss Eames, for all her elegance, wouldn't know what to do with a bogle. A bogle wouldn't be discouraged by clean, polished surfaces or well-aired rooms. It wouldn't be bribed with plum cake or repelled by reasoned argument. When it came to bogles, a lady's only defense was someone like Alfred—with someone like Birdie at his side.

"Oi! Birdie McAdam!"

This time the voice hailing her didn't belong to a shopkeeper. It belonged to a skinny, undersize boy with snapping dark eyes and so much thick, black, shiny hair that his head looked too big for his body. His name was Jem Barbary, and he was a thief. Birdie had seen him about. Unlike most of Sarah's lads, who tended to be rather pale and quiet, Jem was lively, restless, and quick to talk.

He wore a shapeless cloth cap, an oversize flannel shirt,

and striped canvas trousers torn off at the knee. Birdie had always judged him to be about her own age.

"They say you bin mixing with toffs," he remarked with a teasing grin. His teeth were surprisingly good. "Prancing about in hackney cabs, *I* heard."

Birdie sniffed. She had paused for a moment but didn't like being jostled by the crowd. So she began to move on again, anxious not to be seen conversing with a known pickpocket.

Jem kept pace with her, dodging hawkers and porters and piles of manure. He was very quick on his feet. "I got a job for you," he said. "Unless you're too high and mighty to be chasing down work nowadays?"

"I know what *you* call a job," Birdie rejoined, "and don't want no part of it."

"Are you sure? For it's bogling work." Jem smirked as Birdie stopped in her tracks. "That's right," he went on, lowering his voice. "Sal's acquainted with a feller named George Hobney. He's the night porter at the Hackney workhouse and will turn a blind eye to what goes in and comes out, if you know what I mean."

Jem waited, searching Birdie's face with a bright, penetrating gaze. Since he had just confessed that Sarah Pickles was having goods smuggled in and out of an institution specifically designed to feed and house paupers, he may have been expecting Birdie to comment. Birdie, however, was speechless. Any mention of the workhouse always silenced her, because she feared the place as much as she feared prison. From what she could tell, the workhouse was almost as bad as prison. The food was supposed to be dire, the work punishing, and the discipline much too strict.

She knew that she might have ended up in a workhouse if Alfred hadn't plucked her out of the Limehouse canal. And she also knew that she wasn't safe, even now. One stroke of ill luck and she could easily find herself destitute again. If Alfred should die — or if he should one day tell her that she was too old to act as bogle bait — and if she didn't then find work as a match girl, or laundress, or clothes-peg maker . . .

With a shudder she dismissed the thought, turning her attention to what Jem was saying.

"There's four children gone from Hackney spike, and now the workhouse well is beginning to stink," he revealed. "They dragged it and found nothing. No bones. No clothes. The master claims it's proof them children hooked it, on account o' there's *allus* kids running away from that place. But certain people in the workhouse think otherwise. They think it might be a bogle as took 'em. And when Sal heard, she told George to hire a Go-Devil Man."

"Why are you telling me this?" Birdie asked suspiciously, edging away from a coster's donkey that had halted in the middle of the street. "Why not speak to Mr. Bunce?"

"I tried," Jem countered. "He ain't at home. I just come from there."

"He's at the pub," Birdie had to concede. She still didn't like what she was hearing, though. "Why would Sarah Pickles want to tout for Mr. Bunce? She ain't never done it previous to this."

"*She* says it's by way o' payment. For any help she'll need finding her boys as went missing." Jem's face darkened suddenly, and he looked away. For the first time Birdie noticed the graze on his chin and the dark smudges under his eyes.

"Did you know them kids?" she queried.

Jem gave a nod. Studying him, Birdie couldn't help remarking, "You should be careful, then."

"Hah!" Jem scoffed. "Ain't no bogle fast enough to catch *me*."

"Mebbe it weren't no bogle as took 'em," Birdie pointed out. "Don't you think it's queer they was all working for Sarah Pickles?"

Jem scowled. "You'd better stow *that* kind o' talk if you want a quiet life," he snapped, ducking to avoid a wooden beam that was balanced on the head of a passing porter. Though the warning unnerved her, she shrugged off the threat with a fine show of confidence.

"I'm just saying as how you should mebbe give up the work, since it's so perilous," she said.

"And do what?" Jem sneered. "Sell chickweed? Round up stray hogs?"

"At least it would be honest toil."

"So that's what *you'll* be doing, is it? When you get too old for bogling?" Jem's taunt was accompanied by another sly smirk, which annoyed Birdie so much that she set off down the street again.

Jem followed her. "A prig can be any age," he continued. "Ain't *no one* too old for hoisting or tooling—which is a sight easier'n killing bogles."

"I ain't no thief," Birdie spat.

"Are you sure about that?" As Birdie halted again, glaring at Jem, he added, "What is it the parsons say? Summat about not casting the first stone?"

As his gaze slid toward her basket, Birdie's stomach seemed to turn over. With a gasp and a start, she twitched aside the cloth that covered her purchases—and almost fainted.

Emma Bridewell's lace collar was sitting on top of the tripe.

"It's a mortal shame you don't have the chink to *buy* what you want," Jem taunted, as Birdie tried to think straight. How had he done it? Or had someone else done it while Jem was distracting her . . . ?

"You was the decoy!" she blurted out, as white as salt. Looking around frantically, she caught a glimpse of Charlie Pickles, who was ducking behind a nearby dustman's cart.

"That weren't too clever," Jem observed. Though his tone was breezy, he couldn't quite meet her eye. "If I was you, I'd hook it and stay low. On account o' the dealer knows you and how much you like such baubles—"

"Oh, the dealer knows me, all right! She knows me better'n *you* do!" Birdie swung around and began to retrace her steps, ignoring Jem's frantic jabbering. He was telling her that it wasn't worth risking arrest. He was telling her that Emma Bridewell knew where she lived but would *never* find her if Sarah Pickles took her in. He was telling her that if she joined up with Jem and his mates, she could have all the lace collars she wanted . . .

"Emma! Hi!" Birdie called, having spied the slop seller through a screen of moving bodies. As Emma glanced around, Birdie pressed forward—and Jem suddenly melted away into the crowd.

"Why, whatever's the matter with you?" Emma stared at Birdie, who was flushed and panting, with a distraught expression plastered all over her face. "You got a fever?"

"I didn't have nothing to do with it, Emma! It were them lads as took it!" Birdie thrust the lace collar under Emma's nose. "And now I'm bringing it back!"

"Why? What's wrong with it?" the slop seller asked.

Birdie's jaw dropped.

"Did Jem give it to *you?*" Emma went on, with a twinkle in her eye. "He's proper smitten, that lad."

"Y-you mean—you mean—he bought it?" Birdie stammered.

"*And* beat me down on the price. But I'll not hold it against him." Leaning down, Emma put her mouth to Birdie's ear. "You should take it, love, in all good conscience. Don't turn up yer nose at a gift o' the heart. Them tokens'll stop coming to you soon enough! And Jem Barbary's got the makings, beneath all his bluster . . ."

As she talked, Emma gently guided the scrap of lace back into Birdie's basket. Birdie, meanwhile, stood stiff and mute, so angry that she could hardly breathe. She felt like hitting someone. But mixed in with the anger was a kernel of fear. Could Sarah Pickles really be so desperate to recruit her? Had Sarah's three missing pickpockets left a gap so large that she was willing to use a thinly veiled threat to secure Birdie's services—even at the risk of offending Alfred?

I can't tell Mr. Bunce, she thought on her way past a coal merchant's shop. *He'll give Sarah what for, and then she'll get back at him secretly. She'll do worse'n plant stolen goods on him . . .*

Not that the collar *was* stolen. But it could have been; that was the point. Sarah's warning was clear enough. She was saying that she could force Birdie to thieve for her. A well-placed scrap of silk, planted by a deft hand, could put Birdie in danger of arrest — even imprisonment — unless Sarah stepped in to help.

I'll have to be on me guard, Birdie decided. *I'll have to make sure she don't take advantage of me or Mr. Bunce. I've faced down bogles; I can deal with an old toad like Sal. Why, if it comes to that, I'll tell the police she killed her missing boys!*

Turning into her own street, Birdie paused for an instant, scanning every shadow for a trace of Jem or Charlie. Though she couldn't see them, that didn't mean they weren't out there, watching her.

Just in case they were, she tossed the lace collar into a puddle of mud and marched away with her chin in the air.

7

Low Tide

A dozen young scavengers worked regularly around the coal wharf at Shadwell. From the banks of the River Thames they picked up iron, coal and copper, wood and canvas, old lengths of rope, and lumps of fat. Sometimes they found coins or antiquities. If they were lucky, their labors earned them a shilling a day. Each.

So Alfred's fee was completely beyond them. Even after pooling their funds, they hadn't been able to collect more than four shillings and fivepence to pay Alfred for killing the sewer bogle that appeared to be stalking mudlarks along the river flats. Luckily, Bill Crabbe, the tosher, had come to their rescue. Bill had seen the sewer bogle. Though he'd caught only a glimpse of it, he was keen to make sure that he didn't see it again.

"Ah've three children work the sewers and didn't raise 'em to fill the belly of no grindylow," he told Alfred as they stood gazing down at the river. "So ah went to t'other toshers hereabouts, and we stumped up half a crown between us. For there'll be no peace without this thing is nobbled — and right quick, betimes."

Bill was a small man, very thin and yellow, with a bad cough. Despite the heat of the day, he was well wrapped in a tattered oilskin coat over a wool vest and flannel shirt. He had met Alfred and Birdie at a well-known riverside public house, and from there had guided them to the site of "the little lads' doom," as he called it. This was a patch of mud near the very end of Wapping High Street. It was a strange place, busy yet desolate, flanked by a wall of warehouses on one side and a forest of ships' masts on the other. Empty boats littered the mud flats, which smelled very bad in the summer sun. Toiling among the jetties were men too preoccupied to notice a small knot of idlers who were nodding and pointing at the mouth of a nearby drain.

This drain was a perfect bolthole. It lurked behind a barricade of casks, barges, broken crates, and coils of rope. There was enough foot traffic to guarantee a steady supply of food, yet all the business of the riverbank would serve to distract people in the immediate neighborhood. Frightened screams would be masked by the cries of coal whippers and ballast heavers. Brief scuffles would be concealed by overturned keels or piles of fishing nets.

Birdie shuddered as she peered at the rank, boggy, cluttered stretch of riverbank. "That's a sad spot to meet yer end," she observed to the boy standing beside her, who nodded but said nothing. His name was Ned Roach. Having been entrusted with the mudlarks' share of Alfred's fee, he had tagged along with Bill Crabbe to make sure the money didn't go to waste. Birdie wasn't quite sure what to make of Ned. She thought he was probably about eleven. Though plastered with filth and missing a couple of teeth, he was pleasant enough to look at, with his sturdy build and springy brown hair. But he didn't have much to say for himself. At first Birdie had wondered if he was a deaf and dumb—or just stupid. Only after he had corrected one of Bill's statements about the afternoon tides did she realize that he wasn't stupid at all.

He was either afraid of boglers or suspicious of them.

"Did you know the two missing lads?" she asked him, keeping one eye cocked for Miss Eames.

He answered with a nod.

"What names did they go by?"

"Dick. And Herbert." All at once Ned frowned. Following his gaze, Birdie saw that Bill was making his way down to the mud flats, using a short flight of stone stairs.

Alfred was following him.

"Them two'll come to no harm," Birdie assured Ned, "but don't *you* go after 'em, else you might get ate." She smiled up at him and was surprised when he colored. "Did you ever see this bogle yerself?" she queried.

"No."

"Well, I seen plenty, but not one that ever got away. Mr. Bunce knows what he's about." As Ned moved forward to the edge of the quayside, she added, "Mind, now. If you get too close, you'll spring the trap afore it's set."

She was about to say more when she heard the strains of a distant chorus, chanted by rough voices in a mocking tone. *"Abroad I was walking, one morning in the spring, and heard a maid in Bedlam, so sweetly she did sing . . ."* Convinced that this noise meant trouble for somebody, Birdie spun around and spied the singers almost at once. They were half a dozen coarse-looking youths who seemed to be following a madwoman down the street, toward the river. Two of the men had porter's knots tied to their shoulders, suggesting that they had just set down a load of wool, or coal, or coffee. Two of them looked like sailors, and two like off-duty pickpockets. Together they lurched along in a jeering cluster, past tumbledown shoe marts and sailmakers' shops, trying to tread on the skirts of the woman who stumbled along just ahead of them.

"Her chains she rattled with her hands, and thus replied she—I love my love because I know he first loved me-e-e . . ."

It took Birdie a few seconds to recognize Miss Eames, who was dressed in such a motley collection of clothes that she really *did* look as if she'd just emerged from a madhouse like Bedlam. Because her skirt was much too big for her, Miss Eames kept tripping on its hem. Her wide, old-fashioned sleeves were flapping like wings—and they seemed not to belong to the main body of her jacket, since they weren't the same shade of purple. Her straw hat, which sprouted a clutch of mismatched feathers, had the squashed appearance of something recently peeled off a busy road.

Birdie stood for a moment, rooted to the spot, with her mouth hanging open. But then one of the sailors darted forward to tug at the torn veil that dangled from Miss Eames's hat.

"Oi! You leave her be!" Enraged, Birdie rushed to defend the poor lady, dodging a bemused customs-house officer who had stopped to stare at the loud and drunken gang cluttering up the street.

"My cruel parents are being too unkind; they drive and punish me and trouble my mind . . ."

"Oh, Birdie," Miss Eames whimpered. Everything about her was disheveled—her clothes, her hair, the contents of her basket. "They've been following me and I don't know why . . ."

"Well, they'll follow you no farther!" Stepping between Miss Eames and the gang, Birdie put her hands on her hips and cried, "All o' you, go back to yer mumping and yer shirking and let us honest citizens alone!"

"Oh ho!" The largest porter peered down at Birdie, swaying a little, as the song sputtered and died around him. "What's this? Another lunatic?"

"You'd best turn tail or you'll be sorry!" When a burst of raucous laughter greeted this warning, Birdie went on to announce, "I'm 'prenticed to a Go-Devil Man, and he's down there now, on the water! With his bag on his back!"

The two sailors immediately crossed themselves, retreating a few steps. The most sinister-looking member of the gang muttered a curse and slunk away. Only a couple of faces didn't fall. They belonged to a very large porter with an oversize head, and a very drunk lout in a blue neckerchief, who was having a hard time keeping his balance.

"A Go-Devil Man?" the porter brayed. "Then bring him here, and I'll tell 'im to go to the devil!"

"Hsst." His cannier friend prodded him in the ribs. "Careful, matey. Ain't no sense in turning one o' *them* coves against'ee."

"Or he'll open his sack!" Birdie threatened. Then she

turned on her heel and grabbed Miss Eames, who was hovering nearby, looking dumbfounded.

Ned was also within easy reach. It pleased Birdie that he had followed her. "Ain't one o' them lags worth fretting over," she informed him as she led Miss Eames to safety. "But thanks for standing by me, Ned. I'll not forget it."

Ned flushed again. He flicked a doubtful glance at Miss Eames, who said, "Oh, Birdie! I'm so sorry! But I assure you, I never uttered a *word*—"

"You didn't have to. Them clothes was all it took." Studying the crumpled brim of Miss Eames's hat, Birdie had to suppress a smile. "Why'd you dress so glocky, miss? You look like a half-wit."

Startled, Miss Eames peered down at herself. "I was assured that this ensemble would pass muster in the lowest dens," she faltered.

"The lowest dens of Bedlam, perhaps!" Birdie gave a snort. "Whoever told you that was a dirty liar."

"It was a Houndsditch woman," Miss Eames confessed. "A dealer in old clothes."

"Well, miss, it seems like you was the answer to all her prayers," said Birdie. "I'll lay you a shilling that she sold you all the slops she couldn't unload—and charged you double for 'em." Stopping abruptly at the edge of the wharf, Birdie added, "But don't fret. Ain't no one'll trouble you now you're with a bogler's girl."

"Oh dear." Miss Eames was dabbing at her flushed face with a cotton handkerchief. "How dreadful this is! And how sorry I am! You shouldn't be called upon to defend *any*one, not at your age. It shouldn't have happened. Forgive me."

Birdie shrugged. Then she pointed at Alfred, who was down on the mud flats, in front of the drain. "There's Mr. Bunce," she said, "and that's the bogle's lair. You can watch from up here, until Mr. Bunce tells you different." Glancing at Ned, she explained, "If there's too much bustle and chatter, the bogle won't come."

"But what is Mr. Bunce *doing?*" Miss Eames demanded. Ned was also looking puzzled, and even Birdie had to think for a moment when she saw that Alfred was arranging long strips of rag on the ground.

"It's for the salt," she finally declared. "So it'll not get wet from all that mud."

"The salt?" echoed Miss Eames.

"Mr. Bunce always draws a circle of salt," said Birdie. "To trap the bogle in."

"Like a pentagram, you mean?" Miss Eames began to rifle through the contents of her basket as Birdie frowned, unable to answer because she didn't know what a "pentagram" was. "Or perhaps an evocation circle," Miss Eames continued. "Like those used in demonic summoning. Can Mr. Bunce read, by any chance?"

"No."

"I thought not. And yet he is using techniques derived from ancient texts! How *very* interesting!" By this time Miss Eames had extracted a book and pencil from the clutter in her basket. She pushed the basket's handle up over her elbow and began to take notes. "What else does he use, dear? Herbs?"

"No."

"Holy water?"

"A little," Birdie said reluctantly. She didn't know if Alfred wanted her spilling all his secrets.

"Does he bathe beforehand?" Seeing Birdie blink, Miss Eames hastily elaborated. "It needn't be in water. He might use sweet oil, perhaps. Or smoke."

"Smoke?" For the first time, Ned spoke up without prompting. He was staring at Miss Eames as if he'd decided that she really *was* a madwoman.

"Alfred don't hold with baths," Birdie said. She was about to remark that oil was better if burned or eaten when Alfred whistled softly.

It was the signal that she had been waiting for.

"I'm wanted," she informed Miss Eames. "You'd best stay here."

"Oh, but . . ." For a moment Miss Eames was lost for words. Then she rallied again. "It is so very *unwholesome* in that quagmire. Can Mr. Bunce not manage on his own?"

"Of course not!" Birdie almost grinned at the thought.

"Can you swim, though? How thick are your shoes?" Miss Eames kept up her barrage of objections, though she spoke in an undertone. "Look at all the sharp objects sticking out of the mud! What if you impale yourself on one of them?" Hearing Birdie laugh, Miss Eames spluttered, "I'm sure that Mr. Bunce is quite capable of making all the necessary preparations, Birdie!"

"Aye. He is," Birdie agreed. "But he can't bait the trap."

And she went to demonstrate how important she really was.

8

THE SEWER BOGLE

"Keep yer wits about you," Alfred murmured. "For I'm not easy in me mind, on account o' the breeze."

Birdie gave a nod. Though Alfred had used heavy bits of junk to weigh down his ring of rags, a strong gust of wind could easily ruffle it. And if that happened, the salt circle might be broken—in more than one place.

"Bill says as how the wind'll not freshen, but he ain't no seafarer," Alfred continued quietly. "If we wait too long, and too much damp is in the air—"

"We might have to stop," Birdie finished. She knew that their salt had to remain perfectly pure, unadulterated by water or dust or anything else that might weaken its magical properties.

"A strong wind will carry yer voice away, as well as the salt. I told Bill that, but he'd not hear o' waiting." With a glance at the three faces hanging above him, Alfred added in an undertone, "I warned him it'd cost another sixpence to bring us back tomorrow. He never so much as blinked."

By this time Birdie was looking at the muddy patch in the center of the circle. "No shoes for me," she said. "I'll move quicker in this bog without shoes."

"But not so quick that you'll slip and fall," Alfred warned her. "And you should raise those skirts, lass. We mustn't take no chances."

It was good advice. Birdie didn't want her trailing hem to brush against a fold of cloth and dislodge the salt. So she tucked her skirt up into her waistband and took off her shoes—which she then gave to Miss Eames, at the top of the stairs.

"I'd not leave me shoes alone for one minute," Birdie announced. "The rats'd take 'em, if no one else did."

"But what are you *doing?*" Miss Eames demanded in a voice that was much too loud.

Birdie put a finger to her lips. "I'm the bait," she muttered in reply. "I'll draw the bogle into our trap." As Miss Eames blinked and frowned, Birdie softly said to Bill Crabbe, "Mr. Bunce wants you down the street a portion,

Mr. Crabbe, on account o' your coughing will afright the bogle."

Bill scowled. "If ah cannot see thee work," he protested, "how will ah know tha'rt earning thy fee?"

"Because *I'll* be a-watching," Ned piped up. He turned to Birdie and asked, "How will you kill the bogle, once it's bin caught?"

"I'll not kill nothing," Birdie said. "It's Mr. Bunce does all that." She pointed to where Alfred was positioning himself near the sewer pipe, weapon in hand. "He has Finn MacCool's spear, see."

"Finn MacCool's spear?" Miss Eames's expression changed from mild distress to pure astonishment. "You mean the Poisonous Point that killed the fire-breathing Aillen at Tara, in the Irish legend?"

"Umm . . . yes. That's the one." Birdie had never heard of Aillen — or Tara. But she boldly laid claim to them anyway, having decided that Miss Eames probably knew more about ancient history than she did. "Ain't no other weapon in the world could kill a bogle like this'un."

"Must be worth a bob or two," Bill Crabbe remarked. Though there wasn't a trace of calculation in his tone, Birdie glared at him fiercely.

"That spear is poisoned," she hissed, "and needs an artful hand to ply it."

Bill sniffed. Then he turned on his heel and began to

trudge away, coughing as if he had a ball of glue lodged in his throat. Miss Eames, whose forehead was creased into lines of doubt and concern, suddenly said, "And where will *you* be placed, Birdie? In the center of that circle?"

"Yes."

"With your back to the bogle's lair?"

Birdie was surprised. "Yes," she said again, wondering how Miss Eames had worked *that* out.

"So you never even see any bogles?" Before Birdie could explain that she always used a little mirror, Miss Eames continued. "This all seems rather dangerous, dear, even if . . . well . . ." Miss Eames paused for a moment, catching herself on a thought that she apparently didn't want to share. Then she changed tack. "You must get very frightened, at times like this."

"Frightened?" Birdie drew herself up to her full height. "I ain't *never* frightened!"

"Yes, but—"

"I'm a bogler's girl!"

"But a very young one, still. A child of your age—what are you, eight years old? To use an eight-year-old child as bait for a monster—"

"I'm ten!" Birdie snapped.

"Ten?" From the shock in Miss Eames's voice, it was clear that she had been misled by Birdie's delicate bones and small stature. Birdie understood this at once.

"I may be little," she retorted, "but I'm quick and I'm strong! Ain't no bogle never got the better o' me!"

By now Alfred was beckoning to her furiously, so she scampered back downstairs before Miss Eames could delay her with further questions. Though she *was* feeling a little scared, Birdie had no intention of showing it. Despite the fact that she had to pick her way barefoot through an obstacle course of half-submerged splinters, she managed to toss a carefree grin at her audience. And as she removed her little hand mirror from its pocket, she used it to tease Ned, flashing sunlight into his eyes so that he had to shield them from the glare.

Now that she was close to it, the sewer pipe looked bigger than she had expected. It was nearly as tall as she was, and darker than a chimney. But she turned her back on it without a moment's hesitation, keeping her chin up and her shoulders back. Then, mindful of the doubts expressed by Miss Eames, she chose a song as brave as a war cry.

> *"Silvy, Silvy, all on one day,*
> *She dressed herself in man's array,*
> *A sword and pistol by her side.*
> *To meet her true love, away she did ride."*

Framed in her hand mirror, the pipe yawned like a great, wet mouth. Alfred lurked to one side of it, holding his salt and his spear. A trickle of muck had worn a channel down to the water, but this shallow ditch didn't pass through the magic circle. Alfred had been careful to place his trap to the east of the ditch, where no discharge would threaten his precious salt.

Conscious that she was being observed by at least four pairs of eyes, Birdie tried to concentrate on the ones that weren't human. She watched for a glint in the darkness behind her as she sang.

> *"And as she were riding over the plain,*
> *She met her true love and bid him stand.*
> *'Your gold and silver, kind sir,' she said,*
> *'Or else this moment your life I'll have.'"*

Still nothing stirred in the depths of the pipe. The sun beat down. The water slapped and gurgled. The boats and barges plowed past Birdie in both directions, while distant masts swayed gently, like treetops. But Birdie didn't even glance up from her mirror. She stood shifting from foot to foot, making sure to loosen the mud that was sucking at their soles.

Though she could feel an intermittent breeze grazing her cheek, she tried not to worry that it was carrying her voice in the wrong direction. She could hear enough of the hobblers' shouts and ships' bells to know that somewhere in the sewer, hidden away like a snake in a burrow, the bogle must be listening to snatches of her song, even if it couldn't make out every word.

> *"Oh, when she'd robbed him of all his store,*
> *She says, 'Kind sir, there's one thing more,*
> *A golden ring, which I know you have;*
> *Deliver it, your sweet life to save.'"*

There was a stench in the air, as fitful as the breeze. At first it made Birdie anxious. She knew that bogles often stank like a tanner's privy, and she was filled with dread every time the horrible stink assaulted her nostrils. Gradually, however, she realized that the river itself was what smelled so bad. Its evil breath was almost choking her.

But still she managed to sing.

> *"'The golden ring a token is;*
> *My life I'll lose, the ring I'll save!'*
> *Being tenderhearted just like a dove,*
> *She rode away from her true love."*

Birdie was trying not to worry about the river in front of her, even though she couldn't swim. Then, as she paused to draw breath, she noticed something. The muck dribbling out of the pipe was changing color, from greenish brown to pitch-black.

She tensed every muscle, struggling to keep her voice steady.

> *"Next morning in the garden green*
> *Just like true lovers they was seen.*
> *He spied his watch hanging by her clothes,*
> *Which made him blush just like a rose."*

The black tide of sewage was like a carpet unrolling in front of the bogle, which started to emerge from the pipe very slowly and haltingly. It was as if a huge wad of sludge and hair had been dislodged from the sewers, and was now oozing its way down to the Thames, pushed along by a trickle of foul water. Only as it approached Birdie did the big, formless dollop begin to unfurl, sprouting limbs like tentacles.

Birdie, however, stood fast and kept singing—even when she heard someone shriek in the distance.

> *"'What makes you blush, you silly thing?*
> *I thought to have had yer golden ring!*
> *'Twas I as robbed you on the plain*
> *So here's your watch and gold again!'"*

Birdie had learned to keep her eyes firmly fixed on Alfred, so she didn't really get a good look at the thing that was creeping toward her. She saw that it was black, with half a dozen limbs, but she couldn't tell if it was furred or scaly, thanks to the thick layer of slime that coated its misshapen form. It moved as silently as a snail, while Alfred remained motionless.

Come on, she thought. *What are you waiting for?* Then she realized that the bogle still hadn't entered their trap, though its long arms were already reaching for her. And she suddenly wondered: Just how long *were* those arms? Were they long enough to pull her out of the magic circle?

She had to swallow before launching into the next verse.

> "*I did intend and it was to know*
> *If you was me one true love, or no.*
> *For if you'd gave me that ring,' she said,*
> *'I'd have pulled the trigger and shot—'*"

"Now!" Alfred cried, lunging. Birdie broke off. She jumped out of the circle and bolted.

By the time she felt safe enough to look back, the bogle was already dead.

It was melting into the mud like fat in a pan. As the hummock of black slime sank lower and lower, its edges expanded, swamping the ring of salt and forming little pools of stuff that reminded Birdie of creosote, or coal tar. Some of this oily liquid soaked into the ground. Some of it poured down the sewer channel into the river.

Within half a minute there was nothing left of the bogle except a black stain, a faint sizzling noise, and a lingering smell of burnt rubber and rotten eggs.

"Oi! Bunce! Are you finished?" Ned shouted. "For yer friend is taken bad up here!"

Startled, Birdie glanced toward the quayside—where Miss Eames had fainted dead away.

9

THE SCIENTIFIC APPROACH

It was real!" Miss Eames squawked the instant she woke up again. "The monster! It exists!"

She was lying on the ground next to her overturned basket. Her head was pillowed in Ned's lap. Though her hat had fallen off, Ned had picked it up and was fanning her with it.

Birdie knelt close by, collecting all the coins and books and handkerchiefs that had spilled out onto the pavement.

"That's right, miss," she said, then called to Alfred, who was still gathering up his equipment. "You got any brandy, Mr. Bunce?"

"*I* got gin," Bill offered. He had rushed to help Miss Eames. "It's for my cough, like."

"You can't give gin to a *lady*," Birdie growled.

But Miss Eames was already struggling to sit up. Raising her head, she croaked, "I saw it! I saw the beast!"

"Yes, but it's dead now, miss," Birdie assured her soothingly, before rounding on all the strangers who had gathered to stare. "Ain't you got nothing better to do than gawp like dead fish, you pack o' shirksters?"

"It was *there!* It was *real!*" Miss Eames quavered. "I never thought — I didn't believe — oh, Birdie, how *dreadful!*"

"Here." Alfred had reached her side at long last and was trying to thrust his flask of brandy under her nose. "Take a sip o' this, why don't you?"

"No, no." She waved it aside as she struggled to her feet. "I'm perfectly well. It was the shock. *Please* don't make a fuss."

"Got any smelling salts on you, miss?" said Birdie. "Only I can't find none in yer basket."

"Birdie, I have never fainted before in my life," Miss Eames declared. Though her voice was still wobbly, it was gaining strength. She was also standing on her own two feet again — with Bill Crabbe's assistance. "I don't carry smelling salts because I don't generally require them."

"Is there a respectable place hereabouts where she can

lie?" Alfred asked Bill, who frowned and said, "Not that ah know of. The Jolly Tar's a lushery if ever there was one."

"We can't take her to a public house." Alfred directed a baleful look at the dock laborers and watermen hovering in their vicinity. "Not around here."

"I am *perfectly well*," Miss Eames insisted. "All I need to do is sit on that step for a few minutes." She lurched toward the stone stairs that led down to the river, shaking off Bill Crabbe as she retrieved her hat. Birdie followed her. While Alfred buttonholed the tosher, demanding his fee, Birdie joined Miss Eames on the top step, settling down beside her with the basket and a couple of shrewd questions.

"Did you not believe us, miss? Did you think me and Mr. Bunce was running a racket?"

"Oh, no, Birdie, not *you*," Miss Eames replied. "I know you're an honest girl, and a brave one."

"But you thought he were flamming me," Birdie insisted. "Ain't that so?"

Miss Eames shook her head. "Not exactly," she said, reaching for her handkerchief. "Mr. Bunce has a living to make. I never doubted his beliefs. I simply wondered if he might be exaggerating his own abilities . . ." She broke off, then wiped her eyes and blew her nose. "Oh dear, oh dear, what a frightful thing. Remarkable, of course — quite extraordinary — but how horrible, all the same!"

Birdie shrugged. "Ain't no shortage o' vermin in this world. And I'd rather be a bogler than a rat catcher."

"But it's so *dangerous*, Birdie. So *unsuitable* for a child your age!"

Birdie couldn't help laughing. "I'd rather kill bogles than get black lung in a mine. I'd rather be a bogler's girl than work in a match factory and have me jaw eaten away by acid. Or get stuck in a chimney, or drowned in a sewer, or chopped up by a machine—"

"Yes, I understand that there are many children who must do perilous things to earn their keep," Miss Eames acknowledged. "It is a sad fact of life. But surely there must be another way of luring bogles out of their burrows?"

"No." Birdie was adamant. "Bogles eat children. *All* bogles do. Ain't nothing else they like so much."

Miss Eames opened her mouth, then broke off as she spied Alfred shuffling toward them, pocketing his fee. "Mr. Bunce, have you ever thought of approaching your job in a more scientific manner?" she asked him.

He frowned. "Beg pardon, miss?"

"It seems to me that you are putting Birdie's life at risk. Have you considered that there might be other ways of killing bogles?"

Alfred didn't reply. He just stared at her suspiciously. So Miss Eames went on.

"If you knew more about the monsters themselves, you

might be able to kill them more efficiently. The ancient texts tell us that different creatures respond differently to different things. For example, the basilisk is killed by the smell of a weasel. And Finn MacCool himself discovered that an Irish buggane cannot touch water." When Alfred's expression didn't change, Miss Eames began to sound a little impatient. "Do you not see the point I am making, Mr. Bunce? If you were to tell me all the characteristics of a particular bogle, I could perhaps find out what its habits and weaknesses are. Then, if it has a documented taste for gold, or sheep, or something other than children, Birdie wouldn't have to risk death every time she went to work with you."

Birdie couldn't believe her ears. *"Gold?"* she spluttered. *"Sheep?"*

"If you've a purse full o' gold or a spare sheep about you, miss, I'd be happy to take it off yer hands," Alfred remarked, with a gruff attempt at humor. "For now I'll be satisfied with the payment you promised. Two shillings, it was. After the shilling paid in advance."

"Yes, of course." Miss Eames drew her basket onto her lap and began to rifle through it, while Birdie sat and grinned. A sheep, of all things! Maybe Miss Eames wasn't as clever as she looked.

"You should learn to think like a naturalist, Mr. Bunce," Miss Eames continued. "A grindylow is a freshwater monster, so it may differ in its tastes from a saltwater monster like the French Tarasque, or the Irish Formori. And these differences may prove to be very important when you're dealing with it."

Alfred, however, was shaking his head. "A bogle is a bogle," he insisted. "And a child is allus going to lure it into plain sight."

"I see." Miss Eames paused in the act of searching through her basket. She squinted up at Alfred, her lips pursed. "So it doesn't trouble you that one day poor Birdie might be consumed by one of these awful things?"

"No. It don't," Alfred replied shortly. "Birdie won't *never* fall to a bogle. She's fast and she's smart. Which is why I picked her out and trained her up."

"I'll be all right," Birdie promised Miss Eames in a sympathetic yet cheerful voice. "It's a good living, and a respectable one."

"Yes, but—"

"No one ever taunts a bogler's girl, any more'n they'd taunt a bogle. Why, I'm safer than *you* are, miss!"

"Providing that you don't trip and fall on your way out of the pentagram," Miss Eames rejoined. Then she reached up, pressed two shillings into Alfred's open hand, and said, "At least allow me to do some research for your next job. Where will it be, do you know?"

Alfred hesitated.

"I'll pay you another three shillings to attend," Miss Eames said encouragingly. "Sixpence in advance."

At the mention of payment, Alfred buckled. "It's at the spike," he confessed. "In Hackney."

Miss Eames looked confused. "The spike?" she echoed.

"Where the paupers and old'uns go, instead o' starving," Alfred explained. "*You* know. They feed 'em there, and give 'em beds."

"The workhouse," Birdie supplied with a shiver. The very word put a knot in her guts.

"Oh!" Miss Eames was nodding. "The Poor Law Union! I understand."

"There's four children gone from Hackney spike," Alfred told her. "The master claims they legged it, but others blame a bogle in the workhouse well on account o' the stink. And since most of 'em is too poor to stump up for a bogler, it's the night porter and the cook as decided to fork out."

Birdie winced. She herself had mentioned the workhouse job to Alfred, who had then made arrangements with George Hobney, the night porter. But she hadn't said a word about Jem Barbary's cruel little trick, or the threat it implied. Had she done so, Alfred might have turned down a perfectly good moneymaking opportunity—and he couldn't afford to do that.

Still, she didn't like concealing things from Alfred. Nor

was she thrilled about doing business with one of Sarah's cronies. Though George Hobney might be a decent enough man, there was always the other possibility . . .

"Has anyone actually seen this mysterious creature?" Miss Eames was asking. When Alfred gave a nod, she said, "What does it look like? Do you know?"

Alfred shrugged. "A shadow in the dark. A glimpse is all they ever got."

"When are you due at the workhouse?"

It was Birdie who answered. "Saturday sunset."

"I'll be there." Miss Eames stood up. "In the meantime, I shall see if I can identify our quarry. We already know that it's a freshwater monster with a nocturnal habit. The rank smell may also be important."

"Lots o' bogles stink," Birdie pointed out. She, too, had risen. "Ain't nothing special about *that*."

"Nevertheless, it's worth noting." Miss Eames straightened her hat as she glanced around. "Can you direct me to the nearest omnibus from here? I must confess that I'm a little lost . . ."

"You shouldn't be catching no bus," Alfred mumbled. He turned, then scowled. "Where's Bill?" he asked Ned.

"Bill's gone." Ned jerked his chin at the tosher's retreating back.

Like the rest of the dispersing crowd, Bill had long ago

lost interest in Miss Eames — who sighed irritably and said, "I assure you, I shall be perfectly all right."

"Not in them togs, you won't," Birdie retorted. To Ned she observed, "There must be a place hereabouts where you can catch a cab on the fly, like."

Ned pondered for a moment. "There's the wine vaults. And the Queen's warehouse," he finally suggested, in his husky voice. "I seen toffs a-plenty come and go 'round there, in every kind o' carriage."

"Then perhaps you could show me the way?" Miss Eames proposed, scrabbling around in her basket. When she pulled out a penny tip, Ned was quick to accept it.

"That I can," he said. "Stay close, now."

But as they all set off, it was Alfred who helped Miss Eames to wend her way between the piles of rubbish and puddles of brine. Because Ned had offered his arm to Birdie.

10

Bogle Spit

Birdie sat on her little stool, darning a sock and thinking about Miss Eames.

In many ways she admired Miss Eames, who spoke nicely and dressed well. Birdie had even thought her clever, at first, though not so much anymore. Imagine believing that you could kill a bogle by waving a weasel under its nose! Birdie couldn't help smiling when she remembered the weasel. As for the suggestion that Alfred should use gold as bogle bait ... well, that was just absurd. A purse full of gold couldn't move out of harm's way. And what would happen if the bogle swallowed it?

On the other hand, Miss Eames wasn't a *complete*

fool. What she lacked in common sense, she made up for in book learning. She knew all about Finn MacCool, and could probably name every bogle he'd ever fought. She'd mentioned an Irish bogle and a French bogle; she'd talked of grindylows and basilisks. Birdie had no idea what any of these things were, but Miss Eames did. And the more Birdie thought about it, the more worried she became.

There could be no doubt that Miss Eames had hit upon a clever notion, despite all her silly talk about sheep and weasels. What if her books *were* full of scientific advice about bogles and their habits? What if she went away and learned how to distinguish between one type of bogle and another?

What if she discovered that the best bait for some bogles might be roast goose, or a human skull? Where would that leave Birdie?

I'd have no living to make, she realized. *Alfred wouldn't need no 'prentice and would cast me onto the street.*

She shot a worried glance at Alfred, who sat hunched in front of the empty grate, smoking his pipe. Though he seemed no different, Birdie wondered what was going through his head. Perhaps he, too, was anxious about Miss Eames. Perhaps he was concerned that she would figure out how to kill bogles with songs or herbs or charms. Hadn't she spoken of a bogle that couldn't touch water?

"Will you let Miss Eames watch us again, after

Saturday?" Birdie said to Alfred. He didn't reply, so she tried again. "Mebbe you should charge more next time." When he remained silent, puffing away, she added, "Five shillings?"

Alfred removed the pipe from his mouth and cleared his throat. "If I ask too much, I'll scare her off," he growled.

Birdie was about to observe that getting rid of Miss Eames might be a *good* thing when someone knocked at the door. Alfred grimaced. Birdie glanced at him inquiringly, but he shook his head.

"Who is it?" said Birdie, raising her voice.

"Why, it's Sally Pickles. Is Fred Bunce there?"

Birdie froze. It was Alfred who answered.

"What do you want, Sal? I already told you, I ain't got yer boys."

"And I believe you, Fred," Sarah replied. "For I think I know where to find 'em."

Even Alfred seemed startled to hear this. After a moment's hesitation he nodded at Birdie, who stood up and went reluctantly to the door.

This time Sarah was wearing a straw hat instead of her coal-scuttle bonnet. And she was accompanied not by her son but by a tiny, bent old man in rusty black knee breeches. Birdie knew him, though not very well. His name was Elijah Froggett, and he was a caffler, or rag-and-bone man. Birdie had often heard him calling "Ol' cloes! Ol' cloes!" as he wheeled his little cart full of scraps and tatters along the street. He was memorable because he had a long, stringy beard like a piece of frayed rope, and because he had never been known to remove his velvet smoking cap. His nose and fingers were stained brown from years of taking snuff. He wore fingerless gloves, a trailing oilskin coat, and knitted stockings.

Under his arm was a well-stuffed drawstring bag.

"I expect you're acquainted with Mr. Froggett," Sarah remarked as she waddled over to Birdie's stool. Alfred politely inclined his head, though he didn't get up. Birdie, who was taken aback, offered the caffler an uncertain smile. She hadn't known that Sarah Pickles and Elijah Froggett were friends.

"Show 'em what you found, m'dear. Just lay it all out," Sarah told the caffler, who grunted. While he was emptying his bag onto the table, she addressed Alfred in her harsh, flat voice. "Mr. Froggett knows every one o' me boys—by sight, if not by name. Ain't that so, Mr. Froggett?"

Elijah grunted again.

"Which is why, when he bought a bundle o' rags off a muck snipe and reckonized every article, he were downy enough to get more particulars afore he came to me." Watching the caffler as he carefully spread the remains of a striped shirt across the tabletop, Sarah explained, "That shirt belonged to Sam. So did the weskit. The coat were

Nolly's, and the wipe didn't once leave Abel's neck. Them boys might still be missing, but their clothes is found."

"Who found 'em?" Birdie couldn't help asking, in a hushed tone.

Sarah hadn't taken her eyes off the striped shirt. There was a sour look on her lumpy face. "A muck snipe, like I told you. A tramp. A moocher. He said as how he found 'em at the back of a big house, on a rubbish heap. Near a privy."

"In Clerkenwell," Elijah interposed. His voice was creaky and breathless.

"Take a look at 'em, Fred, and tell me what you think," Sarah went on. "Then I'll tell you what *I* think, which ain't pretty, I warn you."

Alfred approached the display of rags, with Birdie close on his heels. Together they inspected thirteen items, all child-size, all smudged, and all covered in a thick layer of greenish slime.

"It's likely them black marks is where someone tried to burn the clothes but couldn't," Sarah observed.

"What's this?" Alfred gingerly touched the gooey green stuff, which clung to his finger like glue. Then he sniffed it and winced. "It don't smell too good."

He was right. It didn't. Though faint, the smell had an ominous quality—like a whiff of corruption carried on a light breeze.

Birdie stepped away from the table, suddenly feeling sick.

"Well, now, Fred, I'm sorry to hear you say that. For I were a-hoping you might know what happens when a bogle eats a boy." As Alfred and Birdie gazed at Sarah with horrified expressions, she said, "See that weskit? I washed that, this morning, in soap and water. You'd never know to look at it, would you?"

Birdie turned her attention to the vest, which had once been quite a handsome garment, made of plum-colored silk. Like the rest of the clothes, it was stained black and coated with slime.

"Whatever that stuff is, it won't be cleaned off. Or burned up. Which is why I've come to think it might be the devil's work." Sarah leaned forward, fixing her eyes on Alfred's face. "If a bogle ate them boys," she said, "and coughed up their dunnage like we'd cough up a nutshell, would its spit be rank and green?"

"That I can't tell you," Alfred gravely replied.

"But you're a bogler!" Sarah snapped. "You *must* know!"

"I only once lost a child to a bogle," Alfred retorted, "and that bogle didn't live long enough to cough up *nowt*. I killed it straight after."

Birdie swallowed. She didn't like to hear Alfred talk

about his third apprentice, whose name had been Henry. Jack had gone to sea, Patrick had returned to Ireland, Tom was working on the railways, and Adolphus had been gaoled for theft. But Henry had fallen to a bogle—and Alfred preferred not to discuss it.

Sarah narrowed her eyes. "Well, well," she murmured. "Now *that* ain't summat I ever knowed." And she glanced at Birdie.

"One thing I can tell you is this," Alfred continued. "If a bogle coughed up them rags, then it's living in the rubbish heap where they was found. Either that, or someone moved 'em there. For no bogle would shift clothes from place to place."

"Mmmph." Sarah nodded in a meditative fashion. "This feller as found 'em—he's one o' them coves they call 'skippers.' He sleeps in sheds and privies and the like. So one night he climbed over a locked gate and saw them rags piled up against the privy wall." After studying Alfred for a moment, Sarah said evenly, "Seems to me, if they was moved, they must have come from inside the house."

"Or inside the privy," Birdie piped up. Bogles were like rats; they favored old privies and earth closets. Birdie had helped to kill at least three privy bogles during her career as a bogler's girl. "Mebbe that's where it lives."

"But the skipper said as how he slept all night in that

privy and weren't troubled, save by rats," Elijah unexpectedly volunteered.

Alfred frowned. "Is he a child, this moocher?"

"No," said the old man.

"Then he'd be safe from most bogles. It's kids they like."

Sarah pondered this for a moment as Elijah began to push the garments, one by one, back into his bag. Birdie watched Alfred, wondering what he was going to do next. She had to admit that it all sounded very odd. On the one hand, she and Alfred had never before encountered anything that resembled bogle leavings. On the other hand, killing bogles often *did* involve a lot of slime and stench — even though these traces tended to vanish pretty quickly once the creature had died.

Birdie tried to imagine a bogle coughing up the silk vest and striped shirt, but her blood turned cold at the thought of it. So she decided to concentrate on what Sarah was saying instead.

"I told you how Nolly were snatched by someone as looked like police," Sarah reminded Alfred. "Now his coat turns up in someone's garden. Could it be the same someone, I ask meself?"

"Perhaps," Alfred agreed cautiously.

"And could that someone be feeding a pet bogle?"

Birdie gasped. Elijah grunted. Alfred sniffed and said, "No."

"Why not?" asked Sarah.

"Because bogles ain't canaries," Alfred rejoined. "I'd sooner keep a bear."

"Bears can be taught to dance," Sarah pointed out.

"Aye. That's why I'd sooner keep one." Alfred shook his head wearily. "I couldn't catch a bogle, Sal. Not without killing it. No one could."

"We'll see." She stood up. "If I was to have that house watched, now, what would the boys be looking for? Aside from a lurker dressed like police."

Alfred shrugged.

"Smoke? Smells? Green lights?" she pressed.

"I don't know, Sal."

"Salt, mebbe," Birdie suggested, before she could stop herself. She then cringed as Sarah's flinty gaze swiveled toward her.

"Salt?" Sarah echoed.

"By the barrel."

Sarah nodded, as if well satisfied with this contribution. To Alfred she said, "I'll not rest till I've an answer, and I know you feel the same. If I was to ask for more help, you'd not be charging me for it, would you, Fred?"

Alfred heaved a sigh. "No, Sal," he muttered. "I

wouldn't take no chink from you." Though he didn't say as much, Birdie knew that he wouldn't dare.

A smile cracked across Sarah's face. "You're a fine feller, m'dear, and straight as they come," she declared. "Rest assured, one day I'll return the favor."

Then she blew a kiss at Birdie, tucked her arm through Elijah's, and shuffled out the door.

After she'd gone, Birdie said, "Mebbe them boys did get lagged. Mebbe they was caught thieving and put in a lockup, and it's a lockup with a bogle inside."

"That don't explain the clothes," Alfred replied brusquely.

"Unless someone working at the lockup lives in that house." Birdie was thinking hard. "A trap or a jack or a beak—"

"Stow it, Birdie." Alfred swung around on his stool so that he was once more facing the fireplace. "Ain't nothing to do with us."

And he refused to discuss the matter again that day.

THE SPIKE

George Hobney introduced himself in a hushed voice as he admitted Alfred and Birdie into the Hackney workhouse. At first sight he looked like a typical night porter, gruff and burly, with a square jaw, a straight back, and a solid frame. But close up, Birdie could see that Sarah Pickles had left her mark on George Hobney—or was it the bogle making him so anxious? His mouth kept twitching. His small eyes jumped around nervously as he ushered his guests through the lobby of the main administrative block, which was a three-story brick building with windows set so high that Birdie couldn't see out of them.

She and Alfred had already spent several minutes trying to find the right entrance. The workhouse itself was a large collection of buildings, ringed by high walls and spread across several acres of land. In the dusky half light, among a tangle of unfamiliar, mean little streets, it had been hard not to get lost.

"The master don't know nothing o' this," George murmured, "so mind you keep quiet." He went on to explain (very softly) that the master was upstairs in his quarters, and that almost everyone else had gone to bed. "But Mrs. Gudge is in the kitchen. It's down that passage, third door on the left."

"Who's Mrs. Gudge?" asked Alfred.

"She's the cook. She'll show you where Fanny saw the . . . um . . ." George hesitated, rubbing his small, neat, gingery mustache. "That thing," he finished, grimacing.

"It's fivepence in advance," Alfred said flatly. "And a penny for the salt."

While George fished around in his pocket, Birdie eyed her gloomy surroundings. The entrance hall in which they stood had whitewashed walls and no furniture. A dark flight of stairs vanished into the shadowy realm above her head. An invisible clock ticked somewhere close by.

"There's a lady coming to join us," Alfred observed. "Name of Eames."

"She's already here." George handed over six pennies. "In the kitchen, with Mrs. Gudge."

So Alfred and Birdie made for the kitchen, leaving George at his post. The kitchen door was standing open, unlike most of the others that Birdie passed on her way down the passage; all Alfred had to do was steer toward the strip of light that lay across the floor ahead of him. Sure enough, when he reached the door through which the light was spilling, he met a woman on the threshold. She was tall and gangly, all elbows and neck, with untidy hair and a scarred face. Her dress looked like a brown paper bag tied around the middle with string.

"Oh!" she yipped. "Is that—are you—?"

"I'm Alfred Bunce."

"And I'm Birdie." Peering past Mrs. Gudge, Birdie saw that Edith Eames was sitting near the kitchen hearth, which was huge and sooty and cavernous. In her subdued gray outfit, complete with kid gloves and a small felt hat, Miss Eames cut a far more respectable figure than she had at her last meeting with Birdie.

"Hello, Birdie," she said. "Hello, Mr. Bunce."

"Hello, miss," Birdie replied warily as Alfred set down his sack.

"I have been talking to Mrs. Gudge about the bogle," Miss Eames went on, her eyes sparkling, her expression keen, "and everything she said confirms me in my opinion.

I believe the creature in question is either a knucker or a hobyah."

Alfred and Birdie exchanged glances.

"Oh, aye?" Alfred muttered.

"According to my research, knuckers are water spirits known for attacking livestock, as well as people. They live in 'knucker holes,' and are native to Sussex. I have been unable to determine whether they prefer hunting at night or during the day." Miss Eames spoke rapidly, as if she sensed that Alfred and Birdie weren't very interested in what she had to offer. "Hobyahs, on the other hand, are nocturnal in their habits. They are from farther north and eat children, though I'm not sure if they attack livestock. I also don't know where they usually live."

"Aye. Well. That's very interesting," Alfred remarked. "But—"

"What I *have* found out," Miss Eames quickly added, without letting him finish, "is how each of these creatures has been captured and killed. And in *neither case*, Mr. Bunce, was a little girl used as a lure."

Birdie scowled. Once again her livelihood was being threatened. Before she could protest, however, Miss Eames continued.

"According to tradition, the knucker at Lyminster was killed by a huge poisoned pie, which was left beside its knucker hole. Then its head was cut off. The hobyahs, on the other hand, are vulnerable to dogs. They have been known to fall victim to large dogs, and to flee from the sound of barking." Miss Eames suddenly addressed the cook. "Is there a workhouse dog, Mrs. Gudge?"

"Ah . . . no." Mrs. Gudge was looking flustered. She kept wiping her bony hands on her apron. "We've a lot o' chickens, see."

Miss Eames shot a triumphant glance at Alfred, who was growing more and more irritable.

"We ain't got all night," he said gruffly. "Birdie'll tire if we don't start soon."

"Yes, but I wanted to tell you that I have brought a pie with me," announced Miss Eames. Stooping to pick up a basket from the floor beside her, she explained, "Though it's not a *poisoned* pie, I thought we might use it to test my theory about alternative baits for your trap."

Birdie could restrain herself no longer.

"You want to put a *pie* in my place?" she squawked, flushing bright red. "You think a *pie* will draw a bogle out of its lair?"

"It's freshly baked," said Miss Eames. And as she flipped back the linen towel that covered her basket, a heavenly aroma filled the kitchen.

Even Alfred seemed impressed.

"That smell's enough to raise the dead," he admitted,

"but I don't know as how a bogle's got the same appetite we do . . ."

"I'll pay you two more shillings," Miss Eames blurted out. "A crown in total. Would that be fair?"

Birdie glared at Alfred, who removed his hat, ran a hand through his hair, and said hesitantly, "Aye. That would be fair, on account o' the risk."

"It's too *big* a risk!" Birdie objected, so loudly that Mrs. Gudge winced and peered anxiously at the smoke-blackened ceiling.

"Shhh! Someone might hear you upstairs!" the cook warned.

Obediently Birdie lowered her voice. "You kill bogles the way boglers always have done, and it works every time!" she hissed at Alfred. "Why change now?"

"Because the old way isn't necessarily the best way, Birdie," Miss Eames broke in. "Certainly not for you."

"It *is* the best way for me!" Birdie snapped. "What do *you* know? *You're* not a bogler!"

"Nevertheless, I believe that I can help Mr. Bunce shoulder his burden in a more *scientific* way—"

"Bogles ain't steam engines!" Birdie interrupted furiously. "Bogles ain't got nothing to do with science!"

"*Please* will you all stop shouting?" Mrs. Gudge begged. She sounded desperate. "You'll have to go if you don't!"

"Our apologies, ma'am." Rounding on Birdie, Alfred fixed her with a warning look, his bloodshot eyes hard and cool. "You shut yer mouth now, or I'll shut it for you."

Birdie subsided. But she sniffed and folded her arms, making it clear that she wasn't happy.

"Now, ma'am . . ." Alfred turned back to Mrs. Gudge. "Would you tell me more about this bogle in yer well?"

"I—I've not seen it," the cook stammered. "Someone else did."

"Where?" said Alfred.

Mrs. Gudge went on to relate that the four missing children had all left their beds late at night. Though the master was stubbornly insisting that they must have decamped from the workhouse, no one else believed it, because the children had been sick and on their way to the infirmary when they vanished.

"The master claims they was never *really* ill, but that ain't so, for how can you fake the flux?" Mrs. Gudge said in a high, breathless, troubled voice. "It's our belief—mine and Mr. Hobney's—that them children passed too close to the old well near the laundry. For that's where Fanny Tadgell saw the shape. And since the well's bin abandoned, it might harbor a shellycoat or some such thing."

"A shellycoat?" Miss Eames repeated with great interest. Then Alfred frowned at her, and she fell silent.

"How long has the well been abandoned?" Alfred asked Mrs. Gudge.

"Oh, for years. Since the new workhouse were built over the old, and that happened before my time." The cook's taut face relaxed a little as she dredged around in her memory. "They say the old cesspit fouled the well, or else some forgotten grave, but why blame a cesspit thirty years old? *I* say it's from the manufactory next door, which is where they boil up skin and bones to make gelatin—"

"Who's Fanny Tadgell?" Birdie interrupted, because she saw that Alfred was getting impatient.

"Fanny?" echoed the cook. "She's one o' the paupers as helps with the sick children. We ain't got more'n two paid nurses, but they're allus so busy with the old folk, there's mortal need for extra hands."

"And where *exactly* did Fanny see the bogle?" This time it was Alfred who cut her off. "How far from the old well?"

Mrs. Gudge seemed thrown by this question. "That I don't know. You'll have to ask her."

"Ask Fanny?" said Alfred. "Now?"

"She's in the infirmary. She took a late shift, in case she were needed." Hearing Alfred grunt, Mrs. Gudge remarked, "I'll not stay much longer meself, for they expect me back here early tomorrow, and how am I to cook all them breakfasts if I ain't slept?"

"But can you show us to the infirmary before you leave?" Miss Eames requested in a briskly confident manner that infuriated Birdie. "And perhaps introduce us to Fanny Tadgell?"

"Oh, I'll do *that,* miss. You cannot be left to wander about on yer own at night." Mrs. Gudge cast a worried glance around the kitchen, as if checking that every dish was washed and every flame extinguished. Then she picked up a glowing oil lamp, clumsily knocking against a shelf as she did so. "I'll take you to meet the girl," she said, "and when you're all done, Mr. Hobney will let you out." On her way to the door, she stopped suddenly and asked Alfred, "It'll not . . . There'll not be too much *noise,* I hope?"

Alfred shrugged. "Bogles ain't loud, as a rule," he replied. "Which is why they escape notice."

"Stealth is their greatest weapon," Miss Eames concurred—almost, Birdie thought crossly, as if she had a right to say anything.

Alfred pretended that he hadn't heard Miss Eames, even though his eyes flickered. "I'd not be surprised if the lass had to sing," he told the cook, much to Birdie's delight, "but she'll do it soft and wake no one."

"Oh dear." Mrs. Gudge sighed before throwing a feebly apologetic smile in Miss Eames's direction. "Could you see yer way to covering that pie, Miss Eames? A smell like that could wake the whole men's ward, never mind any bogle hereabouts."

"Of course," Miss Eames murmured, tucking the linen towel back over her pie.

Then she followed everyone else out the door, down the adjoining passage, and into the garden.

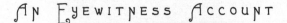

12

An Eyewitness Account

It was still damp outside. Though night had fallen, there was just enough light from Mrs. Gudge's lamp—and from one or two upper windows—to give Birdie a vague sense of how large the workhouse grounds were. The back door of the administrative block opened onto a very spacious garden, which was flanked by two three-story wings projecting from the rear of the main building. And though at first Birdie couldn't see what lay farther to the south, a few glimmers in the distance told her that *something* did.

"That's the men's ward to yer left, and the women's to yer right," Mrs. Gudge whispered. "Keep to the paths, or you'll trample on our carrots."

So it's a kitchen garden, Birdie thought, peering at a wide expanse of dim, feathery shapes. The shadow cast by a ragged scarecrow made her start, then shudder. She felt very uneasy. For as long as she could remember, the workhouse had loomed large in her nightmares. It was the fate that had threatened her since birth. One misstep—one stroke of bad luck—and she would be off to break stone in the workhouse. Birdie had heard all the workhouse stories and believed every one of them. She had heard that workhouse children were starved and flogged; that they were marched in straight lines like soldiers; that they labored from dawn till dusk.

She had always sworn to herself that she would rather die than set foot in a workhouse. And yet here she was.

"Birdie?" Miss Eames stooped to hiss in her ear. "Believe me, I don't want to make your life more difficult. On the contrary, I'm trying to improve it."

"Shhh!" Birdie refused to listen. There was a bogle nearby, so she had to stay strong. She had to forget that Miss Eames was plotting against her. One day, if Miss Eames was successful, Birdie might end up in a workhouse just like this one. But for now she had to pretend that Miss Eames didn't even exist.

So she turned her face away, scowling.

"That's the infirmary," Mrs. Gudge suddenly declared. She had stopped at a fork in the path and stood with her lamp raised, pointing toward another large, dense shape to their right. "You'd best wait here while I fetch Fanny. I'll not be long."

She scurried off with the lamp, which began to illuminate details of the building that finally swallowed her up. A golden gleam bounced off three stacked rows of blank, dark windows. It brushed across brown brick and green paint. For an instant Mrs. Gudge was silhouetted against a rectangle of light as the infirmary door opened and shut.

Shortly afterward she emerged again through the same door, bringing with her another woman carrying another lamp. Or *was* it a woman? Squinting at the newcomer, Birdie decided that she was no more than thirteen or fourteen years old—very young for a nurse.

"This is Fanny," said Mrs. Gudge on rejoining the group in the garden. "Fanny, this is Mr. Bunce, and Miss Eames, and . . . um . . ."

"Birdie McAdam."

Fanny grinned. With her froth of dark curls, her upturned nose, and her plump red cheeks, Fanny looked surprisingly healthy and cheerful. She wore a shapeless striped gown, a dirty apron, a cotton cap, and flapping slippers. Her front teeth were missing.

"Are you the Go-Devil Man?" she asked Alfred.

"Aye." He surveyed her warily. "Are you the girl as saw the bogle?"

"That I am!"

"Shhh! Don't talk so loud." Mrs. Gudge gave the girl's arm a shake. "Do you want to get rid o' this bogle or not?"

"Sorry, ma'am," Fanny said — though she didn't sound very sorry.

The cook sighed. "I'll bid you goodbye now, Mr. Bunce, Miss Eames. Fanny will take you back to Mr. Hobney when you're finished." She shot Fanny a doubtful glance. "You'll do that, Fanny, won't you? You'll be a good girl?"

"Oh, *yes,* ma'am." As Mrs. Gudge turned away from her with a slightly dissatisfied air, Fanny pulled a grotesque face at her back. Only Birdie saw it happen. And when their gazes locked, Fanny winked.

"Should I collect the rest o' the fee from Mr. Hobney?" Alfred inquired of Mrs. Gudge in a low voice, before she could leave.

She stopped in her tracks. "Why, yes. At least . . . did he not mention it? Oh dear," she said, flustered. "I'll ask him when he lets me out."

"It's six shillings more." Alfred was eyeing her with obvious misgivings. "He gave me sixpence in advance."

"He has the full sum, I know," Mrs. Gudge assured Alfred.

But she didn't seem very confident, and after she had walked away into the night, Alfred muttered to himself, "I'll wager he *ain't* got it, or why would she be fidgeting like a cricket?"

"She always does that," Fanny volunteered. "Don't fret — they'll pay you. Otherwise you'll fuss, and the master will find out." She began to giggle, then slapped a hand over her mouth to smother the noise.

Birdie couldn't help smiling. But Miss Eames wasn't amused.

"Can you tell us where you saw the bogle?" she asked Fanny, her tone crisp and impatient.

"I'll *show* you where I saw it," Fanny offered, starting forward. Alfred, however, pulled her back.

"Not yet," he said. "We'll talk here first. Tell me where you think the bogle is."

"Oh, it *has* to be in the well." Fanny eagerly explained that the schoolhouse block occupied its own fenced yard, which had a gate that was locked at night. So the vanished children had been let out by either the schoolmaster or the schoolmistress, both of whom had custody of the keys. "Up to the gate, them kids was safe and sound," Fanny insisted, wriggling with excitement. "Mr. Winch recalls letting 'em out — and Miss Percy, too."

"Is Miss Percy the schoolmistress?" Miss Eames wanted to know.

"*That* she is." Fanny rolled her eyes. "And wouldn't

help a poor, sick child cross the grounds at night—*oh,* no. Every one of 'em had to walk past the laundry all alone, though some was bent double with the flux, poor lambs."

Fanny spoke in a kind of low, pious chant, as if she were imitating someone else. But when she returned to the subject of the bogle, her voice quickened again, becoming squeaky and breathless. "The old well lies between the laundry and the infirmary, though it's closer to the laundry. And its cover's broke in two."

"There's a cover on the well?" Birdie interrupted.

"Of course! D'you think they'd leave an open well among the weeds, to swallow every passerby?" Then, realizing that she was talking too loudly, Fanny began to whisper again. "That stone might be heavy, but two men can raise it. I seen 'em with me own eyes when they dragged the well."

Alfred grunted. After a moment's thought he said, "You found no trace o' the children?"

"Not a hair," Fanny replied with exaggerated solemnity.

"Not even a lamp?"

"There weren't no lamp to find. Two o' the bigger boys had to risk being spiked on a bean stake, for Mr. Winch don't hold with lamps when the moon's bright." Fanny's tone was drenched in scorn. "The other two took candle stubs which weren't never seen again—and don't think we stopped hearing o' *that* in a hurry. The master claims they was stolen. 'No different from stealing a watch,' he says—"

"But *you* saw something." Alfred cut her off. "When was that?"

"Last week," said Fanny. "Two nights after little Matilda went missing. I needed a breath of air, so I came out that door, Mr. Bunce . . ." She gestured at the infirmary. "And I walked down toward the laundry a bit and saw something move."

She stopped, then shivered. Birdie wondered just how scared she really was. For a workhouse girl, anything that broke up the monotony of life would probably be welcomed, even if it *was* a child-eating bogle. Perhaps that was why Fanny seemed almost to be enjoying the drama of the occasion.

As she went on to describe the large, dark, slithering shape that she'd glimpsed in the shadows, Alfred began to frown. When she revealed that she hadn't mentioned it for several days, he fixed her with a baleful look. "You didn't go out for no breath of air," he objected.

"I did!" Fanny yelped, before hastily lowering her voice. "There's sick folk inside, and lots o' bad smells . . ."

She trailed off, because Alfred was shaking his head. "You're little and tender, like a spring lamb," he pointed out. "That bogle were coming for *you*, or you'd not have seen it. But summat scared it off."

"Were you meeting someone, Fanny?" asked Miss Eames. She leveled a bright, accusing gaze at the pauper girl, who bridled and retorted, "What if I was?"

"We won't tell no one." Birdie hastened to assure her before Miss Eames could take Fanny to task and spoil everything. "We just need to know what happened."

"Well . . ." Fanny hesitated for a moment. Then she shrugged, smirked, and proudly confessed, "There's a feller I know from the infirmary. But it's against the rules for us to meet, so we do it in secret."

"And you arrived first, and saw the bogle, but yer friend came along and it disappeared." Alfred had been leaning close to Fanny so that he wouldn't miss a word she let fall. Now, as she nodded, he pulled away from her and rasped, "You can walk me to the well but don't say a word. Don't *nobody* say a word. For it's a quiet night, and this bogle don't like crowds."

"Mr. Bunce." Suddenly Miss Eames weighed in. "Will you please allow me to bait your trap with a pie before you place Birdie at risk? I understand you're both reluctant to change your ways, but I *did* pay sixpence in advance, if you recall."

Birdie felt her cheeks burning. Before she could open her mouth, however, Alfred said to Miss Eames, "I'll take the rest o' that money, then, if you're still of a mind to interfere — though I can't see the sense in it."

"Of *course* not! It's a *stupid* idea!" Birdie was about to say more when Alfred's hand closed on the back of her neck. He thrust his face into hers, so that she shrank away from him, subdued by his stony glare.

"What did I just tell you?" he growled. "Didn't I tell you to hold yer tongue?"

She nodded.

"And is that what you'll do? Or will you keep blabbing till you scare off the bogle?"

"I'll shut me trap," Birdie muttered.

"Good." Releasing her, Alfred addressed Fanny and Miss Eames. "The same goes for the rest o' you. I'll not have a *word said,* or you can hook it. Is that clear?"

Fanny grinned, nodding enthusiastically. Miss Eames took a deep breath, folded her lips into a tense line . . . and swallowed hard before giving a quick little jerk of her head.

Alfred sniffed. "All right, then. You can show me the well now, and mind you tread as soft as a kitten." He was speaking to Fanny, but before she could reply, he abruptly shifted his attention to Miss Eames. "And when the circle's drawn, *I'll* place the pie. I'll give it one hour, and if the bogle don't bite, I'll send Birdie in."

"But — "

"We ain't got all night, miss. You can take it or leave it."

Miss Eames took it. And after giving Alfred his money, she once again bent her lips to Birdie's ear. "If that creature doesn't take the pie, you may eat it yourself," she offered. "My cook makes a *wonderful* gooseberry pie."

Birdie didn't answer. Alfred had warned her to hold her tongue, so she was holding her tongue. Had she been allowed to talk, however, she would have told Miss Eames to stick her pie where it would hurt the most.

I'd like to throw it in her face, Birdie thought.

She didn't say so, however. She just kept stomping along in Alfred's wake, grim-faced and silent.

13

A Taste of the Pie

The abandoned well was tucked between the laundry and the drying lines. Unlike the neat rows of vegetables and clipped fruit trees that led to it, this patch of ground had an untidy, neglected appearance. A pile of old lumber, waiting to be turned into firewood, was stacked against the laundry wall. Weeds sprouted around the heavy slab of the well cap, while the grass under the drying lines was so trodden down that it was scattered with bald spots.

Alfred chose one of these bald spots for his magic circle. In the light from Fanny's lamp, he carefully arranged a ring of rags on the damp earth. Then he poured out his salt and removed the gooseberry pie from its basket.

After placing the pie in the center of the circle, he moved away again. But he didn't join his three companions. Instead, he positioned himself by a rusty washtub that had been dumped near the well, his salt in one hand and his spear in the other.

Watching him, Birdie felt deeply uncomfortable. She should have been out there in the circle, not cowering behind a woodpile. Alfred had given her his dark lantern to mind, just in case. (He always made sure that they had an alternative source of light during night jobs, and the dark lantern, with its hinged shutter, could be transformed instantly from a little black box into a shining beacon.) But this wasn't enough for Birdie. It was as if she'd been demoted. Excluded.

And it was all the fault of Miss Eames.

Not that her silly pie plan was going to work. Birdie kept telling herself this. If the bogle liked pies, it would have been raiding the workhouse kitchen, not picking off children in the dark. The pie was going to fail, and then Birdie would be restored to her proper place at Alfred's side.

In the meantime, however, she had to put up with Fanny. It was hard to concentrate while Fanny was around, because she was fidgety and restless. For all her faults, Miss Eames remained perfectly still as they waited for the bogle. Fanny, on the other hand, kept scratching and sighing and shifting about until Birdie was tempted to jab her in the ribs. But they weren't supposed to be making any noise, and Fanny would probably yelp or squeak if she felt the sharp point of an elbow. Birdie couldn't even *say* anything—not with a bogle listening in. For she had no doubt whatsoever that there was a bogle nearby. She could sense it. She could feel its dark weight in the air. She could smell a faint odor of fish and rotten eggs.

So she tried to stay alert, even though, as the minutes dragged on, nothing happened. The bogle refused to show itself.

At last the workhouse clock struck twelve. Hearing it, Birdie realized that they had been waiting by the laundry for more than an hour. She saw Alfred's head swivel in her direction. Then he jerked his chin. As Birdie rose, Miss Eames couldn't suppress a murmur of protest.

But Birdie's furious scowl quickly silenced her.

Since two of the pauper children had been taken with candle stubs in their hands, Alfred had decreed that Birdie could safely carry a light. Without one, she wouldn't be able to see the bogle coming. So before stepping into the ring of salt, Birdie exchanged her dark lantern for Fanny's lamp. And once she'd entered the magic circle, she set the lamp down beside the gooseberry pie.

Then she raised her mirror, checked Alfred's position, and softly began to sing.

"The Lord said to the Lady, afore he went out,
'Beware o' false Lamkin, he's a-walking about.'
The gates they was locked both outside and in
But for one little hole that let Lamkin creep in."

Suddenly Birdie saw the well cap move. One half of it rose a little, hovering an inch or two above the ground, before it slipped sideways to expose a wedge of darkness. Though the shadows were dense and her view was partly blocked by weeds, Birdie could just make out that a spiky-looking hand, or claw, had lifted the stone cover like a basket lid.

But if the slab made any kind of noise as it settled onto its bed of weeds, Birdie didn't hear it. Her own voice was ringing in her ears.

"He took out a penknife both pointed and sharp
And stabbed the wee baby three times in the heart.
O Nursemaid! O Nursemaid! How sound you do sleep?
Can't you hear them poor children a-trying to weep?"

Gradually the hole in the ground began to extrude something shiny and black and very long, with limbs that kept unfolding from beneath its belly. Birdie couldn't tell if the thing was encased in a giant millipede's shell or in a suit of armor, but she *could* see red eyes glowing beneath what was either a helmet or a hairless skull. The bogle's body was so long that Birdie began to sweat and shake. What if its bottom half was still outside the circle when it reached her? Timing would be of the essence, if she was to avoid being caught.

Birdie focused all her attention on Alfred, bracing herself for his signal. It seemed to be a long time coming. Crooning away, she wondered why he didn't pounce.

"Here's blood in the kitchen, here's blood in the hall:
Here's blood in the parlor, where the lady did fall.
False Lamkin shall be hung on the gallows so high,
While his bones shall be burned in the fire close by."

When Alfred finally leaped forward, so did Birdie. She rolled across the ground. She jumped to her feet. Then something slashed at her cape—and she realized that one of the bogle's razor-sharp claws had only just missed her.

Fanny screamed. There was a smell of hot gooseberries. The lamp went out, and suddenly Birdie couldn't see a thing. But as she cast around frantically, a golden glow flared behind the woodpile.

Miss Eames had uncovered Alfred's dark lantern.

In its pale light Birdie saw that Alfred must have speared the bogle, which was already curling up into a crispy ball that began to crumble away like burnt paper. The pie was a bubbling pool of goo. Fanny's lamp had been knocked down.

Fanny was sobbing but broke off with a startled hiccup when Miss Eames shook her.

"Stop it!" Miss Eames ordered. "Pull yourself together *at once!*"

"Are you all right, lass?" Alfred asked Birdie.

"I think so." Examining her cape, Birdie was grieved to see that the rip was getting bigger. Some kind of poison left there by the bogle's claws was acting on the yellow silk just like acid; its fibers were shriveling and its color darkening.

With a sinking heart, she accepted that she would have to throw away her favorite garment.

"Me cape's ruined," she informed Alfred sadly as she untied the bow beneath her chin. "The bogle tore it, and it's spoiling fast."

"Then toss it in the circle," Alfred advised. So she did. The cape landed in a heap between the melted pie and the toppled lamp. When Alfred sprinkled it with holy water, the browning satin fizzed like soda, then turned into a toffee-like substance that began to melt into the ground.

By this time the bogle itself was just a little heap of black ash, about the size of a dinner plate.

"Oh dear, oh dear." Fanny still sounded shaken. "Mercy, but what a terrible big thing!"

"Shhh. Calm down." Though Miss Eames's voice was

also a little unsteady, she had recovered quite well from the shock of the bogle's appearance. "Here," she said, rummaging through her basket. "This time I brought some smelling salts . . ."

"You there! What in blazes are you up to?"

Somebody was yelling at them. Birdie looked around in surprise but couldn't see any strangers. Then she realized that the voice was ranting away above their heads — and when she turned, she spotted a shining window on the top floor of the infirmary.

A man was leaning out of it.

"Who is *that?"* he roared. *"What the devil are you doing?"*

Fanny didn't answer, having quickly ducked down behind the woodpile. It was Miss Eames who said, with remarkable firmness, "There is no cause to shout, sir, and no need to use such language. Mr. Hobney himself let us in, and we are on the point of asking him to let us out again."

Her cultivated tone seemed to mollify the man in the window, whose own accent was that of a gentleman. He continued more softly, though still with a touch of suspicion, "Well, forgive me for my intemperate language, ma'am, but who *are* you? And why are you here in the middle of the night?"

"My name is Edith Eames. As to my purpose here, I'm afraid I'm not at liberty to disclose the particulars. You'll have to take that up with Mr. Hobney and Mrs. Gudge. Be assured, however, that my colleagues and I are on the premises in a *professional* capacity, with a view to improving conditions for the younger inmates."

To Birdie, it sounded as if Miss Eames was claiming to be some kind of church visitor. The man at the window must have thought so too, because he said, "Hum. I see. But why all the screeching?"

There was a moment's pause as Birdie, Alfred, and Miss Eames all glanced at the woodpile. It soon became clear, however, that Fanny wasn't about to step up and take the blame. So Miss Eames said smoothly, "I'm afraid that was my fault. A rat ran over my shoe."

"Well, kindly have more consideration," the man snapped. "These sick people in here need their rest!" Before Miss Eames could respond, he pulled his head back inside and slammed the window shut.

There was a moment's silence.

"Prating old article," Fanny muttered as her own head popped into view again. "We never told him nothing, for he don't believe in bogles. Doctors never do." Gazing reproachfully at Miss Eames, she added, "Mr. Hobney'll catch it now. *And* Mrs. Gudge. Why'd you give 'im their names, miss?"

"What choice did she have, when you wouldn't speak up?" Birdie snapped, before it occurred to her that she shouldn't be trying to defend Miss Eames, even if Fanny *was* a coward.

Fanny shrugged. "It ain't Miss Eames as would be punished for neglect o' work," she said. "Besides, she didn't need me. She done all right by herself."

"That she did," Alfred agreed. "It were a stroke o' luck you came along, Miss Eames. Thank'ee for yer help."

"Help with the doctor, not help with the bogle." Birdie thought this point worth emphasizing, just in case anyone had forgotten about it in all the excitement. "I knew that pie wouldn't work. If bogles wanted pastry, we'd be finding 'em in bread ovens."

She flicked a triumphant look at Miss Eames, who sighed but wouldn't admit defeat. "Perhaps I misidentified the creature. Perhaps it was a fuath. Fuaths don't like sunshine, though they tend to be found in Scotland . . ."

Alfred, however, wasn't interested in fuaths. "Come along," he said to Fanny. "George Hobney owes me six shillings, and you're a witness to it. I want you there when I claim me dues, just in case he tries to bilk me."

"Oh, he'll not do that, Mr. Bunce," Fanny promised. "But he might faint dead away when I tell him what happened!" She had come out from behind the woodpile so that Birdie could give her the fallen oil lamp. Alfred, meanwhile, was wrapping up his spear, while Miss Eames watched him, crestfallen.

"I hope you haven't lost faith in the scientific approach, Mr. Bunce," she said bravely. "I still believe there might be some merit in it."

"I don't," Alfred retorted. And to Birdie's delight, he went on to declare, "This ain't no game, miss. It's dangerous work and shouldn't be fumbled—not for all the gold in England. You're allus welcome to join us, but there'll be no more pies, nor nothing else as would put us in peril. I'm sorry."

Then he shouldered his sack and began to walk away.

Whatever Happened to Billy Crisp?

Birdie was dreaming about bogles when an urgent *rat-a-tat-tat* jerked her awake. For a moment she lay helpless, confused by the noise and the glare. Then she realized that it was broad daylight, and that she was still in bed because she had arrived home from the Hackney workhouse very early that morning.

I must have overslept, she thought vaguely, turning to look at Alfred's huddled shape on the other side of the room. He was snoring softly in a rat's nest of soiled blankets and unraveling shawls.

Rat-a-tat-tat! "Fred Bunce! Are you there?" a voice demanded. It belonged to Sarah Pickles.

Birdie sat bolt upright. "Mr. Bunce," she croaked, "you'd best rouse yerself."

"Nnnaugh?"

As Alfred coughed and groaned, Birdie lurched to her feet. She hadn't bothered to take off her clothes the previous night, so she didn't have to dress before opening the door to Sarah Pickles—who took one look at her and drawled, "I see you're a lady o' leisure, lying about until noon. Fred must be doing well."

"We got in late from a job," Birdie said hoarsely, blinking up at Sarah and her son. Charlie was looking more ferret-like than ever, with his long neck and beady little eyes. His shirttails were flapping beneath an unbuttoned vest, his sleeves were rolled up, and a blue knitted cap was pulled down low over his ears.

His mother hadn't shed a single layer of clothing since her last visit, despite the warm weather. Like Alfred, she was all wrapped up in greasy old shawls.

But most of Alfred's shawls fell off him when he rose to greet Sarah, revealing that he had gone to bed wearing his green coat over a long nightshirt.

"Ahem ... ah ..." he gurgled, pulling his coat tightly around him. Then he spat on the floor. "What brings you here again?" he rasped, sounding disgruntled. "I've a mind to start charging you rent, Sal."

"And I've a mind to tell *you* there's ladies present," Sarah Pickles retorted. "But I've no time to waste, so I'll not ask you to make yerself decent." She waddled over to the nearest stool, her face darkening, as Alfred dropped back onto his bed. "It's bad news, Fred. The worst. We lost another." She corrected herself, pointing at her son. "*He* lost another, I *should* say."

"It weren't down to me, Ma," Charlie growled. "We done what we was told to."

"I never told you to lose Billy Crisp!" she snapped.

Birdie frowned. Billy Crisp was one of Sarah's youngest employees—a stunted little eight-year-old with a blank, triangular face and blond hair finer than Birdie's. Though she had seen him about, Birdie didn't know him well. She tried to stay away from Sarah's gang. Alfred had always insisted on it.

"Charlie and Billy—they bin watching that crib in Clerkenwell," Sarah was relating. "The one as had them clothes dumped in the garden—"

"I remember," Alfred said shortly.

"I told Charlie to hang about the place and keep his eyes open," Sarah went on, "which he did, well enough, and came back with particulars. There's two people live there: a doctor and his maid of all work, who's an old slavvy as sleeps in the attic. The doctor's young and works regular hours."

"Name of Morton. Roswell Morton," Charlie broke in, a little sullenly. "Last three days he's left the house between nine and ten, returning between six and eight."

"Never in a trap's uniform," Sarah added. "And no sign o' Sam or Nolly or Abel. So yesterday, when the slavvy left for her usual trip to the market—"

"Which takes her two hours each morning, on account o' she's so old and lame," Charlie commented, before a flinty look from his mother silenced him.

"Fred's a busy man and don't need to hear all the particulars," she said, before once again addressing Alfred. "When the house emptied out, Charlie decided to take a tour o' the place. *Uninvited*, so to speak."

Alfred gave a grunt. Birdie looked at her shoes. Listening to Sarah describe how Charlie had spotted an unlatched window at the rear of the house and had made Billy Crisp climb onto the kitchen roof to squeeze through a space the size of a cottage loaf, Birdie wished that she didn't have to hear any of the details. Alfred had warned her, over and over again, that people had gone to gaol for knowing such things. He made a point of not listening when thieves talked about their lurks and capers.

"Billy had to come downstairs and open the kitchen door," Sarah continued, "but he never did. Charlie waited and waited. He waited all night, even after the doctor went to bed, hoping Billy might come out once the house had gone quiet."

"He never showed his face this morning, not even after Morton and the slavvy left again," Charlie revealed.

"Summat happened to that boy," Sarah finished. "Same as happened to the others. And we need to know what, Fred."

Birdie shivered. Alfred sighed. "Someone could have bin skulking in there," he suggested. "Someone Charlie didn't see."

Charlie gave a hiss of dissent, but Sarah nodded. "That's true," she acknowledged, ignoring her son. "Could have bin the doctor's lunatic uncle, shut away behind locked doors. Or a collection o' poisonous snakes. Or a mantrap. Or a greased stair." She narrowed her eyes. "Could have bin a bogle, Fred."

Alfred sighed again. "Sal—"

"I need you to go in there." Sarah's tone was calm and cold. "This time I'll be sending Charlie with a *proper* cracksman, as can get through a door instead of a window. They'll have jemmies and coshes and everything they need to nobble whatever might be waiting for 'em—unless it's a bogle. If it's a bogle, they'll need you."

Silence fell. Birdie chewed on her thumbnail, nervously watching Alfred. So did Sarah. So did Charlie.

Alfred was staring morosely at the floor. At last he said, "You want us all nibbed for housebreaking, is that it?"

"Won't happen," Sarah assured him. "The traps'll never know."

"Speaking o' traps," Alfred began, then changed his mind.

"We can't bring police into it, Fred. You know that as well as I do." To Birdie's surprise, Sarah spoke quite pleasantly. "How can we ask the traps to find a clutch o' young dippers as spent their time emptying the pockets o' *respectable* folk? Why, there'll be questions asked. Objections raised. It wouldn't do at all."

Alfred sniffed. But he didn't comment.

"No traps," Sarah ordered. Then she put out an arm so that Charlie could help her up. "There's a lushery on Clerkenwell Green. The Fox and French Horn. D'you know it?"

"Aye," said Alfred.

"Charlie'll meet you there tomorrow morning, at eight o'clock sharp. You'll need to be at this doctor's crib when the slavvy leaves, and gone again by the time she gets back."

Birdie couldn't help snorting. When Sarah looked at her sharply, Alfred tried to explain why his apprentice had scoffed at the notion of a deadline. "If you want the bogle dead, Sal, you might have to wait for it. You can't set your watch by a bogle."

"Then we'll make sure the slavvy don't interfere," Sarah said with a shrug. "If she's old and lame, the cracksman'll keep her quiet. I'll find you a big one, just to make sure." She bared her gray teeth in an unconvincing smile as she stood over Alfred. "Don't you worry yer head about details of that kind, m'dear. You'll have but one job to fret on and must leave the rest to Charlie. He knows what to do. He's a good boy, same as Birdie's a good girl."

Again she smiled, this time at Birdie—who quickly looked away. Then Alfred said, "If there *is* a bogle, I'll be out o' pocket."

Sarah's smile suddenly vanished. "As will I, Fred. As will I," she rejoined. "The Lord knows, I've already lost all o' Charlie's earnings for a day. But I told 'im if anything takes his fancy in that toffken, he's welcome to it. And I'll tell you the same." With a curt nod, she began to hobble across the room, clearly displeased that Alfred had dared raise the subject of payment. "Just be sure to meet Charlie on time," she added by way of farewell, "and take care not to spout off about this or it might reach the wrong set of ears. We wouldn't want the traps getting ahold of any names, would we?"

She didn't seem to expect an answer, disappearing before Alfred could open his mouth. As the door slammed shut behind Charlie, Alfred and Birdie exchanged a gloomy look.

"At least *some* good may come of it," Birdie muttered at last.

Alfred didn't say anything.

"If Billy's dead or captive inside that house," Birdie went on, "then there ain't no crime in searching for 'im."

"There is if Charlie Pickles hoists a sackful o' silver plate on his way out," Alfred spat. His face was heavy with resentment. "I'll not be lagged for thieving, nor work for nothing. There's only one thing to do. We must take the lady with us."

Birdie frowned. "What lady?" she inquired before the answer suddenly dawned on her. *"Miss Eames?"*

"Aye."

"But—"

"She'll pay to come and will defend us if we're nibbed." Alfred began to nod thoughtfully as he reached for his pipe and tobacco pouch. "I'd trust her to speak for us in any court, afore any beak."

Birdie had to concede that Miss Eames probably *was* a match for any magistrate in London. "But she'll not want to burgle no house, and she *will* want to call in the traps," Birdie protested.

"Aye . . . well . . ." Alfred shrugged. "You'll have to convince her to help us."

"I will?"

"Make her see we ain't got no choice. Even if the traps

believe Sal, which I'm not persuaded of, and even if Sal gives up them clothes, which is our only proof, what do you think the doctor will say when the police come knocking on his door? He'll say someone threw the clothes into his garden. Over the fence."

"But if there's proof inside —"

"If there's proof inside, like clothes or a corpse, well and good — though I'll wager he'll claim that every one o' them kids tried to burgle his house, and who can say different when they was all known thieves? I've heard that more'n one man has killed an armed thief on his property and walked away from a murder charge." By this time Alfred had filled his pipe; now he was fumbling around for matches. "And what if there *ain't* no proof inside?" he argued. "That'll be the end o' the matter — save that our doctor friend'll be alerted and will ensure that no one ever finds out what befell them boys."

Birdie nodded slowly, impressed by Alfred's clear and logical reasoning.

"And if all *that* don't convince Miss Eames," Alfred concluded, "tell her Sal won't never forgive us if we call in the constabulary. Make that very clear." He fixed his apprentice with a grim, dark look while he sucked at his pipe stem. "Tell her what it'll mean, if the matron turns against us."

Birdie swallowed. "Can't *you* talk to Miss Eames?" she pleaded.

Alfred shook his head. "She's more likely to listen if she hears it from you."

Even Birdie had to acknowledge the truth of this. An appeal from Birdie would carry far more weight than an appeal from Alfred.

"You'll come with me, won't you? In case I need help?" Birdie entreated.

"You'll not need help," Alfred said. "And if you're there alone, she'll give you the bus fare back, like as not." Then he dug around in his bedclothes and produced a pair of trousers, which he searched for loose coins. "I've things to buy and debts to pay this afternoon," he revealed, "but we'll eat a good dinner first, so you'll have the stomach to do this job." He tossed Birdie a sixpenny piece. "Here's a tanner. Take it to the pie shop and buy summat tasty. And if there's any change . . ."

He paused as Birdie jumped to her feet. She waited hopefully. Was he about to offer her a penny for her trouble?

"If there's any change, bring it straight back," he finished in a gruff voice.

He was still counting his money when she left for the pie shop.

15

A Very Kind Offer

Someone was playing the piano inside Miss Eames's house.

Standing on the front doorstep, straining her ears, Birdie identified "The Gypsy Girl's Dream." But heavy footsteps soon drowned out the faint tinkling of piano keys, and suddenly Mary Meggs was in front of her, wearing a black-and-white maid's uniform.

"Oh!" Mary sounded surprised. "What are *you* doing here?"

"I came to talk to Miss Eames."

"Did you, now?" said Mary, eyeing her skeptically from head to toe. Birdie flushed. She knew that she wasn't looking her best because she'd had to replace her beautiful yellow cape with an old pink mantle that had been so badly mauled by moths and rats that she'd been using it as bed linen. She was also in a muck sweat, having walked halfway across the city. And somewhere on the trip to Bloomsbury, she'd lost a feather from her hat.

"I've a message from Mr. Bunce," she announced. "Miss Eames will want to hear it."

"I'll see if she's home," said Mary. Then she shut the door in Birdie's face.

Birdie was annoyed, though not surprised. As a bogler's girl from Bethnal Green, she wasn't the kind of visitor that most maidservants would greet with open arms. But she was convinced that Miss Eames would give her a much warmer welcome — and she was right. Barely a minute later Mary opened the door again.

"You're to come in," she said stiffly. "Wipe yer feet first."

Birdie did as she was told, wiping her filthy shoes on the doormat before stepping inside. Her eyes were still adjusting to the dimness when she heard Miss Eames addressing her from the drawing room threshold. "Birdie!" Miss Eames exclaimed. "How nice to see you! Come in and say hello to my aunt."

The music had stopped. Birdie wondered if Miss Eames had been responsible for it but soon saw that Mrs.

Heppinstall was the one seated at the drawing room piano. The old lady beamed at Birdie, patting the seat beside her.

"Come and sit by me, dear. Do you know this song? It's *very* pretty. My dear friend Mr. Fotherington likes nothing else quite as much. I should love to hear you sing it, if you would oblige me."

Birdie hesitated. She glanced at Miss Eames, saying, "I've a message from Mr. Bunce."

"Which I'm eager to receive," Miss Eames assured her. "But perhaps you'd like some tea first. Or something a little colder? Lemonade, perhaps?"

Birdie licked her dry lips. "I'd like a glass of lemonade," she admitted.

"Let me go and tell Mary," said Miss Eames. She vanished back into the hallway, leaving Birdie with Mrs. Heppinstall.

"Do you know this song, my dear?" The old lady struck a few chords. "It's called 'The Gypsy Girl's Dream.'"

"I know it," Birdie said, having heard it many times. Then, as Mrs. Heppinstall kept playing, the lure of the tune became irresistible.

Birdie began to sing.

"I dreamt I dwelt in marble halls,
With vassals and serfs at my side,

And of all those assembled within those walls,
That I was the hope and the pride.
I had riches all too great to count
And a high ancestral name.
But I also dreamt, which pleased me most,
That you lov'd me still the same . . ."

Birdie had often sung to the tune of a hand organ in the street, and had once been accompanied by a fiddle. But she'd never before known the joy of having a pianist gently carry her voice through a song. She forgot everything but the pleasure of the notes, and when the last chord sounded, and silence fell, she was shocked to realize that Miss Eames was standing beside her, applauding enthusiastically.

"Oh, Birdie, that was *beautiful!*" Miss Eames exclaimed. "Utterly flawless!"

"Pitch perfect," her aunt agreed. "What a lovely voice you have, dear."

"Good enough for the stage," said Miss Eames. She exchanged a quick look with Mrs. Heppinstall before adding, "Have you ever wanted to go on the stage, Birdie? Have you ever wanted to be a professional singer?"

"Oh, I'll never be that," Birdie replied. She had once or twice gazed wistfully at the Grecian Theatre, which was often adorned with pictures of lovely ladies singing their hearts out. For Birdie, however, trying to imagine a stage career was like trying to imagine a trip to the moon.

"But would you *like* to be a singer?" pressed Miss Eames. "My aunt and I truly believe that with a voice like yours, and a little training, you could be the next Jenny Lind!"

Birdie had no idea who Jenny Lind was. Seeing this from her blank look, Mrs. Heppinstall explained, "Jenny Lind is an opera singer and concert performer of *great* renown. And she was discovered quite by accident, when she was your age."

"You're pretty enough to act in musical theater," Miss Eames observed. "You have every advantage, except that your speaking voice needs more refinement. And some musical training would not go amiss."

"Even the strongest voice can be grievously damaged unless the singer is properly trained," Mrs. Heppinstall agreed.

Birdie looked from one lady to the other, confused by their eager expressions. What on earth were they trying to say? At last Miss Eames came out with it.

"We have been discussing your plight, Birdie, and would be very happy to arrange lessons with a good singing teacher," she said. "We would foot the bill, of course."

"And find a room for you in this house," Mrs.

Heppinstall promised Birdie, whose mouth had dropped open.

"Yes, you would have to live here," Miss Eames hastily added. "No *reputable* teachers would be available anywhere near *your* home. We would also arrange a general tutor for you, because even the finest singer in the world cannot perform unless she is able to read lyrics and stage directions."

By this time Birdie was backing away from Mrs. Heppinstall's gentle smile and Miss Eames's bright-eyed zeal. "But I'm a bogler's girl," Birdie objected. "Mr. Bunce depends on me."

"Not for much longer, though," Miss Eames reminded her. "What will you do when you're too old to help Mr. Bunce? What will you do when he needs a new apprentice?"

Birdie frowned. Though it was a question she often asked herself, lying awake at night, she tried not to dwell on the future. "Mebbe I'll be trained up," she mumbled. "Mebbe I'll become a bogler in me own right."

"Is that likely, though? With Mr. Bunce still practicing?" Miss Eames was watching her intently, her gaze as sharp as a pin. "And you're a female, Birdie. Don't forget that. Have you ever heard of a female bogler?"

Birdie swallowed, because she never had.

"I only ask out of interest," Miss Eames said. "I'm

still lamentably ill informed when it comes to the bogling profession."

Suddenly Mary appeared with the tea tray. It was loaded with delicious food: muffins, cakes, buns, and biscuits. Birdie's mouth began to water at the sight of so much sugar and starch.

"Here is your lemonade, Birdie," Miss Eames pointed out. "What would you like to eat with it? Some angel cake? A Sally Lunn?"

Birdie wasn't stupid. She knew quite well that Miss Eames was trying to suggest, with this astonishing tea, that more astonishing teas would follow if Birdie agreed to move in. There would be more teas, and more fresh flowers, and more pretty clothes, and more lovely music. It was all very tempting, especially the food. But when Birdie tried to imagine herself living with the two ladies, she found that she couldn't. Everything about them was too strange. The Birdie she pictured sitting straight backed at the piano, with a scrubbed face and a soft voice, wasn't anything like the *real* Birdie. It was a Birdie she didn't understand—and didn't entirely trust.

Besides, she couldn't leave Alfred. Not while he needed her. Not while London was infested with child-eating bogles.

She was perched on an upholstered chair, folding a Bath bun into her mouth, when Miss Eames remarked, "I hope you don't decide to follow in Mr. Bunce's footsteps, Birdie. I'm sure you wouldn't enjoy forcing a poor little apprentice to face death at every turn."

Birdie decided not to take offense. How could she, while eating so much of Miss Eames's rich and sticky food? "*I* do it all the time," she said thickly, with a shrug.

"But while your own courage supports you," Mrs. Heppinstall murmured, "you would hesitate, I'm sure, to demand the same of any other child."

"It would be *wicked*," Miss Eames declared, much to Birdie's annoyance.

"Ain't nothing wicked about it!" Birdie snapped. "Mr. Bunce and me make a decent living! We save lives! We kill monsters!"

"Yes, but—"

"Which is why I came here." Birdie decided that it was high time she delivered her message from Mr. Bunce. "There's four boys gone missing, and we think a bogle might be to blame," she said. "The only trouble is, we cannot *reach* the bogle without entering someone's house uninvited." She went on to relate the story of the doctor's house in Clerkenwell, though she was careful not to name anyone, or provide too many details about the boys' profession. She admitted only that they had been beggars who "sometimes stole." And she insisted that Billy Crisp would not have broken into the doctor's house if he hadn't been trying to find his friends. "They never deserved what befell 'em. Ain't *no one* deserves to be fed to a bogle," she stoutly declared. "That's why we need to kill this'un just as soon as ever we can."

The two ladies listened with many exclamations of shock and horror. Birdie noticed that Miss Eames would sometimes shoot an anxious look at her aunt, as if concerned that such a terrible story would prove too much for her. Certainly the old lady turned very pale and kept pressing a lace handkerchief to her lips. But she never left the room nor asked for her smelling salts. And she didn't suggest that they inform the police.

It was Miss Eames who raised *that* possibility.

"No." Birdie shook her head, wiping the crumbs from her chin. "We can't." She began to list all the reasons why the police should be avoided at all costs. When she mentioned how cruelly she and Alfred would be treated by certain parties if they did approach the police, Miss Eames could contain herself no longer.

"Oh, Birdie, this really is too bad!" she exclaimed. "Surely you must see how dangerous it is to consort with such people? Why would you even *hesitate* to abandon the kind of company you keep in Bethnal Green when you have a chance to improve your prospects immeasurably by living here with us?"

"I can't leave Mr. Bunce," Birdie growled. "Not while he needs me."

She refused to give in. Though Miss Eames peppered her with arguments—though Mrs. Heppinstall gently offered her more cake, new clothes, and an attic bedroom all to herself—Birdie wouldn't budge. She was almost afraid to. Somehow she knew that if she allowed herself even a pang of doubt, there would be no turning back.

Finally Miss Eames had to admit that she was beaten. "Very well. I can see that you're frightened to make a change," she said. "But you must think about it, Birdie. You're a clever girl and will soon see that if you stay where you are, your future is destined to be short and sorrowful." With a sigh she abandoned the subject, turning instead to the job in Clerkenwell. "As for this housebreaking business, I find it *very disturbing.* Since there are lives at stake, however, I understand why Mr. Bunce should have agreed to take part."

"And you, miss?" asked Birdie. "Will you be coming too?"

"*I?*"

"You did us a great service last time. Even Mr. Bunce says so. And I'd be easier in me mind if you *was* there." Watching the effect this remark had on Miss Eames, Birdie suffered a twinge of guilt, ashamed at having uttered such a bald-faced lie just to get her own way. Because for the past few days, she had been telling herself that she wouldn't care if she never saw Miss Eames ever again. And despite the offer that had just been made to her, Birdie was still a little wary of Miss Eames, whose intentions were so hard for her to understand.

But when Miss Eames agreed to meet her on Clerkenwell Green at eight o'clock the next Monday morning, Birdie experienced an unexpected surge of relief. And she realized, with utter amazement, that she hadn't been lying to Miss Eames after all.

16

A Meeting on the Green

Alfred knew that no respectable lady would want to enter a seedy-looking public house like the Fox and French Horn. So he and Birdie arrived at Clerkenwell Green a little before time, to ensure that Miss Eames would not have to wait for them in the rain.

But when he ducked inside to fill his brandy flask, he found that Charlie Pickles was already on the premises. And so was a hulking, grim-faced man who introduced himself as Enoch Moulsdale.

Charlie and Enoch were sharing a nip of gin. They had with them a dirty carpetbag and wore clothes that were a little heavy for the season. Charlie's thin frame was almost lost in an old-fashioned driving coat that had several shoulder capes. Enoch's black dreadnought coat was even bulkier. Their hats had wide brims and were pulled down low. Both men sported neckerchiefs.

Hovering on the threshold, Birdie couldn't see much of Enoch because the taproom was so dark. Only when he emerged into the dull light of the street was she able to determine that she didn't know him—not even by sight. For such a big man, he had quite small features, which were crowded together in the middle of his fat, mottled face. His eyes were bland and lead colored, and his beard was an auburn fuzz.

Spotting the scabs on his knuckles, Birdie immediately looked away.

"I'm expecting one more," Alfred informed Charlie, "and won't go nowhere without her."

"What?" Charlie wasn't pleased. "You didn't say nothing about a third party!"

"Here she is," Birdie announced. Miss Eames was moving toward them across the green, threading her way through the market stalls. She carried a black umbrella. On one side of her loomed a church spire; on the other, the grim façade of a courthouse.

Perhaps it was the sight of the courthouse that made Charlie feel nervous. He let loose a string of oaths.

"Have you lost yer wits?" he demanded of Alfred in a

furious whisper. "This here is a *crack job,* not a picnic in the park!"

"She knows it," Alfred replied.

"She *knows* it?" cried Charlie, appalled.

"She'll not tell the traps," Birdie promised. "She swore on the Bible she wouldn't."

But Charlie was shaking his head. "I don't know what Ma's going to say about this. This ain't what we planned for. This'll be the ruin of us."

"No, it will not." Suddenly Enoch spoke up. He had a deep, dreary, hollow voice, like someone talking from the bottom of a well. "We can use her. She's what you'd call an addition."

Charlie blinked. For a moment he stared at his friend in astonishment. Then he shrugged. "Very well," he muttered. "You're the cracksman. But we cannot walk in step with her. She must keep behind us, all the way."

By this time Miss Eames had joined them. She wore a sober outfit of dark gray, trimmed with black velvet. As she opened her mouth to speak, Charlie said softly, "Have you coins in yer purse?"

"Wh-hat?" Miss Eames was taken aback.

"You should make as if you want to pay us for summat," Charlie advised her in a low voice. "Else why would you be stopping to chat with the likes of Enoch and me? Not to pass the time o' day, I'll be bound." As a flustered

Miss Eames gaped at him, he added, "You must do as you're told and stay quiet, d'you hear? Or we'll all fare the worse for it." Then he glared at her in a threatening manner.

Birdie scowled. "You'll fare the worst of all if you can't keep a civil tongue in yer head!" she snapped. It enraged her that someone like Charlie should be telling them what to do. But she fell silent when Alfred laid a warning hand on her head, reminding her that they were in a public place.

"Begging yer pardon, miss," he murmured, "but you'll need to stay apart from us till we get where we want to go— on account o' the looks we might draw if you're seen in our company."

"Oh! Yes, of course." Miss Eames gave a brave little nod as she pretended to press a coin into Charlie's hand. "You wish me to follow you at a distance. Is that correct?"

"Aye," said Alfred.

"And when we reach the crib, she's to knock on the front door while we hide 'round the back," Enoch suddenly remarked, addressing Charlie as if Miss Eames weren't even present. "As a precaution, like. To smoke out anyone as might still be at home."

"I thought you said the house'd be empty?" Alfred cut in. "Ain't you got a crow there watching it?"

"Jem Barbary's our crow and is on the job now," Charlie said—causing Birdie to blink, then grimace. "But Enoch's right," he added. "You can't never be too careful."

"If no one answers her knock, we'll go in," Enoch finished, still not looking at Miss Eames. Birdie was about to remind him that Miss Eames would be going in with them when Charlie declared that it was time to hook it. The longer they dawdled, he said, the less chance they would have to get away clean.

He then set off down the nearest side street, lugging his heavy bag. Enoch trudged after him. Alfred was about to follow when Miss Eames said, "A word, Mr. Bunce? Before we do this?"

Alfred paused.

"I don't know if Birdie has told you about the offer I made yesterday, during her visit to my aunt's house," Miss Eames continued. "The offer that we pay for her musical education?"

As Alfred frowned, obviously confused, Birdie mumbled, "I never got a chance." She hadn't wanted to consult Alfred the previous evening, which he had spent swigging down cheap liquor. Birdie had learned to tread carefully when he was in one of his morose, gin-affected moods.

"No," he said, "I didn't hear about that."

"Well, I think you should consider it. For Birdie's sake." Miss Eames quickly went on to describe her plan, while rain dripped off her umbrella. She finished by saying, "Birdie insists that she cannot leave you because you need her. Though I'm sure her departure will come at some cost to yourself, I find it hard to believe that you would prevent her from pursuing her chance for a secure and stable future. At the very worst ..." Miss Eames hesitated, then took a deep breath and proceeded bravely. "... At the very worst, and however much I might deplore it, you can always hire another child to take her place."

"No." Alfred's tone was flat. "I can't."

"But—"

"Listen here." He thrust his long, sour face into hers, so that the brim of his hat scraped against the spokes of her umbrella. "I lost one child. Once," he said grimly. "And I ain't *never* going to lose another, so help me God. This one don't make mistakes. She's the best there is. As long as I have Birdie, I'll not ever lose no kid, nor have to live with it after." Straightening, he nodded at Charlie's retreating back. "We'd best get moving, else we'll be left behind. Are you coming with us, or ain't you got the stomach for it?"

Miss Eames didn't answer. Instead, she folded her lips into a stern, straight line. Birdie wasn't surprised to see her hesitate as Alfred shuffled after the distant figures of Charlie and Enoch. She knew Miss Eames well enough by now to realize that she was helplessly seething under her ladylike façade.

She's going to turn around and go home, thought Birdie, feeling an odd pang of regret. But she was wrong. On

Farringdon Lane, Birdie glanced over her shoulder to see that Miss Eames was doggedly pursuing them, at a carefully calculated distance.

This distance grew longer as the way grew steeper. Birdie soon began to suspect that Charlie was trying to shake off Miss Eames by setting a fast pace, and said as much to Alfred, who immediately stopped. When Miss Eames had caught up a little, he moved on again, through narrow, winding, muddy streets lined with rag merchants and beer shops. The air rang with costers' cries and the wails of small children. It smelled of tobacco, boiled horse, and fried fish. At last Birdie became quite anxious about Miss Eames, who was far too nicely dressed for such a quarter.

"She'll be robbed and rolled in a minute, and I don't doubt that's Charlie's plan," Birdie whispered to Alfred, who frowned as he scanned the street. Ahead of them, Charlie looked back and jerked his head in a meaningful way.

"Don't fret," said Alfred. "We've arrived." He didn't pause in front of the house that Charlie had indicated but cast many a quick, sidelong glance at it as he walked past. Then he told Birdie, out of the corner of his mouth, "Run and tell her it's this'un. Pretend you're griddling. I'll be in that lane over there with the other two."

Birdie nodded. She turned around and skipped back down the road, then planted herself in front of Miss Eames with her palm outstretched, as if she were a beggar. "That there's the house, miss," she quietly informed Miss Eames. "You can meet us in the side lane when you're done."

"Oh. Yes. Very well." Miss Eames was a little out of breath. "If anyone answers my knock, I shall pretend that I am looking for a Mr. Potter."

Thanks to the rain, the street wasn't as crowded as it could have been, though there were still a few people about, splashing in and out of nearby courts with their heads down and their collars raised. It was an old, dilapidated street, dotted here and there with ancient buildings like the doctor's house, which was half timbered, with lead-light windows. Birdie had never before seen such a drunken-looking structure. Its second story jutted out precariously, like a hat brim. Its roof had sunk in the middle like an old mattress, so that its dormer windows leaned toward each other. It had crooked chimneys, bowed walls, and a front door that had settled a few inches below street level.

Miss Eames knocked on this door three times, but there was no response from within. So she abandoned her post on the doorstep and joined the others in a nearby lane, where she reported that the doctor's house seemed to be all shut up, with every curtain drawn and every downstairs shutter fixed.

"There *is* smoke coming from the chimney," she

admitted, "but a doused fire can smoke for ever so long, in my experience."

"We'll ask Jem if that slavvy's gone yet," said Charlie. He then led his companions around a corner into the alley that lay behind Dr. Morton's house. Here they were greeted by a young boy in a flannel jacket, who suddenly popped up from behind a rubbish heap.

"*You* took yer time!" he scolded. "She's bin gone a good quarter hour!"

It was Jem Barbary, the black-haired pickpocket. Birdie scowled at him, but he ignored her. He was too busy peering suspiciously at Miss Eames.

"Who's this?" he asked. "I don't know her."

"She a friend o' mine," Alfred rejoined.

"She knocked on the door for us but flushed out no one," Charlie explained, glancing up and down the alley. It divided two rows of small, fenced yards, so it wasn't over-looked by innumerable windows. Furthermore, the dreary weather had emptied it of life. Not even a rat could be seen foraging in the clumps of refuse that were strewn about. "Is there anything we should know of?" he asked Jem. "Any suspicious movement?"

"Not a twitch," Jem replied. "It's a deadlurk. Empty."

"Then let's do this," said Enoch. And without another word, he heaved Jem Barbary over the nearest fence.

17

THE NECROMANCER

Jem quickly unlatched Dr. Morton's rear gate. As it swung open, Birdie caught sight of a privy. But she didn't get a chance to inspect this dingy little hut for bogles. Though the small garden was shielded by the canopy of a stunted, wizened old crab-apple tree, it was still partly exposed to the gaze of any neighbors who might be looking out their upstairs windows. So Charlie wanted everyone inside the house as quickly as possible.

"Don't talk," he instructed under his breath. "Don't move unless you have to."

Charlie himself stood guard while Enoch picked the lock on the kitchen door. As for the others, they were told to huddle against the wall of a tumbledown coal shed. It was a squalid hiding place, but they didn't have to crouch among the sooty weeds for very long. Soon Charlie was hustling them into the kitchen, which was a dank and decrepit addition to the main house.

One look at its dirt floor, antique oven, and stained tabletop was enough to make Miss Eames turn even paler than she already was.

"He *cannot* be a doctor and live like this!" she protested softly, much to Birdie's surprise. She thought the kitchen quite airy and well stocked, though not as clean as it could have been. And there was a definite smell of mildewed potatoes.

She saw Jem surreptitiously whip a handful of almonds into his pocket.

"Enoch'll stay here, in case the slavvy comes back," Charlie whispered. He had put down his carpetbag, though not before removing a crowbar from its depths. "The rest o' you, keep close to me. I don't want no one wandering off. Is that clear?"

"Aye," said Alfred. Birdie grunted. Jem gave a nod, because his mouth was full of almonds.

Miss Eames was gazing fixedly at the crowbar. "Oh dear," was all she could say.

"Everyone take this rag," Charlie continued quietly, removing a tattered old shirt from the same bag that had yielded up his crowbar, "and wipe yer feet on it. Or we'll be leaving our boot marks, which can be traced back to the boots as made 'em. Enoch'll mind this bag. *And* yer wet brolly." He jerked his chin at Miss Eames, who promptly relinquished her umbrella. Her hand was trembling, Birdie noticed.

"We'll follow in Billy's footsteps, but we'll do it back to front," Charlie went on. "Summat happened to him between here and the upstairs window. If we don't find nothing on our way to that spot, then we'll spread out."

"Watch where you're treading," warned Enoch. "There might be a trapdoor."

"Or a bogle," said Birdie.

She began to wring out her wet clothes, while those with dirty boots cleaned off the muck. When everyone was ready, Charlie raised his crowbar. He cautiously pulled open the door that linked the kitchen to the rest of the house — and found himself stepping into a large, low, shadowy room containing a sideboard and a dining suite. The furniture in this room was heavy and dark. So was the paneling on the walls. But the dignity of carved oak and red damask was marred by a mess of paper that overwhelmed almost everything else.

Books and papers were piled high on the dining table. They were scattered over the floor, heaped in drifts on the sideboard, and stuffed into half a dozen wooden chests.

Sheets of paper were nailed to the wall. Rolls of parchment had tumbled off the window seat. Scraps of cardboard were tucked between the pages of leatherbound books, which were stacked in great towers under a forest of melted candle stubs.

"Good heavens," said Miss Eames. While the others gazed blankly at the chaos in front of them, Miss Eames was awestruck as she peered at a book that lay open on one of the chairs. "Someone reads Latin. *And* Greek."

Birdie glanced up at Alfred, who shook his head. There was dust everywhere, but no blood. No slime. No signs of a recent struggle. "Whatever happened to yer boy, it didn't happen here," Alfred told Charlie. And Charlie agreed.

Together they made their way to a door at the other end of the room, trying not to disturb any books or papers. It was very difficult. Birdie kept slipping on loose sheets, while Jem accidentally knocked a large, dusty volume onto the floor. He snickered when he retrieved the book, because it contained a black-and-white print of a naked man with bat's wings.

"Shhh!" Charlie put a finger to his lips. Then he took a deep breath, raised his crowbar a little higher, and gave the door in front of him a tentative shove.

To Birdie's surprise, the dining room didn't open onto a hallway or a stairwell. Instead, she found herself stepping into a very large drawing room, which contained even more dark paneling and heavy pieces of furniture. There was also a big stone fireplace and an odd little boxy staircase that seemed to be built into one wall. But instead of paper, an extraordinary array of other strange things were strewn about: knives and candles, apothecary jars, a bird's claw, a human skull, a carved-stone figure, a shrunken head. There were scrolls made of silk and animal hide. There were slabs of sealing wax and a grotesque feather mask. There were hairless specimens preserved in glass bottles.

A large circle had been painted on the floor, next to a smaller triangle. The circle contained four six-pointed stars; the triangle had a circle inside it. Each shape was decorated with inscriptions, which Birdie couldn't read. But when she looked around for help, she realized that Miss Eames was nowhere in sight.

"Miss Eames?" she said, a little too loudly.

Charlie glared at her. "Shhh!"

"Where's Miss Eames?" Birdie hissed at Alfred, who was pulling his dark lantern out of his sack. The room was very dim because the window was heavily shuttered. The atmosphere also seemed somehow smoky, though the embers in the fireplace were black and cold.

"She's still in the other room," Alfred replied. "Reading a book."

Birdie didn't like the sound of that. Hadn't they been told to stay together? She was retracing her steps when Jem suddenly announced, "Billy would have stopped for these here. He couldn't have passed 'em up—not if his life depended on it."

He was leaning over a small, round table draped in a purple cloth. From where she stood, Birdie couldn't quite make out what had caught his attention. But then Alfred struck a match, and the lantern flared, and she saw a gleam of silver.

"This ain't plate," said Jem. "It's solid sterling. Feel the weight of it, Charlie."

He picked up a silver cup, which flashed and glittered in the lamplight. Drawing closer, Birdie spotted two other silver objects on the table: a man's ring and a large seal, or stamp. Both were solid chunks of metal, highly polished and carefully placed, like sacred vessels on an altar.

Jem was shaking his head. "If Billy ever seen that ring, he would have tried to palm it, no question."

"And he must have come past here," Charlie said thoughtfully, squinting at the staircase on the other side of the room. "Unless he never made it this far."

Birdie studied the silver ring on the purple cloth. All around lay murky, dusty, eerie clutter, but the round table with its display of treasure was clean and bright and attractive. It made her think of Alfred's ring of salt, with herself standing inside. It made her think of baits and traps and bogles.

Only this wasn't a bogle trap. This was a boy trap.

Her gaze drifted around the room, lingering on the dark walls, the wax stalagmites, the cobwebs hanging from the smoke-blackened beams, and the dead things rotting behind smeared glass. They seemed to exude a gloomy aura, like a prison or a graveyard. They made Birdie's heart sink and her courage fail.

"There's a bogle nearby," said Alfred.

He was staring at the circle on the floor. When he looked up and caught Birdie's eye, she instantly believed him. There *was* a bogle nearby. There had to be. All her instincts were telling her so.

"It's close as can be," Alfred continued. Lifting his lantern, he stepped forward to examine the fireplace. "If yer boy stopped for a time in front o' that silver, Charlie, and had his back to the bogle's lair—"

"But where *is* the bogle's lair?" Birdie interrupted. "D'you think it's a chimney bogle?"

Alfred shrugged.

"That chimney's a long way from this silver." Birdie frowned as she tried to calculate the distance. "And in plain sight, for all it's so dark. If Billy stopped here, and the bogle took 'im . . ."

"Mebbe the silver's bin moved," said Alfred. Then Jem, who was still gazing greedily at the cup in his hand, observed, "Mebbe there ain't no bogle. Mebbe the cove as lives here came through that door, saw Billy hoisting his gewgaws, and nobbled him from behind."

"And did what with 'im after?" Charlie demanded. "We ain't seen no corpse leave this house."

"Not in one piece, you ain't." As the people around him gasped and grimaced, Jem added roughly, "It's what doctors do, ain't it? They cut up corpses to learn their trade. They've the tools for it—*and* the stomach."

But Alfred shook his head. "There's a bogle nearby," he repeated. Then he pointed at the circle on the floor. "Why else would this be here? Someone's seen the bogle and is trying to kill it."

"No." Miss Eames suddenly spoke up. She had appeared in the doorway carrying a small, clothbound book. "He is *not* trying to kill it. He is trying to summon it."

Everyone goggled at her. Even Jem wrenched his gaze away from the silver cup in his hand. Charlie, who had been lifting lids and pulling open drawers, scowled and said, "How d'you know that?"

"Because it says so in his journal." Miss Eames looked damp and pasty, like a fillet of fish. But her eyes were blazing. "Dr. Morton considers himself a necromancer," she announced contemptuously. "He wishes to conjure up a demon so that he can make it serve him." As proof, she opened her book and read from it. "'Let me only invoke an aerial spirit of infernal powers, and I shall have the four elements at my command.'"

"But you can't *make* a bogle do *nothing!*" Birdie protested. "Can you, Mr. Bunce?"

"You can make it die," said Alfred.

"No, no. You don't understand." Miss Eames was trying to stay calm, though the strain of it made her voice creak. "Dr. Morton is highly educated. He has been studying ancient grimoires and other texts associated with magic and alchemy. He believes that he can imitate King Solomon, who evoked seventy-two demons with magic formulae, confining them in a brass vessel to work for him."

Alfred gave a snort. "If you ever tried to put a bogle in a brass box—" he began.

"You would fail," Miss Eames finished. "And he did. He failed to conjure up a demon—until he began to imitate Gilles de Rais." Seeing the confusion on every face, she went on to provide more details. "Gilles de Rais was a medieval lord who tried to evoke a demon to do his bidding. When his first three attempts didn't succeed, he was told by a wicked alchemist to make an offering of dead children."

Birdie swallowed hard. Alfred heaved a sigh, and Jem muttered a curse. Charlie sat down abruptly, as if he'd gone weak at the knees.

"It—it says here that the doctor found a boy, though it

doesn't say how," Miss Eames stammered. "He used chloroform, and put the boy on that triangle—"

"We don't need to hear any o' that." Alfred cut her off sharply. "We know what happened next."

"The bogle came," Miss Eames confirmed, blinking back tears. "It came and took him." She licked her lips and said to Jem, "I'm so very sorry . . ."

"But where did it come *from?*" Birdie demanded. "Did he write *that* down?"

"No. He says it . . . simply appeared." Miss Eames was knitting her brows as she leafed through the journal. "He says he conjured it up from the infernal regions."

Again Alfred snorted—just as Charlie raised his hand.

"Uh . . . Fred?" Charlie faltered. "Is this what I think it is?"

His fingers were coated in greenish slime.

18

Bogling

"Where did *that* come from?" Alfred said sharply.

"I don't know." Charlie was already rising from the window seat, looking shaken. "All I done was hold on to the edge . . ."

"Step away." Alfred moved toward the shuttered window as Charlie retreated from it. And while Alfred crouched down to examine the wooden seat in the glow of his dark lantern, Birdie grabbed Charlie's wrist.

"It's the same stuff," she declared. "The same as was found on them clothes."

"Aye." Alfred had already smeared his own fingers with slime, after running them along the lip of the seat. "There's hinges on this. It must be a box, or summat. A place to store things—"

"Don't *touch* it, Mr. Bunce!" Miss Eames exclaimed. Birdie, meanwhile, was trying hard not to vomit. A sudden wave of nausea nearly sent her reeling; only by taking several deep breaths, and focusing all her attention on her feet, was she able to resist the urge to empty her stomach.

Charlie was frantically wiping his hand on his coat. "Is he in there? Is Billy in there?" he squeaked—much to Jem's horror.

"Don't look!" Jem cried. "Don't open that seat, for gawd's sake!"

"I won't." Alfred stood up and stepped back, frowning.

"But is he in there?" Charlie demanded. "Is that where he is?"

"The *bogle's* in there!" Jem snapped. Though he stopped short of calling Charlie a half-wit, his tone was full of contempt. "It's locked in that box!"

"No, it ain't," said Alfred. "You can't lock a bogle in a box."

"It certainly doesn't appear so, from Dr. Morton's journal." Miss Eames was poring over the pages of her book. "On the contrary, he complains that he cannot restrain the creature for any length of time."

"Of course not!" Birdie exclaimed. "Because it's a bogle!"

Alfred, by this time, was tapping on the wooden wall panels. When asked why, he explained that since the window seat was built into the wall, there was probably a hollow behind the panels leading to an old well or spring or cellar under the house. "Which is where the bogle must live," he speculated, "since this seat ain't big enough for a bolthole."

"So it is merely the mouth of the burrow?" asked Miss Eames, earning a surprised, respectful glance from Alfred.

"Aye," he agreed. "Like enough."

"Can you kill it, then?" said Charlie. He was still rubbing his hand on his coat, his face colorless under a sheen of sweat. "Can you do it here? Now?"

"I think so," Alfred replied.

"Then do it. I told Ma you'd do it."

"But it might take a while," warned Alfred.

Charlie shrugged. "We got all day," he said, adding that if the slavvy should return before they'd finished, Enoch would simply grab her and lock her in a cupboard. "She'll cause no trouble if she's old and lame."

Birdie grimaced. She didn't like the idea of manhandling little old ladies. Neither did Miss Eames, who looked up from her book with a furrowed brow.

"I *cannot* condone an assault," she protested. "Housebreaking is bad enough, but when it comes to imprisoning an aged servant—"

"Would you rather have more dead boys?" Alfred cut her off harshly. His face was so grim that Miss Eames fell silent, biting her lip.

Then Jem asked her, "What makes you think the slavvy don't know what's bin going on? What makes you think she ain't a party to all this?"

It was a good question—and it made Birdie feel better about the old lady. Even Miss Eames looked as if she might be having second thoughts, though she did murmur, "I haven't found any mention of the housemaid, in these later entries . . ."

No one paid any attention. Charlie said, "I'll go and tell Enoch what the plan is." As he moved back toward the dining room, however, Jem called after him.

"Ain't we going to check upstairs first?"

"Oh . . ." Charlie paused. He peered at the staircase. "You're right. We should."

"*I'll* tell Enoch," Jem offered. "You check upstairs while Fred attends to his business."

"As for me," Miss Eames declared, "I shall attempt to glean more useful information from this book."

Next thing Birdie knew, people were heading in all directions, busy with their appointed tasks. Even Miss Eames retired to a distant corner, where the light spilling down the staircase allowed her to read without straining her eyes.

Jem vanished into the dining room. Charlie disappeared upstairs. Alfred set down his lantern, took out his bag of salt, and began to cover the painted circle with a magic one.

Only Birdie was left with nothing to do. She stood quietly waiting, as far away from the window seat as possible, wrestling with her fear and her anger. Neither of these emotions would help her to keep her hand steady or her wits sharpened. If she was to do her job, she had to remain calm and clearheaded.

"Jem's gone and hoisted that cup," she told Alfred when her roving gaze finally settled on an empty expanse of purple damask. "The ring, too. I never saw him do it."

"Jem's a downy lad," was Alfred's only response.

Miss Eames said nothing; she was lost in her book. But as Alfred finished laying out his ring of salt, Charlie came stomping back downstairs and announced, "It's all clear up there. Not a living soul. Nor a dead one, neither."

"Did you check the attic?" asked Birdie.

Charlie gave a nod. "*And* in every cupboard." He frowned at Alfred. "Did you kill the bogle yet?"

"Kill the bogle!" Birdie spluttered, outraged. "D'you think it's that easy?"

Alfred fixed Charlie with a sour look. "I ain't started. And I won't till you hook it. Tell the others to stay in the kitchen until they're wanted."

Charlie sniffed. Then his eyes narrowed as he realized

that the silver was missing. "Who took that plate?" he demanded.

"Who do you think?" said Birdie. But Charlie ignored her.

"It weren't you, Fred? Not even the ring?" he asked suspiciously.

Alfred straightened, holding his spear. His expression was thunderous. "I ain't no thief," he spat, in a tone of disgust that took Charlie by surprise. The two of them stared at each other for a moment until Charlie dropped his gaze and marched out the door — which slammed shut behind him.

Alfred scowled at the noise but didn't speak. It was Miss Eames who suddenly said, "I can find nothing here that will help you, Mr. Bunce. For some reason, the doctor barely saw this creature. He certainly gives no coherent description of it."

"If he didn't see where it came from, then he didn't see it clear," Alfred remarked. "But that don't matter. Like I allus say — a bogle's a bogle." He turned to Birdie. "Are you ready now, lass?"

Birdie nodded. She stepped into the ring of salt just as Miss Eames addressed her from the bottom of the staircase. "I'm here, Birdie, if you need my help. *Please* be careful, dear."

"She allus is," Alfred said, before putting a finger to his lips. "Hush, now," he advised. "No more talking. Not until I say so." Then he nodded at Birdie, who began to sing.

> *"There lives a lady in Scotland (who dearly loved me),*
> *And she's fallen in love with an Englishman,*
> *So bonnie Susie Cleland will be burned in Dundee."*

Peering into her mirror, Birdie kept her eyes glued to Alfred's reflection. The lantern was sitting on the floor beside him, illuminating him from below in a way that cast strange and eerie shadows across his face. But even as her gaze shifted to the salt in his hand, Birdie realized that the lantern's soft radiance was dimming. Or was the air growing thicker?

All at once she realized that the room was getting smoky — and that the smoke was seeping through the floorboards. It seemed blacker than normal smoke. Heavier, too.

Though it made Birdie cough, she doggedly kept singing.

> *"The father unto the daughter came (who dearly loved*
>   *me),*
> *Saying [cough-cough], 'Will you forsake that English-*
>   *man?*
> *For if that Englishman you will not forsake*

O I will [cough-cough] burn you at the stake!'
And bonnie Susie Cleland will be burned in Dundee."

Suddenly a gush of smoke engulfed the room. It happened so quickly that Birdie was taken by surprise. Within seconds her view of Alfred was snatched away; she could barely see the mirror in her hand.

She half expected to hear him shout instructions but then realized that he didn't dare, in case he alerted the bogle. So she looked over her shoulder, hoping that he might signal to her. By this time, however, only the faint glow of the lantern was visible through a veil of smoke.

Birdie couldn't tell if Miss Eames and Alfred were coughing or not. She couldn't hear anything through the sound of her own shrill, cracked, frightened voice.

"'I will not that Englishman forsake (who dearly loved me),
Though you should [cough-cough] burn me at the stake!'
The [cough-cough] brother did the stake make,
The father did the fire set [cough-cough],
And bonnie Susie Cleland was burned in'—oh!"

Something had grabbed Birdie's wrist. She stopped singing. She started to scream. As she plucked at the three bony, barbed, coal-black fingers that were tightening their grip on her, she heard an answering cry from Miss Eames.

"*Birdie! Birdie, where are you?*"

"*HE-E-LP!*" The fingers were very strong. They were tugging Birdie toward the dark center of the smoke cloud. Though she dug in her heels, then dropped to her knees, she couldn't stop sliding across the floor. But she did manage to smash her mirror, before using one jagged shard to slash at the thing wrapped around her wrist.

The substance that spurted from the wound was a sticky black vapor, which seemed to evaporate as it hit the air.

"*Birdie!*" Miss Eames lunged out of the wall of smoke. She threw her arms around Birdie and tried to yank her away from the bogle.

Birdie screamed again. She felt as if she were being pulled in half. And when she caught sight of a gaping hole right in front of her—a hole lined with giant, slime-covered teeth—she screamed so loudly that she nearly burst her own eardrums.

Whomp! An eruption of flame singed her hair. The pressure on her wrist eased. There was a flash of intense heat, another gush of smoke that rolled across the ceiling, and a *clunk* as Alfred's spear hit the floor. Birdie could see the spear because the smoke was already clearing. Within seconds it had dissipated, leaving nothing but a huge scorch mark.

The spear lay in the middle of this charred patch, covered in slime. Alfred stood just beyond it, panting heavily. He and Birdie stared at each other, their eyes bloodshot, their chests heaving.

Miss Eames groaned into Birdie's ear. The two of them were all tangled up together, like flotsam on a beach.

"Birdie?" Miss Eames rasped. "Are you all right, dear?"

Birdie's wrist was stinging. When she glanced at it, she saw that the bogle's fingers had left a large bruise like a bracelet, which was beaded with little spots of blood. The wound was already taking on a greenish tinge.

"I — I hope so," she stammered.

Then the door burst open, and Charlie and Jem erupted into the room.

"What the hell was that?" Charlie exclaimed. "What the devil is going on in here? *What in the world are you people doing?*"

19

THE TRIP HOME

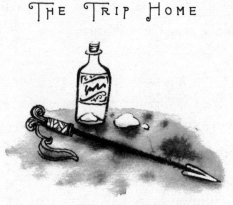

Alfred and Birdie went home in a hansom cab, accompanied by Miss Eames.

They had left Dr. Morton's house together shortly after killing the bogle. No one had said much, at first; Alfred had told Charlie that the bogle was dead, while Miss Eames had suggested in a feeble, breathless voice that they catch a cab. Alfred had then thrust Birdie's injured arm into his bag of salt before packing away the rest of his equipment. He had ignored Charlie's questions. Jem's murmured thanks had elicited no more than a nod and a grunt.

Birdie hadn't felt equal to walking any distance, so Alfred had carried her through the kitchen and out of the house. He had also carried her to the end of the street, which was too poor and narrow to attract many hansom cabs. Luckily, the rain had stopped. And Miss Eames, who had followed Alfred with his sack in her arms, managed to hail a cab almost as soon as they reached the broad sweep of Farringdon Road.

It was only after they had all settled into the vehicle, with Birdie tucked between her two companions, that they were finally ready to speak again.

"Show me that wrist, lass," Alfred said. When Birdie obediently drew her arm out of the bag of salt, he inspected her wound with narrowed eyes. "Mmmmph. That's looking better."

"Is it poisoned?" Miss Eames asked faintly.

Alfred shrugged. "If it is, the salt will draw out the rot." But he sprinkled a few drops of holy water onto Birdie's arm, just in case. "Leave yer hand in the salt," he recommended, "and I'll clap a poultice on it when we reach home."

"Perhaps Birdie would be better off at my house. Perhaps she would be more comfortable there."

Alfred shook his head. "Nay. I've all that's needed for bogle bites under me own bed," he assured Miss Eames.

"Oh, but this ain't no bite, Mr. Bunce," Birdie croaked. "It's claw marks."

"Which is a mercy," said Alfred, "since bites can be fatal."

Silence fell at the sound of the word "fatal." Miss Eames frowned. Alfred sighed. Birdie swallowed and tried to think about something else. It wasn't easy. She kept seeing the gaping mouth in her mind's eye. She kept feeling the weight of black smoke in her lungs.

So she tried to concentrate on the scenery flowing past them: the houses, the churches, the shops, the squares. Everything looked gray and damp and dirty. Flags hung limply from their poles. It had started raining again.

"No wonder that wicked man believed he had conjured up a demon from the fires of hell," Miss Eames said at last. "With all that smoke, I might have thought the same thing."

"Aye." After a moment's pause, Alfred remarked pensively, "I ain't never seen owt like it."

"Really?" Miss Eames sounded surprised. "Never?"

Again Alfred shook his head. "And want to see nowt like it again," he growled. Birdie shuddered.

"Was it *breathing* the smoke?" Miss Eames wanted to know. "Did you see where the smoke was coming from?"

"No," Alfred replied.

"A smoke-shrouded creature . . ." Miss Eames grimaced. "It couldn't have been a dragon, surely? I'm convinced it wasn't *that*."

Alfred said nothing. There was another long silence as they rattled past the Shoreditch Vestry Hall—which looked like a huge, elaborate wedding cake. Then Miss Eames suddenly stiffened.

"Oh!" she exclaimed. "I forgot the journal! I left it there! How *stupid* of me!"

Alfred didn't seem very concerned. He scratched his chin and gave another shrug.

"Maybe we should go back," Miss Eames continued, but Birdie cut her off.

"Go back? Not me!" The thought made Birdie feel cold and sick. "I ain't *never* going back there!"

"Nor I," Alfred agreed.

"But that journal is proof, Mr. Bunce! Proof that Dr. Morton killed all those poor boys!" Miss Eames leaned toward him slightly, raising her voice above the clatter of horses' hooves. "We could show it to the police! It is our *written evidence.*"

Alfred snorted. "Evidence o' what? That a doctor's gone mad and thinks he's a warlock?" Before Miss Eames could protest, he added, "Ain't no trace o' them boys, miss. Ain't no bogle in that house — not anymore. Ain't nothing but rants on a page."

"Which that doctor *might* say is for a penny dreadful," Birdie interposed. While she had never read any of these cheap, flimsy, paperbound books, she knew the kind of sensational stories they told. "He might claim he's writing *The Curse o' the Necromancer,* or suchlike."

"If you tell the traps," Alfred informed Miss Eames, "the first thing they'll do is nib us all for housebreaking. Birdie, too. On account o' Jem'll hoist that silver cup, and I'd not trust Enoch to keep his hands off the rest."

"Then *I* shall speak to the police. Without mentioning any of you." Though Miss Eames spoke bravely, there was a quaver in her tone. "I shall say that the housemaid let me in, and that I saw the journal while I was waiting for Dr. Morton. If the housemaid is very old, she could easily have forgotten that she admitted me into the house. I'm sure the police would give more weight to my account than they would to hers."

Birdie was astonished. "Don't lie to the traps, miss. No good will come of it," she said gravely, causing Miss Eames to flush. The flush deepened as they stared at each other.

At last Miss Eames exclaimed, "I know it's wrong! Of course I do! But something has to be *done!*"

"Something was done," Alfred retorted. "We killed the bogle."

"Which won't kill no one else," Birdie added.

"And Dr. Morton? What of him?" Miss Eames appealed to Alfred. "He must answer for his crimes! He is a *murderer,* Mr. Bunce! He murdered four children!"

"No, he didn't."

"But—"

"It were the bogle as killed them kids, not the doctor," said Alfred. "He just put 'em in harm's way."

These words seemed to hang in the air for a while. Alfred abruptly turned his head and stared out at the passing street—which looked vaguely familiar to Birdie because they were crossing from Shoreditch into Bethnal Green. But she wasn't interested in the cab's progress. She was far more concerned about Alfred. *He thinks he's just like that doctor,* she thought, aghast, and opened her mouth to insist that feeding boys to bogles was *completely different* from using a trained apprentice to lure bogles out of their lairs.

Miss Eames, however, was too quick for her.

"You almost lost Birdie today, Mr. Bunce. Perhaps you should reconsider the offer I made."

Birdie's stomach lurched. There were dozens of things she wanted to say: that she had never *truly* been in danger, that no bogle would ever get the better of Alfred, that Miss Eames was overreacting. But for some reason she found it hard to speak.

So Miss Eames plowed on, addressing Alfred's profile.

"I understand your difficulties. I realize that bogling is your livelihood, and that my experiment with the pie was unsuccessful. But could you at least give some thought to alternative baits? Children's clothes, perhaps?" When Alfred didn't respond, Miss Eames tried another suggestion. "What about hair? Or baby teeth?"

"Baby teeth? For a *bogle?*" Birdie had found her voice at last. "Why not try to catch a whale with a chestnut?"

"I know it sounds odd," Miss Eames argued, "but teeth might have some value as a lure. Baby teeth have been offered up to spirit creatures for centuries, all over the world."

"Not to bogles, I'll be bound," Birdie scoffed.

Suddenly Alfred spoke up. "I might become a rat catcher," he mumbled.

Miss Eames blinked. Birdie gasped. She goggled at him for a moment before recovering her breath.

"*What?*" she squawked.

"You can make a good living out o' rats. There's more rats than bogles in London."

"But you're a *bogler!*" Birdie shrilled. "Bogling's a *respectable* job!"

"Ain't no shame in rat catching," Alfred said.

"Ain't no pride in it, neither!" Birdie couldn't believe her ears. Was Alfred joking? Was he trying to placate Miss Eames? "A bogler's a hero! A rat catcher's like a ferret, or a dog!"

"I think it's a very good idea," Miss Eames interjected.

Birdie rounded on her furiously. "You don't know *nothing!*" she spat, before resuming her attack on Alfred. "What's to be done about all them bogles still in London? Who's going to stop 'em eating kids if you ain't bogling no more?"

Alfred wiped a hand across his tired, morose, pouchy face. He seemed to be wavering. So Birdie went in for the kill.

"People need you, Mr. Bunce! *Children* need you! And you need me!" she cried.

"I don't need you dead, lass." Alfred was shaking his head. Without looking at her, very calmly and quietly, he murmured, "Not you. *Never* you."

Birdie gulped, hiccupped, and burst into tears. It was all too much. She felt as if the foundations of her world were crumbling away. Her wrist was hurting and her stomach was churning and she was shaking all over.

But when Miss Eames tried to wrap an arm around her, Birdie pushed it aside angrily. "Get off!" she sobbed. "I'm tired, is all!"

Then the cab stopped.

"We're here," muttered Alfred.

Miss Eames peered through the rain, toward the crumbling, sooty structure that Alfred called home. "Perhaps I should come in with you."

"No!" Birdie didn't want Miss Eames hovering over her bed, babbling on about police and baby teeth and singing lessons. "Go home. This ain't no place for the likes o' you."

Alfred was more courteous. "Birdie'll be all right, miss. I know how to tend a bogle wound."

"But we haven't finished our talk," Miss Eames complained. "We haven't decided what to do about Dr. Morton."

As Alfred heaved a weary sigh, she said sharply, "He has to pay for what he's done!"

"Oh, he'll pay," Alfred assured her. "There's people will make sure o' that, don't worry."

Miss Eames frowned. "What do you mean? What people?"

"People you don't need to know about." Alfred flicked a warning glance at Birdie, who understood that he didn't want her mentioning Sarah's name. "People as lost an income when they lost them boys."

"Are you talking about Charlie and Enoch?" Miss Eames demanded.

"I'm talking about the person Charlie reports to." Hearing the cabdriver clear his throat impatiently, Alfred pulled the lever to release the door. "Thank'ee, miss. You go home now. Have a cup o' tea — or summat stronger. You earned it today."

"Oh!" Miss Eames gave a start, then fumbled at her waist. "On the subject of earnings, I owe you some money—"

"No, you don't. Forget the three shillings." Alfred paused as he climbed down from the cab. Looking up, his sack on his shoulder, he offered Miss Eames a lopsided smile and said, "I might have lost more'n that if you hadn't bin there."

Then he reached for Birdie.

20

Three Friends

Alfred's poultice was made from a clean rag soaked in salt water and dried herbs.

"A bogle once bit me when I were a boy," he told Birdie as he wrapped the poultice around her arm, "and this is the same dressing I used then." He lifted his trouser leg to show her the faint white scar that ringed his ankle. "Good as gold, see? And a bite's worse'n a scratch."

Birdie nodded. She knew all about the scar, which didn't interest her much. She had other, more pressing concerns. "You ain't *really* going to be a rat catcher, are you?" she said at last, in a trembling voice.

Alfred didn't immediately reply. He was unscrewing the

lid of his brandy flask. "That's for me to decide," he finally answered. "Don't you fuss and fret. I'll do nowt in haste." He offered the flask to Birdie, who shook her head.

"I can't," she admitted. "I ain't got the stomach for it."

"It'll settle yer nerves."

"I'll only bring it up."

"What you need is a coddled egg." Alfred rose to his feet, taking a swig of brandy. "I'll see what I can find while you take yer ease. A day o' rest should see you sprightly again."

He then put on his hat and left the room, and Birdie crawled into bed. She fell instantly asleep and slept for several hours, waking to discover that Alfred had bought her milk, eggs, bread, and tea. Without getting out of bed, she ate the bread soaked in milk while Alfred drank his tea with a drop of brandy in it. Neither of them talked about the future. Alfred was in one of his morose moods, and Birdie didn't feel strong enough to ask any difficult questions. Only by discussing everyday things — like the best way to coddle an egg — could she keep her eyes dry and her voice steady.

When their first visitor knocked on the door, early in the afternoon, Birdie was sure that Miss Eames had come back. "Make her go away!" Birdie entreated, sliding beneath the covers. But if Alfred heard her plea, he gave no sign of it.

"Come in," he growled without getting up.

The door opened to admit Jem Barbary. Though

smelling faintly of liquor, Jem looked more sober than usual. His jaunty air had a battered quality about it, and the smudges under his eyes were darker than ever.

"Good day to you, Mr. Bunce," he said, removing his flat cap. "I came to inquire after Birdie. There's talk that she's bin taken ill."

"She's on the mend," Alfred replied shortly. "Bogle wounds need careful tending."

Jem glanced at Birdie, who glared at him. She was waiting to discover what he *really* wanted, since she couldn't imagine that he was interested in the state of her health.

"Well, that's good," he declared, then dropped his gaze and cleared his throat. "But Sarah wants me to say that if Birdie can't help you no more, on account o' the injury she took, then she can allus find work begging."

Birdie gasped as Alfred raised his eyebrows.

"Sarah says as how a little fair girl will do well on the street, no matter what," Jem continued quickly. "She says when Birdie gets too old for bogling, there's still a good living to be made in scrounging or street singing."

By this time Birdie was red in the face with fury. Before she could even open her mouth, however, Alfred intervened.

"Is that the message Sal charged you with?" he asked Jem.

The boy nodded, rubbing his nose.

"Then you can tell her you did yer job, and no one here is blaming you for it," said Alfred. "As for Birdie, she'll not be needing Sal's help."

"Ever!" Birdie spat.

Jem shrugged. He seemed resigned and a little sheepish. Plucking a fine silk handkerchief from his pocket, he offered it to Birdie with a crooked smile. "I brought this for you. A wipe's more use in a sickroom than anything else, *I* allus think."

Birdie sniffed. "Are you trying to get me lagged again? For harboring stolen goods?" she retorted. But when his face fell, she realized that the gesture had been kindly meant, and she regretted her outburst.

"She's a little feverish," Alfred explained, "and is in no fit state to receive visitors. But she'll be on her feet tomorrow." He fixed Jem with a bleak and knowing look. "You tell Sarah that."

Jem grunted, wordlessly admitting defeat as he stuffed the handkerchief back into his pocket. He then tipped his cap and left the room, though not before winking at Birdie. It wasn't until he had shut the door behind him that she exploded into a furious rant against Sarah Pickles. "Why, I'd sooner be a tosher than work for her!" Birdie cried. "How dare she send me such a message, and make Jem bring it against his will? She's a devil, is what she is! A devil straight from hell!"

"You was too hard on Jem, lass."

Birdie agreed contritely. "I know. It ain't *his* fault. But I don't want nothing to do with no stolen wipe — can he not see that?"

"Mebbe not," Alfred replied. "How could he, when Sal had the raising of 'im?"

Their second visitor knocked when Alfred was lighting his third pipe of the day. Birdie half expected to see Sarah Pickles walk through the door, and was greatly relieved when Ned Roach appeared on the threshold instead. It took her a moment to recognize him because he was so clean, as if he'd never seen a muddy riverbank in his life. His clothes were freshly laundered, his boots were polished, and his face was well scrubbed. Even his hair looked fluffy.

He carried a penny bunch of violets.

"These are for you," he told Birdie. "I heard as how you fell foul of a bogle."

She colored. "Who told you that?" she asked, annoyed that Jem had been gossiping.

"Uh . . . a barmaid I know." Ned glanced uneasily at Alfred, who was puffing away in silence. "She got it from her brother, as got it from Jem Barbary."

"Jem Barbary should mind his own business," Birdie grumbled. But she accepted the flowers, knowing somehow that Ned hadn't stolen them. "Thanks," she muttered. "They smell nice."

"You should sit down, lad." At last Alfred spoke up. "You must be right footsore if you walked all the way from Wapping."

"I live in Whitechapel," Ned explained. "In a common lodging house. It's a deal cheaper than the cribs in Wapping."

"Ah."

"I should move closer to the river," Ned conceded. Then he sat down at Birdie's bedside. There was a long, awkward silence as Birdie remembered that Ned was a boy of few words.

She sniffed at the violets, wondering where he had found money enough to buy them. The thought that he might have sacrificed a meal brought her so close to tears that she became quite cross with herself. *All this crying has to stop,* she thought. *Why am I spouting like a pump well all of a sudden?*

Aloud she asked Ned, "How's business bin, down at the river?"

Ned shrugged. "Not good."

"Oh." When he didn't continue, Birdie tried another tack. "Seen any more bogles lately?"

"No."

Birdie glanced at Alfred, hoping he would say something. But he just sat there, quietly smoking, his eyes on the empty fireplace.

She felt a guilty sense of gratitude when their third and final visitor rapped on the door. By that time even Sarah Pickles would have been a welcome interruption.

"Come in!" said Alfred.

The door opened. Miss Eames entered. She was carrying a covered basket and had changed into her mustard-colored suit, but otherwise looked much the same as she had that morning—pale, agitated, and slightly disheveled. "Oh!" she exclaimed on seeing Ned. "I'm sorry. I had no idea you were entertaining . . ."

Ned jumped up so abruptly that he knocked over his stool. As Miss Eames advanced into the room, he started to edge around her, heading for the dingy hallway outside. Her sudden appearance seemed to have alarmed him.

"Oh, please don't leave on my account!" she implored. "I wish to stay only for a short time."

But he murmured something incoherent and fled. Miss Eames appealed to Alfred.

"What did I do? Have I caused offense in some way?"

"Don't mind him." Alfred had risen to pick up the overturned stool. "I'm persuaded he ain't used to mixed company."

"I see," said Miss Eames, though she obviously didn't. Turning to Birdie, she smiled and asked, "How are you, my dear? How is your wound?"

"Better," Birdie replied, eyeing her warily.

"I've brought you a few things, though I see you already have flowers." Miss Eames unveiled her basket and began to unload its contents onto the table. "Here is a plain cake, and a pot of jam, and some Bath Oliver biscuits, and a jar of beef tea, which is very strengthening. Also, Mrs. Heppinstall has included some stewed apples and a pound of sugar, which I know you will use sensibly."

"Thank'ee, miss," said Alfred, before flicking a sharp look at Birdie.

"Thank you, miss," Birdie muttered.

"My cab is waiting outside, so I cannot linger," Miss Eames continued. "Truth to tell, I wasn't sure how easy it would be to *find* a cab in this district—"

"It ain't." Alfred cut her off. "You did the right thing to keep it waiting."

"I thought as much." Miss Eames hesitated for a moment, her gaze drifting over the cracked ceiling and smoke-blackened walls. She looked profoundly ill at ease. "Have you had any news from your mysterious acquaintance?" she said at last. "About the punishment to be visited on Dr. Morton?"

Alfred shook his head. "I've bin busy with other things," he answered dryly.

"Yes, of course. I understand." Miss Eames glanced at Birdie again. "I'm sorry to see her still laid up in bed.

Should I arrange a doctor's visit, Mr. Bunce? At no cost to yourself, of course."

"Ain't no need for a doctor," Alfred replied. "She'll be on her feet tomorrow."

"Well, if you're *sure*—"

"I'm sure."

Miss Eames nodded. Then she took a deep breath and launched into a speech that sounded well rehearsed. "There is one more matter that I wish to raise before I go," she announced. "I've discussed your situation with my aunt, Mr. Bunce, and we both understand how hard it would be for you to earn a livelihood without a trained apprentice at your side. So I have a proposition to make. If Mrs. Heppinstall and I were to offer you a small stipend over the next three years, would you undertake to devote the greater part of your time toward developing a more scientific way of attracting bogles?"

Alfred frowned. "A stipend?" he echoed, sounding confused.

"A stipend is a regular payment. Like a wage." Miss Eames was watching him closely. "This, of course, would be contingent upon my giving Birdie a musical education. And it would ensure that London's bogles would not be left to their own devices. You would continue to be a bogler, Mr. Bunce, only our aim would be to make bogling a *soli-*

tary pursuit, based on technical advancement and a greater understanding of the natural sciences."

Alfred was staring at her, wide eyed and slack jawed. Even Birdie was speechless. She couldn't believe her ears; was Miss Eames actually offering to pay Alfred for doing nothing?

"I'll leave you to consider my offer. Naturally, I wouldn't expect an immediate decision." Tucking the handle of her basket into the crook of her elbow, Miss Eames began to withdraw. On the threshold, however, she stopped and looked back. "Do remember, though — the longer you delay, the more often you'll put Birdie at risk. And I'm aware, Mr. Bunce, that you would hate to do that."

Then, with a nod and a wave, she departed.

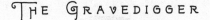

21

THE GRAVEDIGGER

Birdie didn't sleep much that night. She kept wondering how many more nights she would be allowed to sleep in her own bed. She tried to imagine living in Mrs. Heppinstall's house. Would there be cake every day? Would Birdie be allowed to choose her own clothes? How regularly would she be expected to bathe?

She'd never had a bath in her life and was frightened at the thought of taking one. The prospect of school didn't appeal much either. Most of all, though, she dreaded having to leave Alfred.

He can't manage without me, she told herself over and

over again as she lay in the dark. For years Birdie had cooked their meals and mended their linen. She had bought medical supplies when Alfred was ill. She had cleaned and shopped and delivered messages. Who was going to do all that if she left?

And surely Alfred didn't *really* believe that he could kill a bogle without the aid of an apprentice?

When Birdie finally did fall asleep, her dreams were haunted by smoke and slime and bogles. She woke up five times, gasping with fear. Each time, however, she would hear Alfred snoring on the other side of the room—and each time the noise made her feel safe.

In the morning she decided to get out of bed.

"My wrist ain't a bit sore," she declared. "Not a thing is wrong with me. But I *shall* fall ill if I have to lie in this corner, which is so damp and close."

Having checked her arm, Alfred agreed. "This is mending well," he said. It was the only thing he did say for several hours. While Birdie got up and made breakfast—which was bread and tea, sweetened by Miss Eames's jam and Mrs. Heppinstall's sugar—he sat silently gazing at the fireplace, gnawing on the stem of his pipe. He couldn't actually smoke the pipe because he had no tobacco.

Birdie didn't dare break into Alfred's reverie. She knew that he must be thinking about Miss Eames's offer, and she didn't want to make a nuisance of herself. So she bustled about, wiping and sweeping, to demonstrate that she was perfectly well again.

Then somebody knocked on the door.

Alfred seemed as surprised as Birdie was. He snapped to attention, looking at her with raised eyebrows, but she shrugged and shook her head. She wasn't expecting company.

"Who is it?" asked Alfred.

The voice that replied was unfamiliar. It was a man's voice, high and reedy, with a faint Scottish accent. "Would that be Mr. Alfred Bunce? The Go-Devil Man?"

"Aye." Alfred frowned. "And who might you be?"

"Simeon McGill is my name, sir. I need yeer help and will pay for it."

Alfred nodded at Birdie, who went to open the door. When she did, she jumped back with a squeak—because the man waiting in the corridor was enormous. He had to stoop to enter the room, where he stood with his scalp brushing against the cornice. His large hands were seamed with dirt; his large boots were caked with it. He had the broadest shoulders and the widest neck that Birdie had ever seen; yet his head looked a little undersize, as if it belonged to a different body.

"We've got a bogle, Mr. Bunce," he said. "In the Victoria Park burial ground. I'd swear to it."

"Oh, aye?"

"I work there," the big man continued, then paused, as if he didn't know quite how to go on.

"Are you a gravedigger?" Birdie asked him, with a touch of alarm.

When he nodded, she had to force herself not to grimace. Alfred, however, seemed completely unmoved.

"If you've had coffins plundered, you'll not need me," he observed. "Bogles eat living children, not dead'uns."

"Oh, no, sir, it's no' like that." Simeon's squeaky, singsong voice, combined with his blank blue gaze, snub nose, and silky blond hair, gave the impression that he himself was just a child, trapped in a giant's body. He rocked from foot to foot, twisting his rolled cap in his enormous hands. "There's a mortuary chapel in the park, ye see. People sleep there when the weather's bad—"

"At *night,* you mean?" Birdie interrupted, horrified. She would rather have slept in a ditch than in a graveyard at night.

Simeon nodded, glancing from Alfred to Birdie and back again. He seemed quite happy to be answering questions put to him by a little girl. It was Alfred who frowned at Birdie, indicating that he wanted her to keep her mouth shut.

"Though we try to chase 'em out, they come back and break the lock," Simeon continued. "Besides, we cannae work there at night. But now folk say there's a *ciudach* inside the chapel, which ate two bairns. And that's bad for business, Mr. Bunce."

Alfred studied him for a moment, eyes narrowed, brow creased. "A *ciudach*?" he repeated. "What is that?"

Simeon seemed surprised that he didn't know. "Why, a monster. A thing that lives in caves and eats people."

"A bogle, in other words."

"Aye. I'm guessing so."

"And who exactly has bin talking about bogles?" Alfred queried.

Simeon blinked. "Folk. Hereabouts." After a moment's intense thought, he said, "One of the workhouse chaplains."

"Has seen a bogle?"

"Oh, no, sir. But he has heard stories. Even the paupers from the Waterloo Road workhouse dinnae want to be buried at Victoria Park any longer." Simeon went on to explain that sometimes so many coffins were piled up in the cemetery, awaiting burial, that they were attacked by vermin. "When it's rats and dogs, that's bad enough," he confessed, "but folk draw the line at bogles."

"Bogles don't eat corpses," Alfred flatly insisted.

"Uh — Mr. Bunce?" Birdie felt that she had to speak, though she quailed a little as Alfred glared at her. "There ain't no telling what a bogle might do," she reminded him. "*Most* don't eat corpses, the way most don't breathe smoke. But who's to say there ain't one out there with different tastes . . . ?"

She trailed off, knowing that she had made her point. Alfred's fierce expression had already changed to a more pensive one.

"Whether it eats live bairns or dead ones, this bogle is no' a good thing for us gravediggers, sir," their visitor suddenly remarked. "For the park is a business and must turn a profit if me and Mr. Swales are to keep our jobs."

"Is Mr. Swales another gravedigger?" Alfred inquired.

"Aye, sir. There's me and Mr. Swales and the superintendent, Mr. Donohue." Simeon chanted this list of names like a child reciting a multiplication table, his little round eyes fixed blandly on Alfred. "Mr. Donohue lives in a house on the grounds and heard screaming one night, or so he thinks. But he's a tippler and hears strange things on occasion."

"Did he see the bogle?" asked Alfred.

"No."

"Did *anyone* see it?"

"I cannae tell ye that, sir. I misdoubt it."

"What about the missing kids? Can you tell me about 'em?"

"No, sir." Hearing Alfred sigh, the gravedigger added,

"If they were sleeping in a mortuary chapel, they were beggars—or worse."

Alfred pondered for a moment. "Is the park on consecrated soil?"

"No, sir, it is not. Could that be why the bogle came?"

"Mr. McGill," said Alfred, "I don't think there *is* a bogle. Just a lot o' gossip and silliness, which I can't do nothing about."

"Oh, but ye can, Mr. Bunce. Soon as it's known that ye couldnae find no bogle—or that you *did* find one and killed it stone dead—why, then our troubles will be over! For the coffins will start coming back again, praise be."

Catching Alfred's eye, Birdie didn't allow herself to snort or wince. She understood that it wouldn't have been polite.

"You'll be paid for yeer time," Simeon assured them both. "In fact, we'll stump up the full fee even if there's nae bogle. Mr. Swales and me—we agreed that would be fair."

"The fee is six shillings and sixpence, if there *is* a bogle," Alfred warned. But the gravedigger seemed completely unfazed by this sum.

"We'll give ye seven," he promised, staring at Alfred with a slightly cross-eyed intensity. "Seven shillings, no matter what."

Alfred hesitated. He began to chew on his pipe stem— a sure sign of indecision. When he glanced at Birdie, she gave him an encouraging look. Though she didn't like the idea of a graveyard at night, she *did* want Alfred to keep bogling.

His final response was a great disappointment to her.

"The fact o' the matter is, I ain't sure we can do this, Mr. McGill. Birdie's feeling poorly, and I'm ..." Alfred paused, then cleared his throat. "I bin thinking I might retire."

"Eight shillings," Simeon countered. "Half now, half later."

Alfred scratched his nose.

"Eight shillings for a bogle ye dinnae think is there." Simeon was arguing doggedly—tirelessly—like a nagging toddler. "Please, sir. It's our livelihood. How is Mr. Swales to feed his family if Victoria Park closes? What if another bairn is eaten? Who else can help us if you—"

"All right," Alfred said gruffly. He raised his hands in a gesture of defeat. "All right, I'll come."

"When?" asked the gravedigger.

Alfred heaved a gusty sigh. "I don't know ..."

"It's a night feeder," Birdie reminded him.

"That's true. So we'll go tonight." He peered up at Simeon. "When does the park close?"

"Sunset."

"Then we'll meet you there at sunset, Mr. McGill. By

the main gate." As Simeon kept nodding, Alfred extended an open palm. "And we'll collect half our fee at once, if you please."

"Yes, sir. Thank'ee, sir." The gravedigger surrendered his money without a moment's hesitation. He seemed satisfied, but not surprised or delighted. It was as if he'd always anticipated success.

Birdie found his attitude annoying. It was like that of an overindulged child. After he had gone, she said, "Someone that big—he must get his own way in everything."

"Mebbe," Alfred conceded. His expression was so glum that Birdie tried to cheer him up. She reminded him that he now had money enough for tobacco. She even offered to go buy some.

"No," he replied. "I'll go." Then, to her astonishment, he murmured, "Miss Eames ain't going to like this."

"Like what?" said Birdie, though she knew perfectly well what he meant. And when Alfred shot her an impatient look, she cried, "Miss Eames don't have to know about it! Since when did Miss Eames become our lord and master?"

"Since she offered us a decent living." Alfred stood up suddenly, pocketing his pipe and reaching for his hat. "You'll not find a stauncher friend than that lady," he declared. "And the sooner you realize it, the better I'll be pleased."

"But—"

"You're to think about what she said, lass. Good and hard. Because I shall."

He was out the door before Birdie could think of a smart rejoinder.

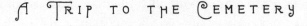

22

A Trip to the Cemetery

The entrance to Victoria Park burial ground was a stone archway that looked like a church front. Embedded in a high brick wall, it had carved corbels and two little matching towers like giant gateposts.

Silhouetted against a rapidly darkening sky, it made Birdie shiver.

Beyond the pointed archway lay a murky expanse of mounds and ditches, hemmed in by a canal, a railway line, and a cluster of tall, black factory chimneys. Two glowing windows marked the location of the superintendent's house. Otherwise, the only light in the whole cemetery came from the lantern that Simeon McGill was holding as he trudged toward Birdie and Alfred.

The gravedigger was easy to recognize, even though he was thickly plastered with filth. There was no mistaking his great height, his small head, or his broad shoulders. "Ye're late," he said, unlocking the iron-barred gates from the inside. "We were worrit you weren't about to come."

"I allus hold to me word," Alfred replied shortly. "Now, where is the chapel?"

"Over this way." After relocking the gate, Simeon guided Alfred and Birdie down a rough dirt path between ranks of headstones. Birdie tried not to look at them. She was aware of an ominous smell that made her breathe in shallow little gasps. At one point she even grabbed Alfred's coat for reassurance.

They quickly came to the superintendent's house, where Mr. Donohue was "soused in a dram or two of whiskey," according to Simeon. Birdie couldn't see much of this house in the darkness, though from the shape of its lighted windows, she deduced that it was probably built like the gate, in a Gothic style, out of stone. Simeon didn't even pause as he passed its entrance. "Mr. Donohue," he explained, "is no' a party to this matter and wouldnae wish to learn of it."

He then led Alfred toward the mortuary chapel, which

stood quite close to Mr. Donohue's house, with its back to the cemetery's western wall. Birdie was surprised at how small the chapel seemed to be. It was like a pocket-size church.

"This here is Mr. Jubez Swales," Simeon suddenly announced as another man emerged from the shadows. Unlike his partner, Jubez Swales was small and dark and stocky, with a full beard. His eyes were so deep set that they were impossible to see under his bushy eyebrows, and his face was like a root vegetable, all lumps and bumps and odd, sprouting hairs.

He carried a gravedigger's shovel and wore a grimy bowler hat that he tipped as he greeted Alfred. "Mr. Bunce," he growled in a nasal voice. He didn't even look at Birdie. "You got the keys there, McGill?"

"Aye." Simeon handed over a clanking bunch of heavy iron keys, and Jubez promptly inserted one of them into the door of the chapel. Though the building was wrapped in gloom, Birdie caught a glimpse of Gothic tracery and pointed arches. The light from Simeon's lantern bounced off a lead-light window. It lingered on a marble step.

But Birdie wasn't interested in the building. She was more concerned about its contents.

"Wait," said Alfred. He set down his bag and began to rummage through it, while Jubez stood with his hand on the door, ready to push. At last Alfred found his dark lantern and safety matches.

"You'll have nae need of that," Simeon piped up, indicating his own lantern.

"I *shall* need it," Alfred replied gruffly, "for you're all to stay out here while I go in." As Birdie opened her mouth to protest, he shot her a warning glance. "I'll not be long. Don't talk in the meantime. We don't want to scare that bogle — if it exists."

He nodded at Jubez, who gave the chapel door a shove. It creaked open to reveal a solid wedge of darkness. Alfred raised his uncovered lantern, then marched forward, straight past Jubez, into the void.

Birdie held her breath. She could see nothing of the building's interior. She could hear nothing except the pounding of her own heart in her ears.

Then a hoarse yell rang out.

"Mr. Bunce?" Birdie cried.

She darted forward just as Jubez plunged into the chapel ahead of her. But before she could reach the door, Simeon grabbed her from behind. One arm clamped around her waist. One hand was clapped over her mouth.

Next thing she knew, she was inside the mortuary chapel. It happened so quickly that at first she was quite confused. She thought she must have been dragged in there by a bogle — until she realized that Simeon was holding her high off the ground. Then she saw that there *was* no bogle. The octagonal space that she'd entered contained only an altar, a ring of stone sarcophagi shoved against the walls like benches, and four grown men.

One of these men was a stranger.

"Tie her up," said the stranger breathlessly, smoothing his ruffled hair with one hand as he offered Simeon a coil of rope with the other. "Use this."

He had the voice of a gentleman, very clipped and quiet. He was also dressed like a gentleman, in a handsome frock coat and a black silk cravat. A gold watch chain glittered on his waistcoat. A pair of steel-framed spectacles sat on his nose. Though small and slight, with a pale face and a modest mustache, he had a commanding presence — perhaps because his large eyes were the bleached and chilly color of river ice. His slicked-back hair gleamed like jet in the light of Alfred's lantern, which was now sitting on the tiled floor.

Alfred himself lay beside it, motionless.

When she saw him, Birdie screamed. But her scream was muffled by Simeon's hand.

The gentleman looked at her and said, "If you make another sound, little girl, you will suffer the same fate as your master. And this time I *may* misjudge the dose. It's a very easy thing to do with small children." As Alfred groaned, the gentleman turned to Jubez. "Tie him up. Now. The effects of chloroform are not long lasting."

Birdie's eyes widened as she stared at the stranger, shocked into silence. She knew something about chloroform. She understood that it was a chemical used by doctors to make people fall asleep during surgery. She realized that it must be the source of the strange, sweetish smell that was tainting the air.

Alfred had already begun to move a little. His eyelids were fluttering. But by the time he opened his eyes, his hands were being trussed behind his back.

"Tie her up!" the gentleman snapped, thrusting his rope more urgently at Simeon. "She won't make any trouble. And if she does, I'll use my chloroform on her." He shifted his pale, expressionless gaze toward Birdie. "Then I'll throw her into one of the stone coffins and leave her there."

Birdie tried not to flinch. She was quite sure that if she were ever imprisoned inside a sarcophagus, she would instantly go mad. So she kept her mouth shut when Simeon uncovered it. And she didn't struggle when he bound her hands and feet.

At the back of her mind she was nursing a vague hope that if she cooperated, her captors might stop paying attention to her. Once that happened, she might be able to escape — or at least raise the alarm. But she had to watch for her chance. She had to concentrate, the way she always did when she was gazing into her little hand mirror, waiting for a bogle to appear.

This ain't no worse than a bogle, she told herself over and over again. *I've faced up to a bogle, so I can face up to this.*

She knew that if she didn't concentrate hard, she would panic. And she couldn't afford to panic. That was the most important lesson Alfred had ever taught her: to keep calm and courageous during moments of great stress.

She had to think about why this was happening and what she could do to stop it. Who *was* this person? What did he want with Alfred?

"Wha . . . ? Norr-r-r . . ." Alfred gurgled, then coughed and groaned again. Only Birdie even glanced his way. The others were too busy talking.

"Did he bring any equipment?" the stranger asked Simeon, who nodded.

"It's out there," Simeon replied.

"Then bring it in. *With* your lamp. And shut the door behind you."

"I'll do that." Simeon propped Birdie against a sarcophagus, arranging her like a rag doll. Then he went to fetch Alfred's sack. Meanwhile, Alfred was struggling to sit up as Jubez stood over him with a raised shovel.

"Whatcher . . . whozat?" Alfred croaked, blinking groggily up at the frock-coated gentleman. When he realized that he couldn't move his hands, however, his gaze skittered away. "What is this?" he mumbled, craning his neck. "Birdie?"

"I'm here," Birdie squeaked.

The gentleman ignored her. "Mr. Bunce," he said, "my name is Morton. We haven't been introduced, but I'm informed that you visited my house yesterday."

Birdie gasped. She'd been too scared and confused to start wondering who the gentleman was. Now that he'd revealed his identity, however, it made perfect sense.

"I've also been informed that you killed a demon in my study," Dr. Morton continued. "And I must confess that I found this news far more distressing than my informant's attempt to blackmail me. Oh, yes. Didn't you know? Your friend Mrs. Smith is a blackmailer."

Birdie couldn't suppress a whimper of dismay. She guessed that the doctor was referring to Sarah Pickles, though it was hard to believe that even *Sarah* could do something so appallingly, unspeakably wicked as to betray them.

Alfred rasped, "Mrs. Smith ain't no friend o' mine." He was writhing and jerking as he tried to free himself from his bonds.

The doctor watched him for a while, dispassionately, the way a scientist might watch a specimen squirming at the end of a pin. At last he said, "I see. But you do know Mrs.

Smith, do you not? Or perhaps you know her by another name. I realize, of course, that she was using an alias."

Alfred didn't reply. Having wrenched a muscle trying to escape, he lay on the floor, panting and glaring.

Dr. Morton waited for a moment. "Perhaps we'll return to that subject a little later," he conceded at last. "For the time being, let us call the woman 'Mrs. Smith.' Since no better alternative has been suggested." He sat down carefully on one of the sarcophagus lids, adjusting the knees of his trousers. "Yesterday evening Mrs. Smith approached me in my own home. She threatened to go to the police with certain clothes and documents that she'd found unless I paid her a very large sum of money."

Birdie was taken by surprise. Though she'd assumed that Jem must have taken the silver from Dr. Morton's house, it had never occurred to her that he might have taken the doctor's journal as well.

"I'm sure the lady expected me to pay up like a meek little city clerk," Dr. Morton said. "When I warned her against interfering with my research, she jumped to conclusions. She assumed I was so defiant because I believed myself protected by the demon that I had been conjuring up. So do you know what she did, Mr. Bunce?"

"I do *not* know," Alfred spat, "and neither do I care!" He squinted at Birdie. "Did they hurt you, lass?"

Birdie shook her head.

"You're mad." Alfred turned back to the doctor with a look of savage contempt and said, "Which ain't news to me, for I've seen where you live, which is a nest o' lunacy. But *you* . . ." He wriggled around to address Jubez. "Are *you* mad? People know we came here and will ask for us if we don't return! What are you going to say to 'em then?"

Jubez stared blankly. It was the doctor who replied, "I'll answer that question in a moment, Mr. Bunce. For now, let me finish my story." He leaned forward, with a smirk that made Birdie's blood run cold. "You'll find it very illuminating, I promise."

23

The Most
Peculiar Proposition

Simeon suddenly appeared again, carrying his lantern in one hand and Alfred's sack in the other. He dropped the sack at Dr. Morton's feet but kept the lantern.

"Thank you." The doctor spoke like someone thanking a housemaid for bringing in the mail. His voice was perfectly calm as he peered into the sack. "Are these the tools of your trade, Mr. Bunce?"

Alfred didn't reply. He simply spat on the floor.

"Hmm." Dr. Morton reached down and produced Alfred's bag of salt, which he opened by loosening the drawstring. "How interesting," he murmured. "Salt is incorruptible—did you know that? Hence its potency as an antidemonic substance."

"You'd best be careful!" Birdie cried. She couldn't stop herself; she hated to see Alfred's possessions interfered with. "There's stuff in there can kill you! Touch it and you'll rue the day!"

She was lying, of course, but the doctor wouldn't know that. When he turned to look at her, something about his colorless regard made her cringe.

"If the contents of this bag *were* dangerous, then I very much doubt you'd be alerting me to the fact," he remarked. "However, a gentleman really shouldn't be seen in public while incorrectly dressed."

Dr. Morton proceeded to don a pair of tailored leather gloves, which he took from a neat pile of objects that lay on the sarcophagus lid beside him. These objects included a top hat, a walking stick, an overcoat, a tin box, and a doctor's leather bag.

"As I mentioned before," he said, "your friend Mrs. Smith seemed to think that my refusal to accept her offer stemmed from a misconception. She tried to alarm me with the news that my demon was no more. It had been killed by someone she described as a 'bogler.' Only imagine my surprise, Mr. Bunce! I had never heard of a bogler. I had no idea that unlettered men such as yourself had been grappling with infernal spirits for untold centuries." Suddenly he gestured at Jubez, who was still standing over Alfred with a raised shovel. "Mr. Swales did, though. He and Mr. McGill have been in my employ for several years. It can be very difficult for a doctor to acquire human body parts for dissection. Occasionally I've been forced to seek help from those whose livelihood depends on the disposal of corpses. It has been a most profitable partnership on both sides."

Alfred muttered something under his breath. Birdie noticed that his gaze wasn't fixed on the doctor but was flitting around the chapel, from object to object. She guessed he was searching for a means of escape.

"Mr. Swales had heard of you, Mr. Bunce, and kindly made further inquiries," the doctor continued. "He soon discovered your whereabouts. But I suspected that you might not agree to an interview, so I was forced to invent an elaborate story to lure you here. As you may have guessed, no demon has been eating children in this chapel." Once again he plunged his arm into Alfred's sack, drawing out the bundle that contained Finn MacCool's spear. "Now, what could *this* be?"

Birdie was visited by a sudden, fierce hope that he would poison himself on the spear's sharpest edge. He didn't, though. His fingers were too deft.

"Well, well," he murmured as the rags fell away to reveal a polished shaft with a stone point. "Is this for demons, or for people?"

"It'd slice through *you* like butter," Alfred snarled.

"I'm sure." Dr. Morton began to examine the spear very carefully, cradling it in both hands. Then he fixed his bland gaze on Alfred. "If it's designed to kill demons and I use it on this little girl, then it won't hurt her, I daresay. Or will it?"

Alfred swallowed. "It's for bogles," he said quickly.

"So this is what kills them?" Dr. Morton asked. "This spear?"

"*That* doesn't," Birdie retorted. "Mr. Bunce does."

Again the doctor looked at her, his pale eyes unreadable in the lamplight. "And what do *you* do while Mr. Bunce is killing demons?" he wanted to know.

"I'm the 'prentice."

"I see." He pondered this for a moment. Then he turned back to Alfred. "Is she your bait? I can only assume she is."

"What do you want?" was Alfred's harsh rejoinder. "I know you want summat. Tell us and be done."

"Very well." As he spoke, Dr. Morton gingerly laid Alfred's spear on the floor and began to rummage in the sack again. "I do want something. And if you can supply it, I may give you something in return. Because I'm a great believer in negotiation, Mr. Bunce." Suddenly he pulled a little glass bottle from Alfred's sack. "Hmm," he said. "Would this be holy water, by any chance?"

"Mind it don't burn you," Alfred growled, eliciting

another smirk from the doctor, who uncorked the bottle and sniffed at it.

"Odorless. So it can't be ether, or alcohol, or anything of that sort." As he resealed the bottle and set it to one side, Birdie cast a quick glance at the gravediggers. Both were watching him unload the sack, like children watching their mother empty a basket in the hope that she might produce a tasty treat. They weren't paying any attention to Birdie.

So she began to bend her knees, pushing her feet closer and closer to her bound wrists. Since her fingers were dangling free, she thought she might be able to untie the rope that had been knotted around her ankles.

"The fact is, you appear to have deprived me of my demon, Mr. Bunce," Dr. Morton was saying. "And if that *is* the case, then you owe me another one."

Alfred glared at him. "You ain't making no sense."

"I'm asking you to find me another demon. And to capture it." Dr. Morton pulled Alfred's brandy flask from the bottom of the sack. "Aha," he said.

"But you can't capture bogles!" Alfred objected.

"Maybe *you* can't," the doctor replied, unscrewing the lid of the flask. "*I* can, however, as long as you help me." He sniffed. "Brandy," he concluded, then replaced the lid, setting the flask beside the bottle.

Birdie noticed that Simeon and Jubez were both

watching the flask with covetous eyes. Taking advantage of this, she began to pluck at her ankle ropes.

"I want you to notify me the next time you receive a call for help," the doctor went on. "Do that, Mr. Bunce, and you will be handsomely rewarded."

Alfred frowned. "Is that all?" he asked suspiciously.

"That is all," the doctor confirmed. "Give me the details, join me at the site, and you will receive a finder's fee of twenty pounds."

"Twenty pounds?" Alfred echoed. Even Birdie was amazed—amazed, but not impressed. As far as she was concerned, those twenty pounds would be blood money. What about Abel, and Nolly, and Sam? Did the doctor really think that Alfred would accept money from the very person who had killed those poor boys?

"All right," said Alfred. "Done."

Birdie's jaw dropped.

"Next time I'm on a job, I'll send you word. I'll tell you the time and the place," Alfred agreed. Birdie was about to protest when she caught his eye—and knew at once that he was making empty promises. He simply wanted to get them both out of there and would say anything to do it. She could understand that.

Unfortunately, so could Dr. Morton.

"Good," he said, pulling a wad of clean rags out of the

sack. "In the meantime, of course, I shall keep your kit—and the girl. They'll serve as a guarantee."

Birdie gasped. Alfred stiffened.

"But—"

"It's a form of insurance," the doctor explained gently. "Obviously I wouldn't want you communicating with the police, or revenging yourself on me, or Mr. Swales, or Mr. McGill—or even Mrs. Smith. If you do any of these things, Mr. Bunce, then you'll lose both your equipment *and* your apprentice."

Birdie could restrain herself no longer. "I ain't going with you!" she cried. "You ain't taking me *nowhere!*" Then she yelped as Simeon gave her a cuff on the ear.

"You touch her again and you're dead!" Alfred roared. He was red in the face. "D'you hear me? You'll be digging yer *own* grave!"

"Kindly keep your hands to yourself, Mr. McGill," the doctor warned. "Or I shall dock your pay." He turned to Alfred. "Your apprentice will come to no harm, I promise. Just as long as you do the right thing."

"And what might that be?" Alfred demanded through his teeth.

"Why, exactly what I told you before. I'm interested in your technique, so I want to know where and when you expect to encounter your next demon. Then I'll join you there with your kit and hand over the twenty pounds when our goal is accomplished."

"And Birdie?" Alfred's voice was strained. "You'll need to bring Birdie."

"No." The doctor shook his head.

"I'll do *nowt* without Birdie!"

"Mr. Bunce, you must understand that Birdie is like an insurance policy for me. Suppose I appear at our rendezvous and it's an ambush of some kind? I have to be sure that you won't kill me or hand me over to the police." Having satisfied himself that Alfred's bag was now empty, Dr. Morton began to replace all its contents, item by item. "I'd be a fool to take you at your word. Surely you can see that? I'm convinced you'd do the same if you were in my position."

"But Birdie—"

"Will be well looked after," the doctor insisted.

"You want me to believe that?" Alfred scoffed. "You must think *I'm* the fool!"

Dr. Morton paused in the act of rewrapping Alfred's spear. "If you wish," he said with a sigh, "I can bring you a letter from her—"

"Except that I can't write!" Birdie interrupted.

"Then you'll be taught to." Dr. Morton dropped the spear into Alfred's sack. "I don't intend to keep you in a box under my bed. Suitable arrangements will be made. Insurance policies are always carefully guarded."

"Listen here." Alfred was on his knees by now, having struggled into a position that was more or less upright. "I can't do me job without Birdie. Without her, there won't *be* no bogle. It won't even show itself!"

"Oh, but it will," the doctor assured him. "You see, when Mrs. Smith tried to blackmail me, she asked for a hundred pounds. In response, I offered her *two* hundred if she would bring me a child whenever I might need one for my work. She was quite amenable to that, and now we have an agreement. So you see, Mr. Bunce, you won't be needing Birdie anymore. When you next require bait, Mrs. Smith will supply it. At no extra cost to yourself."

"She's a witch," said Alfred, almost choking with rage, "and you're the devil."

"No," the doctor replied serenely, "I am merely a man who wants to harness His infernal powers." He rose suddenly, handing Alfred's sack to Jubez. "I'm going to leave you here now, Mr. Bunce. No doubt your cries will be heard by the next group of mourners who pass by, and they will rescue you." Ignoring Alfred's spluttered protests, he reached for the small tin box that was sitting next to his hat, on the sarcophagus lid. "Need I remind you that if you publicly blame Mr. Swales or Mr. McGill, your apprentice will suffer the consequences? I'm sure I don't have to, since you strike me as an intelligent man, if woefully uneducated."

"God damn you to hell!"

"Not to say profane." Dr. Morton had opened the tin box, from which he extracted a small brown bottle and a large wad of cotton gauze. Immediately the room filled with the strange, medicinal odor that Birdie had smelled upon first entering it—and her stomach clenched as her eyes widened.

"Now," the doctor continued, "I'm going to ask you to take a sniff of this, Birdie. You mustn't be afraid. It won't hurt."

"No!"

"It will simply put you asleep for long enough to ensure that you don't make a fuss on your way out. I couldn't bring my carriage onto the grounds, you see. I had to leave it out on the road. And since it happens to be a *hired* equipage—well, you can understand my difficulties . . ."

24

Restraint

Birdie was moving. She was being carried. No—she was bouncing around but not in someone's arms. And she couldn't move her *own* arms. She was trapped. Trapped and bouncing . . .

"Augh," she groaned. Her stomach heaved; she was going to be sick. She coughed and gagged and then a sack was shoved under her chin.

As she vomited into it, she noted somewhere at the back of her mind that it wasn't Alfred's sack. It was larger and rougher, like a potato sack.

"It's all right, Leticia," a calm voice said. "You won't be ill for very long."

Birdie didn't know who Leticia was. She tried to wipe her mouth, but her arms were clamped across her chest. The wounded one was aching.

She was wriggling around, trying to free herself, when someone dabbed at her face with a perfumed handkerchief. "Shhh," he said. "Calm down."

It was Dr. Morton. Birdie recognized his voice. She uttered a great, gulping cry—and suddenly realized that she was in a moving carriage with him. He was sitting beside her, tying something around the mouth of the sack. She couldn't see exactly what he was using as a tie, because it was too dark.

"Help!" she screamed. *"Help me!"*

"That won't do any good," the doctor calmly declared. As he placed his sack on the seat opposite, Birdie grasped that they must be in a four-wheeled hackney carriage. The light of the carriage lamps, filtering through a grimy set of rattling windows, picked out the cracks in the leather upholstery.

"He-e-elp!" she shouted, leaning toward the driver's box. But she couldn't move her arms to tap on the glass.

Looking down, she was puzzled by the strange garment that had been wrapped around her. It was a kind of stiff, white jacket, covered in buckles and straps. No matter how frantically she struggled, she couldn't release herself from its grip.

"Get me out of this!" she screeched. "Let me go!"

"I'm afraid I can't," the doctor replied. "You might injure yourself."

"He-e-lp!"

"Take my advice and save your breath. As long as you're wearing a camisole restraint, no one is going to pay the slightest attention." Feeling the carriage slow, Dr. Morton peered outside. "Ah," he murmured. "Here we are. And not a moment too soon."

"Where are we?" Birdie was almost hysterical with fear. "What are you doing?" Remembering suddenly that the carriage was a hired one, she raised her voice again. *"Help! Help me!"*

Dr. Morton clicked his tongue and shook his head. "Poor girl," he remarked, before pushing the door open.

As he hopped down onto the road, Birdie thought, *This is my chance.* She lurched to her feet, hoping to escape through the door on her own side of the carriage. But she couldn't open it because she couldn't move her hands— and when she dropped to her knees, hoping to use her mouth, she slammed her face against the door panel, making herself dizzy.

Then her stomach heaved again, protesting against the sudden jolt. All at once she was vomiting onto the floor.

Next thing she knew, someone was trying to drag her sideways.

"No!" she gurgled. "Help!"

"Shhh. It's all right, dear. It's all right . . ."

The sound of a woman's voice calmed Birdie. She assumed that a passerby must have heard her frantic shouts. "Get this off!" she groaned. "I can't move! He tied me up!"

But other people were also talking, and they didn't seem to hear.

"Take her inside," said the woman, very softly. "We'll clean her up in there."

"Which room, ma'am?" A male voice spoke somewhere over Birdie's head. It belonged to the very tall, rawboned, gray-haired man who had pulled Birdie from the carriage. Now he threw her over his shoulder like a sack of coal.

Suddenly Dr. Morton began to speak.

"That girl needs to be in seclusion," he announced. With a squeak of alarm, Birdie craned around to see that he was offering a handful of coins to the cabman. "I'm sorry about the mess. This is for your trouble."

"No!" she yelled. *"No-o-o! I want to go ho-o-ome!"*

She kicked and bucked, but the man who held her was very strong. His grip tightened; he pulled her legs down and clasped them against his chest with iron fingers.

"Help! I've bin snatched!" she wailed. *"The doctor done it! Help me!"*

"The restraint room, Mr. Doherty, if you please," said the soft-voiced woman, who was standing close by.

"Aye, ma'am."

Suddenly Birdie found herself bouncing along again—only this time she wasn't in the carriage. This time she was moving *away* from it. She could see one of the carriage lamps shining down onto Dr. Morton's head. He and the soft-voiced woman were conversing together gravely while the cabman climbed down from his box with a handful of cleaning rags.

"I'm afraid she won't even answer to her own name," the doctor was saying. "She adheres with an almost desperate stubbornness to this false history she's created for herself. Her family have been coping as best they can with her lies and abuse and episodes of self-harm, but when she absconded from their care, they realized that they could no longer ensure her safety, and applied to me for help."

"Poor child!" his companion exclaimed. She was quite tall, for a woman—as tall as the doctor—with a long, yellowish face and a beaky nose. She wore an old-fashioned, wide-skirted black gown topped off by a white shawl collar. Her dark hair was streaked with gray. "You can see the refinement in her features, beneath all that grime and filth . . ."

"Self-applied, I fear. She refuses to wash, or to change her clothes—"

"Is she a danger to others?"

"In one of her fits, she may be. It is not out of malice, you understand. She has uncontrolled episodes. They are part of her madness."

At that precise moment Birdie suddenly realized what was happening. They were talking about *her!* They were calling her *mad!* But as she opened her mouth, a door swung shut in her face. It blocked her view of the street and everything in it: the stationary carriage with its muddy yellow wheels, the dim line of townhouses across the road, the glowing lamps, the patches of cobblestone, the woman in the black gown, the evil doctor beside her. All of it vanished behind the big, dark, heavy door, which closed with a slightly hollow *thunk.*

Birdie screamed again. Her head felt as if it were going to burst, because it was hanging upside down. And when she tried to lift it up, her neck ached horribly.

"Hush, now," Mr. Doherty said, "or ye'll be waking the others."

"Let go!" Birdie implored. "You have to let me go!"

"I'll do that presently."

"Now! *Please!* Before the doctor comes!"

"Katie-Ann." They halted. "Have ye the key to the restraint room?"

A girl's voice answered from somewhere beyond Birdie's line of sight. "No, of course not. You must ask Mrs. Ayres for *that* key."

"But I just left her. She's outside with Dr. Morton. She never gave me the key nor mentioned it."

There was a sharp, impatient sigh. "The room must be standing open, then. You go in."

As Mr. Doherty shifted position, a pattern of colored floor tiles spun before Birdie's eyes. Then she spotted a blue skirt and white apron rustling past.

"Wait!" she wheezed. "Please, miss — you've got to help me! I've bin kidnapped! The doctor's a murderer! *Please*, miss!"

But Katie-Ann ignored her. And Mr. Doherty said reproachfully, "A fine thing 'tis, telling such lies about Dr. Morton, who only wants to help ye."

"*No! Let go!*"

"If ye weren't out o' yer senses, I'd call ye wicked, so I would." Suddenly a strange, unearthly moan sounded somewhere in the distance. It rose to a shrill scream, then broke on a sob — making Mr. Doherty click his tongue. "There, now," he said crossly. "Ye've gone and wakened the others with all yer noise and fussing."

Birdie whimpered. She could hear two more voices joining the first in a kind of urgent, howling chorus. "Oh, please," she croaked. "I ain't mad. I don't belong here, I *don't . . .*"

"Mebbe not," Mr. Doherty replied. "But I'm just the night porter, so it's not for me to say."

He began to move down a long hallway, past a massive flight of mahogany stairs. From her upended viewpoint, Birdie couldn't see much—just floor tiles, skirting boards, and the claw-footed legs of occasional tables. Everything was very well lit, by paraffin or gas lamps that hung from the ceiling. Soon the tiles were replaced by flagstones, and the wallpaper by scuffed paint. Mr. Doherty then turned a couple of corners, plunging into the depths of what seemed to be an enormous house full of closed doors.

With her arms crossed against her chest, and her head dangling like a piece of fruit on a branch, Birdie was finding it increasingly difficult to breathe. That was why she finally stopped yelling as the porter reached the end of a long corridor and carried her into a very strange room. In the dim light filtering through its small, high window, she saw that its walls were covered in canvas and stuffed with something like horsehair. Even the back of the door was padded.

A paillasse lay on the floor next to a chamber pot.

"There, now." Mr. Doherty set Birdie down on the paillasse. "That's a bit better, wouldn't ye say?"

Gulping down a few lungfuls of air, Birdie waited for her head to clear. Then she tried to get up—but without the use of her hands, it was very difficult.

"Please," she gasped, "*please* let me out o' this thing!"

"That's for Dr. Morton to decide."

"No!" In a flash, Birdie realized that the more she ranted and raved, the madder she would look. So she tried to speak calmly—reasonably—even though she wanted to scream and shout and bite and kick. "Dr. Morton is lying. He wants to lock me up because he killed four boys. He put 'em in the way of a bogle. I'm a bogler's girl, see, and the man I work for found a bogle in Dr. Morton's house . . ." Seeing the expression on Mr. Doherty's flushed face, she trailed off.

He didn't believe her.

"It's true!" she exclaimed, tears spurting from her eyes. "I swear it's true! I'm Birdie McAdam! Ask anyone in Bethnal Green! Where is this place? Where am I?"

"Hackney," the porter replied.

"Hackney?" Birdie's heart leaped. "Then we ain't far from where I live! Go and find Mr. Alfred Bunce—*he'll* tell you! Ask Mr. Bunce!"

Mr. Doherty was standing by the door, looking nervous. At the sound of approaching footsteps, however, the anxious lines on his brow relaxed.

"Here's Mrs. Ayres," he announced. "She'll know what to do."

"I'm a-telling you what to do! Send word to Mr. Bunce!" Birdie cried. "I work for him! I live in his house! *He'll* tell you I ain't mad!" But the porter had vanished, yielding his place to the soft-voiced woman in the old-fashioned gown. She stood for a moment, framed in the narrow doorway, holding a bunch of keys.

"Now, Leticia," she chided gently, "you know very well that you live with your mother and your aunt. It's thanks to *their* generosity that you're here at all—for London House isn't a charitable institution." As Birdie stared at her, open mouthed, she added, "Why not think about that for a while? Think about how worried they must be, and how much you owe them. And perhaps when I come back, you'll have decided to be a good and grateful girl, rather than a foolish and ungovernable one."

Then she retreated from the room, locking the door behind her.

25

THE SINGING PRISONER

Left alone in the dark, Birdie had to swallow the scream that was building inside her. She knew that if she howled and moaned like some of the other inmates, she would never be released. So she sat quietly on her paillasse, looking up at the window and thinking.

She was in Hackney. That was good news. She hadn't been spirited away to Kensington, or Wandsworth, or even farther afield—into the country, for instance. She was in a private lunatic asylum called London House. That *wasn't* such good news, especially since Dr. Morton seemed to be on the hospital's staff. He had planned everything very cleverly. What better place to hide a hostage than in a madhouse? It was like a private prison, where the doctors were all-powerful. No matter what Birdie said, Dr. Morton would deny it — and everyone, but *everyone*, would believe him.

Birdie whimpered. The full horror of her situation was overwhelming. But then she told herself, as she always did, *This ain't no worse than a bogle. I face up to bogles, so I can face up to this.* She took a deep breath. She thought about Alfred, who would certainly be looking for her. *He'll find me,* she thought. *He'll check every hospital until he does.* Meanwhile, it would be her job to get out of the locked room, into something that was more accessible from the outside.

By the time Mrs. Ayres returned, with Katie-Ann at her heels, Birdie had decided to be as good and grateful as anyone could possibly wish.

"Now, Leticia," said Mrs. Ayres, who was carrying a nightdress and a towel, "my name is Mrs. Ayres, and I want to give you a sponge bath and some clean clothes. Once you've washed, you may have your tea. But only if you behave like a sensible girl and don't make a fuss — is that clear?"

Birdie nodded.

"Very well, then." Having put down her armful of linen, Mrs. Ayres began to unbuckle Birdie's camisole restraint. The relief of having her arms freed was so great that Birdie barely noticed that her clothes were also being removed. It was only after the numbness and tingling in her hands and wrists had stopped that Birdie saw Katie-Ann dip one of the towels into a basin of steaming water that had been placed on the floor nearby.

"Look at this pretty little face, all covered in dirt," Mrs. Ayres remarked as she pushed the fine, gold hair out of Birdie's eyes. "It seems a terrible shame, doesn't it, Katie-Ann?"

"Yes'm."

"And whatever happened to this arm? We'll have to change the dressing; it's *filthy* . . ."

Birdie allowed herself to be scrubbed from head to toe. She allowed herself to be called "Leticia" without uttering a word of protest. She donned her new nightdress obediently and let Katie-Ann carry away her dirty clothes — though not without a pang of regret. When Katie-Ann returned, bringing a laden tea tray, Birdie drank every drop of the tea that was offered to her and stolidly ate four thick slices of bread and butter.

She didn't mention bogles. She didn't abuse Dr. Morton. She didn't insist that her name was Birdie McAdam. But as Mrs. Ayres began to leave, having promised nothing more than a visit the next morning, Birdie could remain silent no longer.

"Mrs. Ayres?" she blurted out. "Could you pass a message to a friend o' mine?"

The woman paused. "Not if you insist on speaking in that silly way," she rejoined. Seeing Birdie blink, she added, "You know perfectly well that you can talk like a proper lady, Leticia. You were raised to it, after all. That common accent is another one of your wicked lies."

"But it ain't, ma'am, I swear!"

"Nonsense. Of course it is. And I cannot help you if you keep lying."

Birdie was dumbfounded. How could she talk like a proper lady? She wouldn't be able to, no matter how hard she tried.

Frantically she tried to think of something clever to say before Mrs. Ayres left the room. Katie-Ann had already vanished, along with the basin of dirty water. When Mrs. Ayres began to jingle her keys, Birdie jumped up from the paillasse and cried, "Please, ma'am, will you not speak to Mr. Bunce? Mr. Alfred Bunce of Bethnal Green—*he'll* tell you who I am!"

"Forgive me, Leticia, but I know all about your wanderings," Mrs. Ayres said reproachfully. "According to the doctor, you have made many low acquaintances in the most *unsavory* slums and rookeries. He insists that none of these wretched people should be allowed anywhere near you."

"But—"

"If you object to this, you must apply to him personally. He'll be doing his rounds tomorrow afternoon." Mrs. Ayres began to shut the door, then stopped to give Birdie one more piece of advice. "And I would recommend that you address him in a proper way, instead of using that false and vulgar tongue. Otherwise, he will simply decide that you are still favoring fantasy over the truth and won't listen to a word you say."

Bang went the door. *Clink* went the key in the lock. As Mrs. Ayres retreated briskly down the corridor, carrying the tea tray, Birdie shouted after her, "*He's* got the false tongue, not I! He's a liar and a killer! *He's the one you should lock up!*"

But Mrs. Ayres wasn't listening. And after Birdie had kicked the padded door a couple of times, she lay down on her paillasse and wept.

Though she was angry with herself for crying, she found that she couldn't stop. Her head was aching and her arm was sore and her stomach didn't feel right—she had packed too much bread into it. She was also scared, though not as scared as she had been. Alone with Dr. Morton, she'd been very scared indeed. Now she felt a little braver, because none of the other asylum staff seemed to be wicked or cruel.

They're just stupid, she decided. *They're stupid for not seeing how bad that man really is.* And she realized that if they *were* stupid, she might get the better of them, Dr. Morton or no Dr. Morton.

She was still wondering how to escape when she fell asleep and dreamed that a bogle was trying to get into her room, through the door. No matter how loudly she called for help, no one answered. So she tried to climb out the window, but it was much too high. And then she realized that there was *another* bogle waiting for her in the garden, disguised as a rag-and-bone man. "Ol' cloes! Ol' cloes!" it was yelling.

Birdie woke with a start. For one confused moment she didn't know where she was. But by now the sun had risen, and the room around her was full of light. It didn't take her long to recognize the padded walls.

"Ol' cloes! Ol' cloes!" someone chanted. The noise was filtering through the window from the street outside. Birdie sat up suddenly. *So there is a street outside,* she thought. Listening hard, she found that she could recognize other noises: the clip-clop of horses' hooves, the distant puff and clatter of a train, a baby crying, a torrent of oaths. But it was the cry of the caffler that really caught her interest. "Ol' cloes! Ol' cloes!" he intoned as he pushed his barrow past London House. Birdie didn't recognize his voice. She doubted very much that he was Elijah Froggett.

Even so, she jumped to her feet — and was about to scream for help when suddenly she had second thoughts. Screaming might not be a clever thing to do. Screaming might confirm that she was a lunatic. The people on the street would certainly think her one. Birdie didn't want to be strapped up again. She didn't want to be gagged or restrained.

She stood for a moment, biting her thumb. How was she going to attract attention while making absolutely sure that she didn't upset Mrs. Ayres? Pondering this, she heard a hawker's cry floating high and pure above the muffled clamor of the street. "Ripe strawberries ripe! Sixpence a pottle, fine strawberries ripe!" And in a flash, she had her answer.

All she had to do was sing.

She had neighbors who worked in Hackney. She'd met people who lived there. She and Alfred had killed bogles all *over* Hackney—in a coal hole, a crypt, a wine cellar, and a disused pottery kiln (not to mention an old workhouse well). Perhaps if Birdie kept singing, some passerby would recognize her voice.

So she sang "The Unquiet Grave" from start to finish. Then she followed it up with "The Three Butchers," "The Barkshire Tragedy," and "Robin Hood's Death." She had just started warbling "Down Among the Dead Men" when Mrs. Ayres appeared, carrying a bundle of clean clothes.

Katie-Ann was with her.

"Here is your breakfast, Leticia," Mrs. Ayres announced as Katie-Ann set down a tea tray and picked up Birdie's chamber pot. Seeing Katie-Ann clearly for the first time in broad daylight, Birdie realized that she was very beautiful, with luxuriant chestnut hair and luminous skin.

Mrs. Ayres looked rather puffy around the eyes, perhaps because she hadn't slept well. She didn't appear to have changed her clothes. Birdie wondered if she'd been to bed at all.

"You've a pretty voice, Leticia, but Dr. Morton won't be pleased to hear that you have been singing such nasty songs," Mrs. Ayres continued. "You must try harder if you're to be let out." Laying down her bundle, she added, "Your family hasn't sent us your clothes yet, so you must borrow these for a time. They will suffice, I'm sure. And if you eat all your porridge, Dr. Morton will be very pleased, and may consider placing you in a room upstairs, where you will have a proper bed and a nice view of London Fields."

"London Fields?" Birdie echoed. "Are we near the park, then?"

"Leticia." Mrs. Ayres looked down her long nose at Birdie. "What did I tell you about that silly, vulgar accent? Unless you abandon it, the doctor will not let you read or sew."

Birdie wanted to say that she couldn't read, but she knew it would be foolish. So she sat mutely as Mrs. Ayres shook her head, gave a disappointed sigh, and withdrew. Katie-Ann didn't leave, though; she stood waiting while

Birdie choked down her breakfast. Perhaps she was afraid that Birdie might smear the walls with porridge or try to fashion a knife from the tin plate.

When the plate was clean and the teacup empty, Katie-Ann helped Birdie to get dressed—for the borrowed gown had buttons all down its back, and the borrowed petticoat needed adjusting.

"It's all a mite too big," Katie-Ann remarked after surveying her handiwork with her head cocked, "but never mind. Yer own clothes'll be arriving soon."

"No, they will not," Birdie retorted. Standing there, almost lost in a mass of stiff, blue serge, she looked Katie-Ann straight in the eye. "Them clothes you took last night is all I got in the world."

They stared at each other for a moment. Then Katie-Ann glanced away, a delicate flush staining her cheeks. "I'll take this," she said, stacking the tea tray, "but you should keep the nightdress."

"You know it's true," Birdie insisted, for she had seen something in Katie-Ann's face: a startled flicker. A fleeting concern. "You *know* I ain't quality."

"It's none o' my business," Katie-Ann replied.

"But—"

"I'm a maid, not a nurse. I do what I'm told, and so should you," said Katie-Ann. Then she picked up the tea tray and departed, though not without locking the door behind her.

Birdie sighed. She felt as if she'd taken aim and missed by an inch. Nevertheless, she sensed that she might have a future ally in Katie-Ann. So she turned back to the window with a much lighter heart.

And though her voice was already roughening from overuse, she launched bravely into "The Three Ravens."

"*There were three ravens sat on a tree.*
They were as black as they might be.
Then one of the ravens said to his mate,
'*Where shall we our breakfast take?*'
With a down derrie derrie down down . . ."

26

A Visit from the Doctor

Dr. Morton returned that afternoon, while Birdie was singing "The Death of Parcy Reed."

She heard footsteps in the hallway. One set belonged to Mrs. Ayres, who jangled keys and rustled a lot of starched petticoat when she walked. The other set wasn't muffled by layers of fabric; it was a man's tread, firm and brisk, but not as heavy as Mr. Doherty's.

Then, as Birdie fell silent, the sound of a muted conversation reached her ears.

". . . been singing all day long," Mrs. Ayres was saying. "I thought you would have no objection, though they tend to be rather *low* songs—"

"Exactly. That is *exactly* why I must forbid them. If she has to be gagged, Mrs. Ayres, I will not have her singing those songs."

It was Dr. Morton speaking. Birdie's heart skipped a beat, then began to pound like a hammer, in double-quick time.

"Have any of her rough friends appeared on the doorstep?" he asked, his voice growing louder with every step.

"Oh, no. I would have told you."

"Well, be on your guard. They are people of the very worst type and would not think twice about breaking into this house. I believe they were befriending her for the purpose of extracting money from her relatives — a form of ransom, if you understand me."

"How dreadful!"

"It *is* dreadful. You can sympathize with her family's desire to place her in a secure location. Eventually they hope to find a suitable house in the country. But of course one has to be *very* cautious when it comes to rural asylums."

The footsteps stopped outside Birdie's door. Someone fumbled with the lock. Looking around wildly for a place to hide, Birdie saw only the chamber pot and the paillasse.

When the door swung open, she was squatting in a corner, scowling.

"Here is Dr. Morton, Leticia," Mrs. Ayres announced.

"I told him you have been very good, though he wants you to stop singing those nasty songs."

"Hello, Letty." Dr. Morton's tone was calm and light, with just a touch of silkiness. He was looking very dapper in a three-piece suit; his mustache was curled, his hair was oiled, and he smelled faintly of lime and sandalwood. "How are you today?"

Birdie said nothing. She just glared at him, hoping that she hadn't gone pale.

"Cat got your tongue?" he murmured with a glint in his eye. Then he turned to Mrs. Ayres. "Might I have a chair, please? I wish to talk to Miss Partridge and would prefer not to stand."

"Yes, of course, Doctor! I'll fetch one straightaway."

But before Mrs. Ayres could withdraw, Birdie jumped to her feet and cried, "No, ma'am! Please don't leave me with *him;* he's a devil!"

Mrs. Ayres hesitated. "Now, Leticia—"

"It's true! I swear! He's killed four kids already and is like to kill me!"

"Nonsense. You mustn't tell such monstrous lies."

"I ain't lying, ma'am!"

Mrs. Ayres clicked her tongue. "You sound like a street hawker when you talk that way," she said. "Now, behave yourself, for I shall return directly. And I can *promise* that you will still be alive when I do!"

She marched off as the doctor stood watching Birdie, his gaze bleached of all color and emotion. There was something very chilling about it. But Birdie wanted to demonstrate that she wasn't a bit scared, so she squared her shoulders and snarled, "You ain't the only one as knows a bit o' magic. Mr. Bunce can lay as many curses as there are ailments. He's laid a curse on *you* by now. You'll be feeling poorly afore the day's over, I expect."

A smile tugged at the corner of Dr. Morton's mouth. Leaning against the doorjamb, he smoothly replied, "Let me tell you something, little girl. I could have killed you in the cemetery, along with your master, since there are any number of places to hide a corpse in a graveyard. But I didn't. And the reason I didn't is that I want to know how to catch bogles."

He paused, glancing over his shoulder into the hallway. Birdie was about to fill the silence with a scathing remark when he raised his hand and said, "Let me finish, please. I didn't simply ask how it's done, because I knew that your master would lie to me. Sheer malice would have prompted him to do it, even if he hadn't been eager to protect his secrets. That is why I have arranged to be with him on his next job. So I can witness the master at work, so to speak."

"I already heard this," Birdie countered. "Whyn't you tell Mrs. Ayres, if you're so damn proud o' yerself? *She'd* be a good deal more interested than *I* am!"

"Ah — but there is something you *don't* know, my dear." The doctor leaned forward, lowering his gentle voice until it was little more than whisper. "You see, Mr. Bunce's next job will be his last."

Drawing his head back, he regarded Birdie with a satisfied but expectant look, as if waiting for her to erupt.

She gaped at him. "Wha — wha . . . ?" she bleated.

"And once I am rid of your master, then I shan't need *you* anymore. Shall I?" Dr. Morton raised a quizzical eyebrow. "Perhaps I'll tell Mrs. Ayres that I'm taking you to a well-regarded country asylum, where it won't be *my* fault if the staff are negligent, the food insufficient, or the medical facilities inadequate — "

"You don't scare me," Birdie interrupted. She knew that he was goading her, though she couldn't understand why. "You'll never lay a *finger* on Mr. Bunce. He's too smart and too strong. He'd make short work o' you, for all he's much older!"

"Oh, I've no intention of challenging him to a duel," Dr. Morton replied, in the very mildest of tones. "We'd be sadly ill matched, for I daresay he favors fisticuffs, while my strengths lie more in swordplay. No, no. You see, when I return his equipment to him, there'll be an extra drop of something in his brandy flask. Something with a bit of a kick to it." He smiled suddenly. "If you get my meaning."

Birdie gasped. But as she darted forward with a cry of

outrage, the doctor stepped neatly into the hallway and shut the door in her face.

"No-o-o!" Birdie screeched. *"You devil! You dog! Come back—you bloody bastard—I'll kill YOU! I'll KILL you!"*

She kicked and pounded, yelling at the top of her voice. Then she heard Dr. Morton call for a key as he held the door shut.

"He's going to kill Mr. Bunce!" she bellowed, her voice cracking on a sob. *"Please, ma'am, we've got to stop him!"* The clatter of footsteps and the jingle of keys galvanized her; she started to hammer on the padded canvas, hurting her injured arm. *"Let me out! LET ME OUT! I must tell Alfred, PLE-E-EASE!"*

"If you don't stop this, Letty, I'll have to prescribe a camisole restraint," the doctor warned.

"Damn you to hell!"

"Leticia!" a shocked Mrs. Ayres exclaimed.

"He's gammoning you! Can't you see that? Are you blind?" shouted Birdie. She felt like punching someone. "He's going to poison Alfred! *He told me so!*"

"I'm afraid I must have challenged her one too many times," the doctor sadly informed Mrs. Ayres. "You can see what her family have to put up with."

"I'll do you down!" Birdie roared. *"I'll set a bogle on you!"*

"Sometimes I fear that she'll never be cured." Dr. Morton was addressing Mrs. Ayres again. "It would be pointless to attempt anything now. I shall return tomorrow."

"*Aaagh!*" Furious, Birdie threw her whole body against the door.

"Shall I dose her with laudanum?" asked Mrs. Ayres, sounding worried.

"No, no. We'll let her tire herself out, I think." Dr. Morton raised his voice. "I'm leaving now, Letty! I shall see you again tomorrow afternoon!"

"*Yer days are numbered, you dimmick!*"

"Try to be a good girl for Mrs. Ayres. She has only your best interests at heart."

To Mrs. Ayres the doctor said, "You see our problem. She can be quite amenable for a few hours and then — *pff!* Up she goes. It makes her difficult to treat."

"*You pile o' pig guts!*" Birdie bawled.

"Control yourself, Leticia, or you'll have no supper today."

It was Mrs. Ayres speaking. But before Birdie could answer, the *click-clack* of retreating footsteps made her pause.

Mrs. Ayres and the doctor were walking away.

"*No! Wait! Come back!*" Birdie shrieked. When no one responded, she kicked the door several times. Then she burst into tears and threw herself down onto the paillasse.

She wept herself dry, cursing and howling and drumming her feet on the floor.

She wanted to kill Dr. Morton. She wanted to kill Mrs. Ayres. She wanted to smash down the door and charge out into the street, waving Finn MacCool's spear. At one point she jumped up defiantly and started to sing, but her voice was thick with sobs and hoarse from screaming. Even if a friend in the street *did* hear her, there was a very good chance that she wouldn't be recognized.

By the time Katie-Ann appeared with her supper, Birdie was lying on her paillasse, staring blankly at the ceiling.

"Now, Miss Leticia," said Katie-Ann, "Mr. Doherty is here, on the mistress's orders, and if you don't eat up like a good girl, we're to put you in a restraint and feed you ourselves. So you'd best tuck in."

"I ain't hungry," Birdie growled, rolling over to face the wall.

"Ah, now, ye can take a bite o' stewed pear," Mr. Doherty wheedled. "There's sugar in it."

"If you don't eat, they'll stick a tube down yer throat and pump you full of beef broth," Katie-Ann warned Birdie, who winced. Force-feeding didn't sound like a pleasant experience. So she sat up and began to eat her supper while Katie-Ann and Mr. Doherty stood waiting for her to finish.

"Dr. Morton is going to kill Mr. Bunce," Birdie told

them between mouthfuls. She tried to keep her tone even. "Will you warn Mr. Bunce o' that? Will you tell him the doctor's planning to poison his brandy flask?"

The maid and the porter exchanged glances.

"Mr. Bunce lives in Bethnal Green," Birdie went on. "Off Club Row. Ask anyone living there—they'll tell you where to find 'im." When no one replied, she added, more urgently, "He cannot read a letter! He needs to be told!"

"Eat up, now," Mr. Doherty mumbled. Katie-Ann said nothing.

"If he dies, then you'll be to blame!" Birdie cried. "I hope you can live with yerselves, knowing as how you killed a man through not lifting one finger!"

"Lass," Mr. Doherty murmured, "I've a morning off each sennight, and *that* not for another five days. When am I to spare the time for a trip to Bethnal Green?"

Birdie gazed pleadingly at Katie-Ann, who had crouched down to stack the tea tray. But Katie-Ann refused to look up.

"I'll tell Mrs. Ayres you've bin good as gold," she said. "Mebbe that'll count for summat, though I cannot promise it will. If you're to get out o' *this* ward, you must be civil to the doctors."

Then she rose to her feet and left, taking Mr. Doherty and the camisole restraint with her.

No one else came to Birdie's room that evening. She

was forced to sleep in her blue serge dress because she couldn't undo all the buttons down its back. Troubled by these buttons, which dug into her spine—and by the terrifying images that infested her dreams—she passed a long and restless night, punctuated by fits of teary-eyed sleeplessness.

It wasn't until long after sunrise that Mrs. Ayres appeared again. She burst into the room, rousing Birdie from a fitful doze, and announced that she had a visitor.

"It's your aunt," Mrs. Ayres revealed. "Quickly, now! You don't want to keep her waiting . . . Letty? *Leticia!* It's your *aunt Hortense!*"

27

An Invitation to Breakfast

Birdie couldn't understand it. She didn't *have* an aunt.

"Wha—who?" she muttered, sitting up groggily.

"Your aunt is here, Leticia! Wake up!" Mrs. Ayres flicked off her blankets. "Come along!"

"What aunt?" said Birdie.

"Mrs. Snodgrass, of course. She brought you these clothes, which you're to put on at once." Mrs. Ayres dumped an armful of lace and ruffles onto Birdie's paillasse. "Dear me, didn't Katie-Ann help you to undress last night? I must have a word with that girl . . ."

Birdie didn't say anything more. Shock and confusion

had rendered her speechless; she allowed herself to be pushed about like a little rag doll as Mrs. Ayres replaced the borrowed outfit of blue serge with a dress of pearl-gray silk—which had pink trimmings and embroidered insets and a beaded sash and was altogether the most beautiful dress that Birdie had ever seen. It came with white silk stockings, gray kid boots, and a pink hair ribbon.

The boots were a fraction too large, but everything else fitted perfectly.

"Your hair needs washing," said Mrs. Ayres as she hurriedly tidied Birdie's wayward curls. "Have you eaten breakfast? No? What *has* that girl been doing? *Katie-Ann! Where are you?* Come along, Leticia. Don't dawdle."

Clasping Birdie's arm, she hurried into the hallway—where she nearly collided with Katie-Ann. "*There* you are!" Mrs. Ayres exclaimed. "Take away those clothes I left on the floor. Not the nightgown—the others."

"Yes'm."

"Does Mrs. Snodgrass want any tea?"

"No, ma'am, but—"

"I can't stop. Tell me later." Pushing past Katie-Ann, Mrs. Ayres hustled Birdie toward the front of the building, where there were no padded rooms or long, empty hallways covered in scarred paint. Now that she was on her own two feet, and it wasn't the middle of the night, Birdie could see much more of London House—which was richly endowed with fine plasterwork and polished joinery. Glimpsing her reflection in a gilt-framed mirror, she saw a pale, shocked face and staring eyes.

Then Mrs. Ayres yanked her through an open door, into a big room lined with velvet curtains, plush carpet, and damask wallpaper. Near the extravagant marble fireplace, which had tinsel in its grate, sat an old lady wearing a vague, sweet smile. She wore a black gown and a white cap, and she wasn't Mrs. Snodgrass.

She was Mrs. Heppinstall.

"Hello, dear," she said to Birdie. "How nice you look."

"Hello . . . Aunt," Birdie mumbled. She flicked a glance at Mrs. Ayres, her heart beating wildly.

"I hope you've not been misbehaving," Mrs. Heppinstall continued. "Have you been saying your prayers?"

Birdie nodded. The old lady's tranquil tone amazed her. Could this really be a brazen rescue attempt, or was there something going on that Birdie didn't understand? Mrs. Heppinstall seemed so *calm*.

"Leticia looks rather pale, Mrs. Ayres. Has she been eating enough meat?"

"Well—she has been with us for only two nights, Mrs. Snodgrass—"

"What about eggs? Did you give her an egg for breakfast this morning?"

Mrs. Ayres hesitated in a way that filled Birdie with a

ferocious sense of satisfaction. "She hasn't eaten breakfast," Mrs. Ayres had to admit.

Mrs. Heppinstall clicked her tongue. "Dear *me*. Then I suppose I must feed her myself."

"Oh, but —"

"Come, Leticia." Rising awkwardly, with the aid of a wooden stick, Mrs. Heppinstall extended a hand toward Birdie. "I'll take you to the Holborn Restaurant, so that you may have a nice chop."

"But Leticia's treatment has barely begun, Mrs. Snodgrass! I don't know what Dr. Morton will say about a trip to a chophouse."

"My niece may be intractable, Mrs. Ayres, but that does *not* mean she ought to be starved," was Mrs. Heppinstall's mild rejoinder. "I'm sure I don't know what her mother will say if you drive the roses from the poor girl's cheeks. This child has a very delicate constitution." She smiled at Birdie, her blue eyes wide and innocent. "If we go to the Holborn, dear, you *will* be a good girl, will you not?"

Birdie nodded vigorously, taking the old lady's proffered arm.

"Uh — Mrs. Snodgrass?" Mrs. Ayres scurried after them both, across the threshold and into the entrance hall. "When can we expect Leticia back?"

"Oh, when she becomes fractious, I daresay," Mrs. Heppinstall replied. She had paused to let a flustered

Katie-Ann open the front door for her. But to Birdie's intense frustration, the old lady didn't head straight out into the fresh air and sunshine. Instead, she turned back to Mrs. Ayres and said, "Incidentally, the Holborn is not a chophouse. It is a *restaurant*, and perfectly respectable. I often eat there."

"Yes, of course." Mrs. Ayres smiled bravely, but Birdie could tell that she was anxious. While Mrs. Heppinstall made her way down the front steps, Mrs. Ayres stood in the doorway, staring after her. Birdie didn't like that stare. It had a suspicious edge to it. So she remained utterly silent as she helped Mrs. Heppinstall into the carriage that was waiting in the street.

Luckily, it was a private carriage—not a hired one—and that must have reassured Mrs. Ayres. As soon as Mrs. Heppinstall had disappeared into it, Mrs. Ayres promptly turned around and let the big, blank, gray façade of London House swallow her up. Even so, Birdie didn't say a word until she had shut the carriage door behind her.

Then she rounded on Miss Eames, who was skulking beside Mrs. Heppinstall, and squeaked, "How did you *do* that? How did you *know*?"

Miss Eames opened her mouth. But before she could answer, the carriage gave a lurch and began to move. Mrs. Heppinstall immediately grabbed Birdie, who had nearly fallen across her lap. "Can you squeeze in, my dear?" the old lady inquired. "I'm afraid it's rather cramped. Mr. Fotherington was *most* kind to lend us his brougham, but it's not a very roomy vehicle."

"I can fit," Birdie assured her, wriggling down between the two women. She couldn't believe how deliriously happy she was to see Miss Eames (Miss Eames, of all people!), though her happiness was overshadowed by a dreadful, gnawing fear that caused her to blurt out, "Dr. Morton plans to kill Mr. Bunce! He told me so!"

"What?" Miss Eames frowned at her from beneath a tilted hat brim.

"He's going to poison his brandy flask! We have to warn Mr. Bunce!" Birdie peered out the nearest window. "Where are we going? Back to Bethnal Green?"

"Wait a minute." Miss Eames laid a hand on Birdie's arm. "What brandy flask? Explain."

Birdie took a deep breath. "Mr. Bunce puts his flask in his sack," she revealed. "But now Dr. Morton has the sack and will poison the brandy afore it's returned—"

"Samuel!" Miss Eames cried suddenly. She grabbed her aunt's stick and leaned forward, rapping it against the front window. *"Samuel, stop! STOP!"*

The carriage jolted to a standstill so abruptly that everyone was nearly flung onto the floor. Then Miss Eames turned to Mrs. Heppinstall, saying, "We cannot go home. We must go straight to Mr. Fotherington's house."

"Yes, of course," Mrs. Heppinstall faltered. "Oh dear. Oh dear me."

"*To your master's house, Samuel!*" Miss Eames bellowed. "*Do you hear?*"

"Aye, miss!" The driver's muffled voice only just managed to penetrate the little wheeled box. "Back to Mr. Fotherington's, is it?"

"*Yes, please!*"

Birdie, meanwhile, was glancing from face to face, looking for an explanation. "What's wrong?" she demanded. "Who *is* Mr. Fotherington?"

"He is a very old friend," said Mrs. Heppinstall. "When I pleaded with him to give us the use of his townhouse for a few hours, he generously agreed to spend the day at his club—"

"It's a trick," Miss Eames interrupted. "Mr. Bunce and I have laid a trap for Dr. Morton. But if what you say is true . . ." She paused for a moment, shaking her head. Her face looked quite drawn, and her dark eyebrows stood out more starkly than usual—perhaps because she was so pale. "If what you say is true," she finally muttered, "then we may have made a terrible mistake."

As the brougham bounced and swayed through the streets of Hackney, heading west, Miss Eames proceeded to tell her tale. She had decided to pay Birdie another visit and had taken a cab to Bethnal Green at about noon the previous day—only to discover that Birdie wasn't at home. Alfred was, though, and he was in a dreadful state, pacing and muttering and wringing his hands.

"He wouldn't stop talking," said Miss Eames. "He told me how Dr. Morton kidnapped you, and how he himself had been locked in a crypt—"

"It weren't a crypt," Birdie interposed. "It were a chapel."

"Well, whatever it was, he had been released from it by some unfortunate mother who had come to mourn her dead child." Miss Eames went on to describe how her frantic conversation with Alfred had been cut short by the unexpected arrival of Elijah Froggett, the rag-and-bone man. Elijah had been at the Hackney workhouse that morning, and in the course of a business transaction had heard a young inmate talking about Birdie McAdam. "It was that foolish girl Fanny, who showed us the disused well," Miss Eames explained. "She had been sent out on an errand earlier in the day and had heard you singing, Birdie, inside a house that she *knew* to be a private lunatic asylum. Though she herself regarded the whole incident as an amusing piece of gossip, Mr. Froggett thought it very strange indeed. He made a point of reporting it to Mr. Bunce, who instantly realized what it meant."

Though Alfred had wanted to rush off and rescue Birdie

at once, Miss Eames had cautioned him against it. A man of his description was unlikely to get beyond the front door of London House — and if Dr. Morton had been on the premises, he might somehow have spirited Birdie away before Alfred gained entry.

"I thought it wise to send someone whose respectable appearance would reassure the staff of the hospital," Miss Eames confessed. "But after I heard from Mr. Bunce about that monstrous Pickles woman, and what she had done — "

"Betrayed us to Dr. Morton!" Birdie cried.

"Exactly. I wasn't sure if her son had told her about me, or how much she might have passed on to Dr. Morton. So instead of seeking admittance myself, I sent Mrs. Heppinstall. I borrowed Mr. Fotherington's house for the same reason; I simply don't know if the doctor has my address." She suddenly reached over and patted her aunt's hand. "You did so *very* well, Aunt Louisa. I cannot thank you enough."

"Think nothing of it, my dear," the old lady replied.

"But how did you *know?*" asked Birdie. "How did you know the doctor told 'em I had a rich aunt as put me in there?"

"Oh, I didn't," said Mrs. Heppinstall.

And Miss Eames added, "We knew that the hospital sheltered only well-to-do patients, so we assumed that Dr. Morton must have told lies about your background. And we were hoping that if a rich great-aunt *did* appear, she would be difficult to turn away. Especially if she brought clothes of exactly the right dimensions."

"Which I *did* enjoy buying. They suit you very well." Mrs. Heppinstall smiled at Birdie, then addressed Miss Eames. "I didn't ask for her by name, you know. I no sooner mentioned that my niece had been placed there two nights previously than the silly woman actually *gave* me her name. 'You mean Leticia Partridge?' she said. So foolish!"

"But what about Dr. Morton?" Birdie still couldn't understand how the two women had pulled off such an audacious plan. "If the doctor had been there—"

"We knew he wouldn't be. That's the problem." Miss Eames took a deep breath, looked Birdie straight in the eye, and gravely admitted, "At this very moment Mr. Bunce is with Dr. Morton. At Mr. Fotherington's house. Pretending to catch a bogle." As Birdie gasped, Miss Eames said, "I'm sorry. It was the only way. And how was *I* to know about the poison?"

28

TO THE RESCUE

Birdie's stomach seemed to do a somersault. "Mr. Bunce is with the *doctor?*" she squawked. *"Now?"*

"We had to make sure that Dr. Morton wouldn't be at the hospital when you left," Miss Eames explained. "So we arranged a diversion."

"But what if he gives Mr. Bunce that sack?" Birdie began to panic. *"There's poison in the brandy flask!"*

"Which is why we are heading *straight* to Mr. Fotherington's house." Miss Eames took Birdie's face between her hands. "Look at me. Birdie? Listen. When does Mr. Bunce normally drink his brandy? Before or after he kills a bogle?"

Birdie had to concentrate. Her head was in a whirl. "After," she said at last. "He don't hold with tippling on the job."

"Then there's a very good chance that he is still safe," Miss Eames pointed out. "He was to stay in the house with Dr. Morton, pretending to work, until I sent word that you were free. I doubt Mr. Bunce will even *touch* his flask until someone knocks on Mr. Fotherington's front door—and perhaps not even then."

"But what if Mr. Bunce is driven to it?" Birdie wailed. "He might if he's bin fretting! And it's all on account o' me!" Tears spilled from her eyes as she wrenched her face away from Miss Eames.

Mrs. Heppinstall, meanwhile, had been quietly pondering. She suddenly said, "Why did the doctor tell you this, Birdie?" And when Birdie didn't reply, she added, "Why would he reveal his plans for Mr. Bunce? It seems very odd—not to say foolish. Why would he risk being overheard by staff at the asylum?"

Birdie swallowed a sob. In a wobbly voice she answered, "It were a trick. He wanted me to scream like a bedlamite so they'd keep me locked up." She had realized this the previous night and was ashamed of the way she'd played into his hands. "It worked," she admitted. "I lost me head and didn't find it again for hours."

"Then his threat may very well have been a sham,"

Mrs. Heppinstall suggested, earning a quick, grateful look from her niece.

"Aunt Louisa is right. The doctor may have other plans for Mr. Bunce and might have lied about the poison to upset you, Birdie."

"Yes ..." Though not really convinced, Birdie knew that she couldn't afford to break down. Not yet. Not until they had saved Alfred. "Where does yer friend live, miss?" she said with a hiccup, wiping her damp cheeks. "The one as lent you his house?"

Miss Eames explained that Mr. Fotherington lived near Regent's Park, in a large house staffed by a cook, a butler, a valet, a housemaid, a kitchen maid, and Samuel the coachman. "But they all have been sent out for the day, and Ellen Meggs has consented to take their place," she told Birdie, who frowned.

"Ellen Meggs?"

"Our own maid's sister. It was through their association that I first heard about Mr. Bunce—"

"Oh, Ellen *Meggs!*" All at once Birdie remembered. "That girl as had the chimney bogle in Westbourne Park!"

"The very same," Miss Eames confirmed. She went on to relate that Ellen had jumped at the chance of earning half a crown by pretending to be Mr. Fotherington's housemaid. "Mr. Bunce thought it wise to use someone who'd already had experience of a chimney bogle, and would know what to say. That is why we decided to give Mr. Fotherington's servants a day off. In case they were not good liars."

"And Ellen's answering the door?" asked Birdie, interested despite herself.

Miss Eames gave a nod. "Exactly. Ellen was instructed to behave just as she did when you first called on her, in Westbourne Park. You see, Dr. Morton has been told that there is a bogle in Mr. Fotherington's chimney, and that Ellen summoned Mr. Bunce to get rid of it. This isn't true, of course. Mr. Fotherington has never been troubled by missing sweeps' boys."

"I must say, I'm glad we employ Mary Meggs," Mrs. Heppinstall suddenly remarked. "Her sister's talent and enthusiasm for lying makes me wonder if Ellen is entirely trustworthy as a maid."

"Ellen should have left the house by now," Miss Eames continued, ignoring her aunt. "We didn't want her running any risks. Dr. Morton is a dangerous man, and there is every chance he might try to involve her in some dreadful scheme—"

"But what about the bait?" Birdie interrupted.

"Oh, you needn't worry about that," said Miss Eames, waving the question aside in a way that alarmed Birdie—who was struck by a terrible thought.

"You ain't gone to *Sarah Pickles* for a kid?" she demanded shrilly.

"Of course not!" Miss Eames sounded hurt. "We would never dream of it!"

"There's a brave little boy who volunteered to help," Mrs. Heppinstall broke in. "Edith was quite taken with him — weren't you, dear?"

Miss Eames nodded. "He arrived at your house while Mr. Bunce and I were making our plans and insisted that he play a part," she revealed. "Mr. Bunce could *not* dissuade him —"

"Who is it?" Birdie cut her off. "Not Jem Barbary?"

"I believe his name is Ned," Miss Eames replied.

"Ned Roach?"

"He came to visit you, Birdie, knowing that you were ill. He hadn't heard about your abduction, needless to say." After a moment's hesitation Miss Eames carefully observed, "He seemed a nice enough boy, and very brave, though not — not a *refined* person, of course."

"Perhaps we should say that he is one of Nature's gentlemen?" Mrs. Heppinstall daintily proposed. "He did, after all, bring Birdie a bunch of violets."

"Ye-e-es . . ." Miss Eames hesitated long enough for Birdie to jump in.

"You mean Ned wants to be a *bogler's boy?*" she yelped. "But he never opens his mouth!"

"He doesn't have to, Birdie. There *is* no bogle, remember?" Though Miss Eames spoke gently, Birdie detected a hint of reproof in her tone. "All Ned has to do is stand and wait until word arrives that you have been rescued. Though *now*, of course, there has to be a slight change of plan . . ."

She glanced out the window, as if checking their progress, while Birdie felt a pang shoot through her like a needle to the heart. Distracted by her conversation with Miss Eames, she had briefly forgotten about the peril hanging over Alfred's head. This sudden reminder made her panic all over again.

"Where are we now?" she asked breathlessly. "How far away?"

"We're very close." Miss Eames had her nose pressed to the glass. "I think we just turned off Great Portland Street— oh!" Without a word of warning, she almost jumped out of her seat, then hurled herself forward and pounded on the roof. *"Stop! Samuel! STOP!"*

"Whoa!" Samuel's cry reached Birdie's ears as the brougham jounced to a halt, throwing her sideways. Before she could ask what had happened, Miss Eames was pushing open the carriage door and shouting at the top of her voice.

"Ned! Ned Roach!"

"Edith, *really!*" Mrs. Heppinstall was scandalized. "You're making a spectacle of yourself!"

"Ne-e-ed!" Miss Eames was now hanging out of the carriage, attracting a lot of attention. From behind her, Birdie caught a glimpse of faces turning toward them in the

crowded street, which was lined with handsome shops and houses.

But Birdie couldn't see Ned. Not with Miss Eames blocking her view.

"I don't think he heard me! Oh dear. *Ne-e-ed!*"

Birdie was fast losing patience. Pushing Miss Eames aside, she stuck her fingers in her mouth and unleashed a deafening whistle that made Miss Eames clap her hands over her ears.

"Oi! Ned!" Birdie waved her arms—and soon noticed someone waving back. It was Ned, all right; she recognized his blunt nose, broad face, and springy hair.

By this time a few vulgar remarks were being made by passersby. One man even offered to take Ned's place. But a gruff voice invited him to stow it, and the next thing Birdie knew, Ned was sticking his ruffled head into the carriage.

"Get in," she told him as Miss Eames cried, "What are you *doing* here, Ned? You should be with Mr. Bunce!"

"I got sent away," Ned gasped. He was damp and red faced, as if he'd been running. "Mr. Bunce told me to hook it . . ."

"But why?" Miss Eames demanded. Before Ned could explain, however, Mrs. Heppinstall appealed to her niece.

"For pity's sake, Edith, will you *close the door?* It's so vulgar to attract attention like this!"

So Miss Eames pulled Ned into the carriage and

slammed the door behind him. There was a brief moment of confusion while Ned cast himself onto the little fold-out seat that was tucked away opposite Miss Eames, facing backwards. Though he wasn't *that* big, Ned seemed to fill the whole carriage. Perhaps it had something to do with his dirty clothes, or his rough voice, or the faint, swampy smell that hung about him, which made Mrs. Heppinstall shrink back into her seat.

"I were looking for a policeman," Ned rasped. "There's a lockup in Great Marlborough Street—"

"A *policeman?*" Miss Eames echoed. And Birdie clutched his arm.

"What happened?" she quavered. "Is—is he dead?"

"Who?" Ned stared at her in confusion. "You mean Jem?"

"Jem?" Birdie didn't understand.

"Jem Barbary. Sal Pickles must have sent 'im." All at once Ned launched into a long and slightly garbled explanation, which burst out of his mouth like soda from a siphon. "That doctor knew he were on his way, but I don't think Jem knew much, or he never would have come—"

"But what *happened*, Ned?" Birdie cried impatiently, making him scowl.

"I'm a-telling you, ain't I? That doctor—he arrived in a cab, carrying a box. A big brass box. He said he'd be catching the bogle in it. Mr. Bunce said, 'How?' But then someone knocked on the door, so the doctor said, 'I'll show you,' and went down to let Jem in." Ned winced as Birdie's grip on him tightened—but he didn't try to loosen it. "Me and Mr. Bunce followed a little behind, so we didn't see Jem get jumped. It's my belief the doctor put cloor-a-form on a wipe and laid it across Jem's face as he stepped inside. For when *I* first saw Jem, he were being dragged across the kitchen floor like a drunken sailor."

By this time Mrs. Heppinstall had covered her own mouth with both hands, which were clad in fingerless gloves made of black lace. Miss Eames said, "Oh, how wicked!" Birdie was chewing her knuckles.

"He put Jem in the brass box," Ned continued, "and told Mr. Bunce the bogle would be caught when it went in after 'im—"

"Devil!" Birdie croaked.

"—and when Mr. Bunce objected, the doctor said Birdie would suffer if Mr. Bunce kicked up a fuss." Ned paused for a moment to draw breath; not being a talkative person, he was already beginning to flag. "Now, Mr. Bunce, knowing as how there ain't no bogle in that house—and *not* knowing if you'd bin rescued, Birdie—"

"Went along with it," Miss Eames finished.

"He did," Ned agreed. "And sent me off home, out of harm's way. But I don't like it, miss. Jem Barbary's bin as good as kidnapped, and drugged besides—"

"And you think it best to summon the police." Miss Eames nodded briskly. "You're right. The time has come. We have a drugged boy and a possible case of poisoned brandy. If we summon the police now, that monster will be caught in the act."

"But Mr. Bunce might die in the meantime!" Birdie protested. Releasing Ned, she grabbed Miss Eames, saying, "*You* go and fetch the police, miss. Me and Ned, we'll run back to the house. We'll hide, we'll watch, and we'll wait. But we'll also make sure that *nothing happens to Mr. Bunce.*" She then turned back to the hot, begrimed, breathless boy sitting opposite her and barked, "Come on, Ned! Let's go!"

29

Mr. Fotherington's House

Birdie didn't want to waste any time. When Miss Eames began to argue that two lone children shouldn't be entrusted with such a dangerous mission, Birdie's answer was to push open the carriage door and ask, "Where *is* Mr. Bunce?"

"Birdie—"

"The house ain't far," Ned volunteered, interrupting Miss Eames. "I'll take you there."

"Let *me* go!" Miss Eames tried to grab Birdie's pretty beaded sash. "Ned and I can protect Mr. Bunce while you and Aunt Louisa alert the police."

"Oh, but Edith . . ." Mrs. Heppinstall looked aghast. "I

have no *idea* what's going on! You never told me about this Pickles woman. I know nothing of Jem Barbary—"

"And *I* ain't going to no lockup," Birdie snapped. She eluded Miss Eames by jumping to the ground, where she landed near a pile of horse manure. "Them traps won't listen to me. Nor to *him*, neither." She jerked her chin at Ned, who had just joined her on the road. By this time Miss Eames was hovering in the doorway, glancing from her aunt to Birdie and back again. It was hard to judge who needed help the most; though Birdie was just a little child, Mrs. Heppinstall was as frail as a stick of rotten wood.

Seeing Miss Eames hesitate, Birdie made the choice for her—by moving away from the carriage.

"Wait! Birdie!" Miss Eames tried to call her back. And when that failed, she added, "Take the front-door key! You might need it . . ."

She tossed the key in Birdie's direction, so that it flashed through the air like a silver dart. Ned caught it. Then he offered it to Birdie, who waved it aside because she didn't have a pocket.

"Which way?" she asked him.

"Next left," he answered. Behind them, Samuel was cracking his whip.

"Look after her, Ned!" Miss Eames exclaimed. "I'll be there directly, as soon as I find a policeman!"

She slammed the door shut as the brougham began to roll forward.

Ned and Birdie took off down the street, which was flanked by very wide pavements. For once, Birdie didn't feel out of place among all the gentlefolk parading up and down—not in her expensive, brand-new clothes. But she was running with a badly dressed boy, and they made such an odd couple that they attracted quite a lot of attention.

Rounding a corner, she almost collided with a nursery maid pushing a pram.

"Beg pardon, miss!" Birdie gasped. She saw that she was now on a quieter, narrower street where the terraced houses were all five stories high, with white porticoes, black railings, and tall, stately red-brick façades. At number six a maid was sweeping the front steps. At number nine a footman was helping a lady into a cab.

"It's over there," Ned suddenly announced, pointing. "Twelfth one along."

Birdie stopped in her tracks. "Tell me where Mr. Bunce is."

"In the parlor."

"Aye, but where's that?"

Ned haltingly explained that the front door of Mr. Fotherington's house opened into a wide entrance hall with two large rooms off it. The parlor window looked out onto the street and was divided from the dining room by a pair of wooden folding doors. When prodded by Birdie—who found it hard to get information out of him—Ned explained that the bogle was supposed to be hidden in the parlor fireplace.

"So they're all in the front room?" asked Birdie, her face falling.

"It ain't as bad as it sounds," Ned assured her. "The window's shuttered, and them rooms . . . they're *big*." He racked his brain for a comparison. "Like a church."

"But they'll hear us if we go through the front door. They're bound to." As Ned shrugged, Birdie pondered. "And we can't see through the window, on account o' the shutters being closed."

Ned gave a nod.

"Where's the kitchen?" Birdie queried.

"In the basement. You can reach it from the open area under the front steps." After a moment's thought, Ned continued, "There's a mews out back, for the horses, but I ain't bin there. It's all locked up, I expect."

"We'll try the kitchen first," Birdie decided.

She took the lead, marching along with her head held high because she was as well dressed as any child in London, and saw no need to skulk. Ned, on the other hand, followed her with his head down, casting nervous glances from side to side.

"You look like a princess," he mumbled, making Birdie flush.

"If I were a princess," she replied in a low voice, "I'd be wearing a hat and gloves." Abruptly she halted again. "Is this the house?"

"Yes."

"Are you sure?" They all looked the same to her. "How do you know?"

"I told you. I counted."

They were lucky. There wasn't a soul near the place. What's more, the drawing room window was set quite high; even if it hadn't been shuttered, anyone inside would have had to stand very close to the glass to see Ned and Birdie pass underneath it into the area. A simple latch opened the gate, which swung smoothly on well-oiled hinges. A short flight of stone steps led down to the basement door. No stray leaves or nuggets of coal crunched under Birdie's feet as she padded across the area flagstones. No curious neighbors hailed her from the street to ask why such a respectable-looking girl was ushering a common beggar (or worse) into Mr. Fotherington's house.

When Birdie tried the basement door, its knob turned cleanly in her hand. Someone had left the door unlocked. Dr. Morton, perhaps? After he let Jem in? As Birdie slowly pushed her way inside, she gritted her teeth in fearful anticipation. But the door was as well oiled as the gate and hardly made a sound.

All at once she found herself in a generous scullery, complete with four stone sinks. The room was deserted save for a ginger cat, which was sunning itself on the window-sill. Silently it watched Ned follow Birdie over the threshold. The door clicked shut behind him, making him wince. Across the room another door was standing ajar. It led to the kitchen, which was enormous but very dingy.

It, too, was uninhabited.

Mr. Fotherington ain't short of a quid, Birdie thought, noting the fine array of copper pots stacked on a dresser. She threaded her way between the table and the bread oven, her gaze lingering on bowls full of candied peel and great bunches of fresh parsley. The floor was damp. There were no windows. The larder was a dismal rat hole, and the lime-washed walls were gray with soot. Yet the shelves groaned with spices, a whole brace of partridges hung from the ceiling, and a fancy dumbwaiter had been built into one wall, ready to transport food directly upstairs at the pull of a chain.

One of the doors beyond the larder was a pitch-black rectangle. Birdie could only guess that it led to a root cellar. Though she caught barely a glimpse of it in passing, even that quick glimpse filled her with dread. Was there someone inside? Someone she couldn't see? Telling herself that this was a foolish notion—that Miss Eames had given all the servants a day off—Birdie rushed up the kitchen stairs as if pursued by a man with a meat cleaver. She didn't know why she was so unnerved. The danger lay ahead of her, not behind. Yet the more distance she put between herself and that dark hole, the better she felt.

She stopped only when she reached the top of the staircase, which didn't creak as much as she had expected it to—perhaps because it was built to muffle the footsteps of servants at dawn. Ned caught up with her as she was yanking off her boots. From the ground-floor stairwell they stepped straight into a kind of butler's pantry full of crockery and linen. This pantry, in turn, opened onto the main entrance hall, which was separated from the servants' quarters by a cloth-covered door.

Birdie placed one hand on the green baize padding and gave it a gentle push. Then she peered into the hallway. Like the kitchen, it was empty. The front door was shut. There were only two other access points: the parlor door, which was also closed, and the dining room door, which stood slightly ajar.

Somewhere out of sight, a voice was squeaking wordlessly in fear or anger. Or was it desperation?

"That's Jem," Ned breathed into Birdie's ear. "Sounds like he's bin gagged."

She nodded. Thanks to Ned, she knew that she would

see something of the front parlor if she stuck her head into the dining room—because the folding doors between the two rooms had been pushed apart. So she crept forward on stockinged feet, passing lightly from oilcloth to polished parquet. But then the floor creaked behind her, and she glanced around.

Ned was standing frozen, with one foot raised. He looked both guilty and apologetic. When she motioned for him to stay put, he gnawed at his lip and pulled an anxious face. He didn't, however, try to follow her across the hall, which was wider than Birdie's whole house and crowded with all kinds of strange things: a carved grandfather clock, a hat stand made of horns and antlers, a barometer inlaid with mother-of-pearl, a painting of a tiger eating a wolf. The dining room door was squeezed between the grandfather clock and a lacquered cabinet full of strange wooden masks. When Birdie peered around the doorjamb, the first thing she saw, in the middle of the room, was a long table draped in green cloth. Behind it was a fireplace. To the left was a sideboard, with the dumbwaiter hatch inserted into the wall just above it. To the right, one of the folding doors projected slightly, forming a strange little stub of a wall that partially blocked Birdie's view of the parlor.

But though she couldn't see much of the room to her right, she *could* see Alfred. He had stationed himself beside the parlor fireplace, which shared the same wall as the one in the dining room. Visible in front of him was a triangular wedge of parquet floor, together with a small portion of the salt circle he'd laid out. Birdie could also see half a painting, half a side table, and a very large book cupboard.

She couldn't, however, see Dr. Morton. If he actually *was* in the parlor, he had to be tucked away out of sight, near the front window. Jem was also hidden from Birdie, though she could hear him well enough. The sound of his muffled squawks made her blood run cold. She guessed that he was in the middle of the magic circle — most of which she couldn't see.

She was craning her neck to get a better look when Alfred suddenly spotted her. His eyes widened. His face stiffened. Birdie quickly put a finger to her lips, before encircling her wrists with her fingers, to signify handcuffs. Then she jerked her head toward the street. She was trying to tell Alfred that the police were coming.

In response, he blinked. Birdie instantly understood that Dr. Morton must be in the room with him — somewhere in a corner, out of sight — and that she would have to be very, very careful. So she went on to explain, in sign language, that Alfred shouldn't drink anything. First she pointed in his direction. Then she mimed a bottle. Then she shook her finger at him, after which she clutched her throat with both hands, as if she were choking.

Again Alfred blinked. Twice. He had been darting little

glances at her; now he fixed his gaze on the parlor fireplace, as if trying to allay any suspicions that the doctor might have. Birdie was satisfied. She knew that Alfred had understood. And since she was becoming more and more overwhelmed by a kind of creeping dread (which she blamed on Dr. Morton's close proximity), she decided it was time to retreat.

She was slowly edging backwards when her eyes strayed toward the dumbwaiter. For an instant her heart seemed to stop. The little hatch was open. It had been closed before, and now it was a gaping hole.

But it wasn't the hole that frightened Birdie. What gave her the shock of her life — what made her freeze, then gasp, then jump backwards — was the thing bubbling *out* of the hole.

It moved silently, like a cloud. It was large and dark and oily, like a surge of coal-black soapsuds. And it was growing bigger by the second as it slurped down onto the floor . . .

30

A Terrible Shock

Birdie didn't know how long she stood there, paralyzed, with her hand over her mouth. Time slowed to a crawl. She could see Ned trying to attract her attention, his face a mask of anxiety. He wanted to know what was going on.

Then she heard a muffled shriek—and snapped out of her daze. There was a bogle in the next room! A *real* one! And here she was, a bogler's girl, cowering like a mouse in a bread bin!

It's only a bogle, she told herself, before taking a deep breath and charging back through the dining room door.

She was confronted by a scene of pure chaos. The bogle was now heading for the parlor. It was a huge mass of warts—or were they boils? Or bubbles? Birdie couldn't tell; while the lumps *did* pop like bubbles, they also oozed like boils. And because of all these eruptions, it was hard to make out the bogle's exact shape, though it did have a couple of gnarled, twisted, leprous-looking horns, and some kind of dragging tail that left a sticky black residue in its wake.

It also had two very long arms, with claws at the end of them. And just as Birdie crossed the threshold, one of these arms shot toward Alfred—who couldn't quite dodge it in time. Perhaps he'd been deliberately looking away from the dining room, so that Dr. Morton wouldn't be tempted to glance in that direction. Perhaps he wasn't as alert as usual because he hadn't been expecting a real bogle to descend on them.

Whatever the reason, he was taken by surprise. Before he could even aim his spear, the bogle seized a clump of his shirtfront and jerked him into the air like someone lifting a pint pot. The spear was knocked from Alfred's hand. Birdie saw it hit the floor. She darted forward to grab it, but the bogle was in her way.

Behind her, Ned cried, "Birdie!" Jem was squealing; from where she now stood she had a clear view of the salt circle and the brass box, which was quite big, though not big enough for Jem. His feet and head were sticking out of the box, which could have been a coal box except that it was embossed with strange symbols instead of miners, or knights, or jolly drinking scenes. There was a strip of cloth tied across his mouth. His legs were bound with thick, hairy twine.

Beyond Jem, near the parlor window, stood Dr. Morton. He was reading aloud from a leatherbound book, his voice raised in a monotonous chant that was barely audible over all the shouts and screams. Since he seemed to be fully absorbed in his task, and wasn't threatening anyone, Birdie made a snap decision to ignore him.

She was busy enough already.

Suddenly the bogle plowed forward, into the magic circle. Alfred still had his bag of salt but couldn't reach down to close the circle because he was being jerked around like bait on a hook. The bogle grabbed Dr. Morton's brass box, upending it so that Jem tumbled out. Jem groaned. His dark eyes were bulging with fear. Dr. Morton gave a shout of protest when he saw that his trap had been sprung.

The bogle didn't pay him any mind, though. It grabbed Jem around the ankles. And as Birdie watched, horrified, it plucked him from the floor so that he was dangling upside down. Then the bogle turned again, spinning around on a kind of oil slick. It held Jem and Alfred suspended, one in each hand, like the dead pheasants downstairs.

Birdie was now standing between the bogle and the dumbwaiter. Luckily, help was on its way in the shape of

Ned Roach, who had entered the dining room and was sidling in her direction. "The spear!" she told him hoarsely. "Get the spear!" As soon as he nodded, she gulped down a lungful of air and began to sing.

> "Hold up thy hand, most righteous judge! Hold up thy
>   hand awhile.
> For here I see me father dear come tumbling o'er the
>   stile."

Her own voice astonished her; it was clear and pure and strong, cutting cleanly through all the commotion. It mesmerized the bogle, which became so still that Birdie finally got a good look at it. She realized that its dragging tail was actually a pair of long, wet, leathery wings. Its legs were rotting stumps. It had the crinkled muzzle of a bulldog, topped by a cluster of lidless eyes. When it suddenly bared its teeth—which sprang up in double rows like blood-drenched spikes emerging from a black, muddy bog—Birdie's breath caught in her throat. But after a moment's pause, she kept on singing.

> "Oh hast thou brought me silver or gold or jewels to set
>   me free,
> Or hast thou come to see me hang? For hanged I shall
>   be."

Ned was edging toward the fallen spear, using the table and chairs as cover. Jem's gag had fallen off. He was twisting and writhing and yelling for help at the top of his voice. Birdie wished that he would stop. It was hard enough trying to be heard over Dr. Morton's strange, monotonous chanting. The doctor had picked up his brass box; he was standing behind the bogle as if he expected it to climb inside. But the creature didn't seem to notice him at all.

Alfred, for his part, was trying to empty his bag of salt onto the bogle. He missed because its arm kept flailing around, knocking him against the wall, the ceiling, the book cupboard, the mantelpiece. His face was turning purple, thanks to the bogle's tight grip on his collar. He couldn't speak. He'd lost his hat. As the bogle surged forward, his knee bounced off the folding door.

Birdie retreated a step. Then another. Then another. But she didn't for one moment stop singing.

> *"If I could get out o' this prickly bush that prickles me heart so sore,*
> *If I could get out o' this prickly bush, I'd never get in it no more."*

By now Ned was squatting behind the folding door to Birdie's left. She could tell that he was biding his time, waiting for the moment when he could throw himself at Alfred's spear without getting too close to the bogle. So she began to move in the opposite direction, edging closer and closer to the dining room door.

Her plan was to lure the bogle away from Ned, then make her escape into the entrance hall while Ned grabbed Alfred's spear. Even as she sang to the bogle, she was looking at Ned and miming a stabbing motion. But would he understand what she was trying to say? He was as white as Alfred's salt beneath the smears of soot and mud that adorned his face.

> *"Oh, I have brought no silver or gold, nor jewels to set thee free.*
> *But I have come to see thee hang, for hanged thou shalt be."*

Suddenly the bogle dropped Alfred. She saw him bang to the floor and reach for his spear. Then a giant claw snapped at her, missing her by inches. She screamed and threw herself backwards just in time. When the claw lunged again, she dodged it by falling over. Rolling onto her stomach, she heard Ned shout.

Next thing she knew, she was sailing into the air, screeching like a parrot. The bogle! It had her! It was going to eat her!

And then, all at once, it popped.

She didn't realize what had happened at first. She heard a strange noise and felt a warm shower of goo as she hit the floor with a *thump* that shook every bone in her body. Despite the pain in her arm, however, she immediately jumped up and hurled herself into the entrance hall.

"Birdie! Wait!" It was Ned's voice, coming from behind her. She was about to respond when she spied Dr. Morton, who was also in the hall. He yanked open the front door, then shut it again in a panic—though not before Birdie spotted a policeman on the doorstep.

Dr. Morton slammed the bolt home, turned on his heel, and charged toward Birdie. He was probably making for the kitchen stairs, and the look on his face was so frightening that, just for an instant, it drove every other thought from Birdie's head. She froze in terror. And by the time she found her courage again, Dr. Morton was almost on top of her.

Someone else reached her first, though. As the policeman hammered on the front door, and Jem let loose a torrent of oaths, and Ned burst out of the parlor, Alfred suddenly appeared beside Birdie, carrying his spear. He scooped her up with one hand; with the other, he shoved his spear at Dr. Morton's throat.

"Take one more step," he said in a harsh, icy voice, "and I'll slice you in two."

The doctor had skidded to a halt. He thrust an open palm at Alfred, as if ordering him to back off, and began to recite something in a foreign tongue. But Ned had already unbolted the front door, which banged open to admit a very tall, burly police constable.

"Now, then!" the policeman boomed. "What's going on, here?"

"There he is!" a familiar voice cried. It belonged to Miss Eames. She was hovering behind the constable, pointing down the hall. "Dr. Roswell Morton! I accuse that man of murder, attempted murder, kidnapping, and false imprisonment!"

Dr. Morton spun around to face her. He wasn't looking quite as suave as usual, because his oily hair was in disarray and his clothes were disheveled. Even so, when he addressed the constable in his calm, dry, slightly bemused tone, he sounded very convincing—or so Birdie thought.

"Constable, I was called here for a medical emergency and immediately found myself threatened by a low type with a spear. I believe he and his cohorts were robbing the place . . ."

By this time Alfred had let Birdie slide to the floor. She was still plastered to his side, though, and could feel him take a quick, deep breath. But before he could say anything, Jem cut him off.

"Help! *Help!*" Jem cried. "Untie me, damn you!"

He was still in the parlor. As the police constable

swerved toward it, Birdie tugged at Alfred's coat. "Is it dead?" she squeaked. "Did you kill the bogle?"

"Aye, lass," Alfred replied, without taking his eyes off Dr. Morton. Though Miss Eames had followed the policeman into the parlor, Ned had stayed behind; he was guarding the front door, which was shut again. Birdie could see him out of the corner of her eye, standing there with his legs apart and his arms folded. He looked very frightened, despite his brave stance.

"I thought there *weren't* no bogle!" Birdie exclaimed.

"So did I," said Alfred—and the doctor gave a little start. Birdie saw him do it. Alfred must have seen him too, because he smiled sourly and tapped Dr. Morton between the shoulders with the point of his spear. "Aye, that's right. We lured you into our trap, just like a bogle. You're not the only one as can set a snare." Before the doctor could do more than hiss, Alfred laid his free hand on Birdie's head and muttered, "It just goes to show, lass, that you can't never be too careful. Not where bogles is concerned." And he finally added, in a preoccupied tone, "That bogle must have come out o' the basement and used the dumbwaiter to get up here. I wonder if Mr. Fotherington ever lost a boot boy?"

Meanwhile, the noise from the parlor had been increasing, with Jem and Miss Eames both jabbering away at once. Birdie caught the words "chloroform," "brandy," and "poison." It crossed her mind that the doctor's bottle of chloroform had to be somewhere in the house. And although every trace of the bogle was rapidly evaporating, she suddenly felt quite sure that proof of the doctor's wickedness would soon be found—and that one day it would be used against him in a court of law.

Then the police constable reappeared with Jem in tow and Miss Eames tagging along behind them.

"All right," the big man trumpeted, "I don't know what this is all about, but I can see that something isn't right, here. And I intend to get to the bottom of it, even if we have to spend the *whole day talking* . . ."

31

Four Months Later . . .

Alfred's new address was on the sixth floor of a big old house off Drury Lane. To reach it, Birdie had to climb flight after flight of rickety stairs, past rooms full of crying babies, grubby children, toiling dressmakers, quarreling grandmothers, and pale-faced girls with chesty coughs. They all stared at Birdie, who had come straight from her singing lesson in a dress of plaid poplin under a velvet mantle trimmed with silk.

Some of the children started to follow her, whining for money, until she told them to hook it. "I ain't no blooming toff," she snapped, "and I've *just* enough for me bus fare home. So you might as well save yer breath."

Startled by her Bethnal Green accent (which was sharply at odds with her Paddington Green appearance), the children fell back, allowing her to trudge on alone. Alfred's room was a former servant's garret, high up under the roof. By the time she knocked on his door, she was red in the face and puffing like a pair of bellows. *If he ain't home,* she thought, *I'll be blowed if I'll come all this way again!*

But he was at home. And he smiled at the sight of her.

"Hello, Birdie. Does Miss Eames know you're here?"

Birdie chose not to answer his question. Instead, she folded her arms and scowled. "Why didn't you tell me you'd left the old place?" she demanded. "I had to find it out from Ned!"

Alfred shrugged. "I thought Miss Eames might not want you to know . . ."

"Miss Eames ain't got nothing to do with it!" Birdie exclaimed, before correcting herself. "I mean, she *doesn't* have nothing to do with it." Still this sounded wrong; after a moment's reflection, she added, "*Anything* to do with it."

Alfred raised his eyebrows and wiped a hand across his scrubby chin. "Well, now you're here, at last, you'd best come in," he said, stepping aside to let Birdie cross the threshold. "You look a picture, lass. Like you was born to a life o' luxury."

Birdie snorted. "Luxury! Hah!"

Alfred raised an eyebrow. "Ain't you getting enough jam tarts?" he asked in a dry voice that made Birdie blush.

"There's no end o' food," she admitted. "I've all the clothes I want, and I ain't got to cook or clean or carry—"

"Which sounds like a throne in paradise to me."

"It is. And I'm grateful. Truly I am," Birdie mumbled. Then she burst out, "But there's so much else I have to do! The reading and the writing and the singing and the speech training . . ." She shook her head, trying for the moment to banish all thoughts of her new life. In so many ways it was easier than her old life, because she no longer had to help kill bogles. In other ways, though, it was much harder. Sometimes she felt as if her head were going to explode with all the information that had been stuffed into it: information about grammar, music, the alphabet, clothes, table manners, ladylike deportment . . .

It was quite a relief to find herself in a place where she didn't have to keep her back straight or her voice hushed.

"Is that where Ned sleeps?" she asked, gazing at the heap of old shawls and coats and blankets that occupied one corner.

"Aye," said Alfred.

"How's his cooking?"

Alfred gave her another crooked smile as he closed the door. "Not too good. But Ned's doughty on them stairs. Especially with bags o' coal."

Birdie grunted. She had been half hoping that Alfred's new living arrangements would fail. It had annoyed her when he'd offered to house Ned, rent-free, in exchange for the boy's domestic services—though she understood that both of them would benefit. Ned would no longer have to pay threepence a night for a bed in a common lodging house, and Alfred wouldn't have to darn his own socks. But while she liked Ned well enough, and was glad that Alfred had someone to look after him, she couldn't help feeling that she'd been replaced like a worn-out shoe. Especially now that Ned had started exhibiting an interest in bogles.

"Is *that* Ned's?" she asked suspiciously—for there was a large and very beautiful doll sitting in one corner. It had a china face, blue glass eyes, and real hair coiled into ringlets. It wore a dress of white muslin and a straw hat.

"Nay," Alfred replied, settling himself onto his old stool. "That's Jem's."

"Jem's?"

"He says he came by it fair and square, though I ain't convinced." Watching Birdie approach the doll, Alfred remarked, "If you tip it over, it makes a noise."

He was right. The doll bleated "Mama" when Birdie picked it up—almost causing her to drop it again.

"I'll be . . ." she murmured. "But why did Jem bring it here?"

"Oh, Jem had a notion it would make good bogle bait, no matter who might be holding it." As Birdie frowned, trying to imagine what would happen if you put a little old woman in a magic circle with a talking doll, Alfred continued, "Jem's forever coming here with ideas like that. If you ask me, he ain't finding a delivery boy's life so congenial. You know he's 'prenticed to a grocer now?"

"Yes," said Birdie. She knew all about Jem because Miss Eames had taken an interest in his progress. After Jem had angrily denounced both Dr. Morton and Sarah Pickles to the police — thereby triggering the doctor's arrest and Sarah's sudden disappearance — his sad story had found its way into the newspapers, and had aroused the sympathy of an Islington grocer named Barnabus Leach. Mr. Leach had thought Jem a promising lad, bright and quick though badly raised, and had offered to take him in off the street. At the time, Jem had been at a loose end. Sarah had either gone to ground or been killed for betraying one of her own boys (no one seemed quite sure which), while Jem had been too widely known, by then, to earn his bread picking pockets. So he had agreed to work for Mr. Leach.

"Jem says as how I should start bogling again, but I've a suspicion it's *him* as wants to be a bogler," Alfred went on. "Ned, too. They never leave me alone — allus going on and on about bogles . . ."

Birdie was well aware of this. Ned had twice waylaid her outside her singing teacher's house with the news that Alfred had turned down *yet another* bogling job. After Dr. Morton's trial had been reported in the newspapers, Alfred had become something of a household name. Appeals had started flooding in from all over England. A village in Cornwall had lost a couple of children in a large pond; a coal mine in Yorkshire had mysteriously mislaid four of its hurriers, or coal-dragging girls; six children had disappeared in the vicinity of Maidstone, Kent, over the past three years.

But for every appeal there had been half a dozen insults. While accusing Dr. Morton of being an evil and deluded maniac, the newspapers had also condemned Alfred for defrauding bereaved working folk of their hard-earned wages with his stories of child-eating monsters hiding in chimneys. After two members of the Victoria Institute had interviewed him and had come away scoffing at his claims, people had begun to abuse him publicly — though not, for the most part, in his own neighborhood. The inhabitants of Bethnal Green knew Alfred well enough to defend him when nosy journalists, drunken thrill seekers, and prying folklorists came poking around, asking questions.

Even so, Alfred had decided to move. Too many strange people had found out where he lived and were soon waylaying him in the street, or knocking on his door, demanding bogle slime for their potions or offering to save his soul from the devil. He wasn't comfortable in the limelight and wasn't happy talking to gentlemen who used long, scientific words. What's more, he had decided to give up bogling after his discovery that *some* bogles were actually desperate enough to attack an armed grown-up. How could he protect his apprentices if he couldn't protect himself? Miss Eames had been right, he said. Bogling was not safe for apprentices, and until an alternative bait could be found, he wasn't about to put any more children in danger — no matter how many times Jem or Ned might plead that bogling was better than picking pockets, or sifting mud, or cleaning bacon slicers.

"But what about all the missing kids in Yorkshire and Kent and Sussex?" Birdie inquired as she inspected the talking doll. It had ruffled pantaloons, silk stockings, and white leather boots. "Don't you care about *them?*"

"Not enough to throw more kids into a bogle's mouth."

"But what if you don't have to?" Birdie put the doll back down before focusing her attention on Alfred. "See, I came here to tell you summat — *something* — that I heard today at me singing lesson. There's a cove in France has used a machine to copy part of a song onto a cylinder. So it won't be long before there's a machine as can record songs *and play 'em back!* Like a self-playing piano . . ."

"What's that got to do with me?" Alfred queried.

"Well—if you had a machine as could sing like a child, you wouldn't need a real child no more!"

"And how much do you think this new machine'll cost, when it's finally invented?" Alfred asked in a dry voice.

"Oh, that don't matter." Birdie dismissed the question impatiently. "Miss Eames'll buy it for you."

"I think she'd prefer it if I didn't bogle at all," said Alfred, plugging his old clay pipe with tobacco. "Which I won't if I have to wait for a machine that ain't even bin invented yet."

"Then how will you *live?*" Birdie had been worrying more and more about Alfred, who had refused to take money from Miss Eames, and who was fast running through the fees paid to him by various journalists. According to Ned, Alfred's first foray into rat catching had left him with an infected bite that had put him in bed for a week. "You ain't no vermin hunter; you're a hero!" Birdie cried. "You'd be wasted as a rat catcher, or a night watchman or—or—" She was suddenly interrupted by a tentative tap on the door. "Who is it?" she barked.

There was a brief pause. Then a startled voice said, "Birdie?"

"Come in, Ned." Alfred's tone was long suffering. "You *know* you ain't got to knock."

"Yes, but I brought a visitor," Ned explained as he

sidled into the room. Behind him was a swarthy young navvy wearing moleskin trousers, hobnailed boots, and a velveteen coat. A gaudy handkerchief was tied around the navvy's neck; he carried a white felt hat that he kept rubbing between thick, nervous fingers.

"This here is Fettle Joe," Ned announced awkwardly. "He works on the London and North Western Railway."

Fettle Joe bobbed his head, which was crowned by a dense thatch of black hair. More hair covered his throat, jaw, arms, hands, and upper lip. His brown eyes looked softer than the rest of him.

"Me ganger sent me to find you, Mr. Bunce," he said. "We heard all about that wicked doctor as went to gaol on account o' you."

"Oh, aye," Alfred replied in a noncommittal way.

"It's just . . . well, we've got boys working alongside us in the tunnels, see, and some no more'n ten years old. But two of 'em vanished last week. We ain't seen hide nor hair of 'em since, though I did hear one scream afore he disappeared."

"They work underground," Ned interposed. "And bogles like deep holes."

"Alfred knows what bogles like!" Birdie snapped. But Alfred said nothing.

"We thought as how you might help if there's a bogle

dogging us," Fettle Joe continued. "Which we're inclined to believe there is."

Alfred hesitated. "I don't kill bogles no more," he growled at last. "'Tis a thankless job."

"I can appreciate that, sir, but they was stout little lads, one supporting a sick mother with his wage and the other learning to read." Seeing Alfred frown, the navvy softly pleaded, "Will you not take pity on the other boys, Mr. Bunce? Who must give up either their lives or their livelihoods?"

Everyone stared at Alfred—including Birdie. He wouldn't look at her, though.

"We'd pay double," Fettle Joe added.

"And I'd be yer boy," Ned volunteered, much to Birdie's disgust.

"You!" She couldn't contain herself. "What do *you* know about bogling!"

"Not much," Ned had to concede. He fixed his clear, trustful gaze on Birdie. "You could teach me, though."

Birdie glanced back at Alfred, who was shaking his head. "If there's smoke again, or summat worse . . ." he began. But she forestalled him.

"We'd have more'n one lure, to protect ourselves," she pointed out. "Say there was three of us, widely spaced. You saw what happened at Mr. Fotherington's; the bogle didn't know which of us to eat first. Suppose there *is* smoke, which I doubt, since you've seen only one smoking bogle in yer whole life. We can slow the bogle by confusing it with *three different voices*: Jem's, Ned's, and mine."

"Not yours, lass," said Alfred. "Miss Eames wouldn't like it."

"Miss Eames needn't know," Birdie retorted. "And it's only this once."

"*I'll* do it," Ned cut in. "And so will Jem."

"Please, Mr. Bunce," begged the navvy.

"The next boy who's taken will be on yer conscience if you don't help," Birdie warned Alfred. "Can you live with that? For *I* cannot!"

"And me and Jem—we need the experience," Ned mumbled. "We've our hearts set on bogling. 'Tis a respectable trade, and mudlarks don't make old bones."

"There's no one can do this but you, Mr. Bunce," Birdie argued. "And there's still more underground lines to build, with boys slated to work 'em. Ain't that right?"

She appealed to Fettle Joe, who nodded gravely. Meanwhile, Alfred sat hunched in his old green coat, sucking on his pipe, looking tired and worn and grim but somehow indomitable, like an ancient ruin. At last he pulled the pipe from his mouth.

"All right," he said. "I'll do it." Before the navvy could

thank him, however, Alfred addressed Birdie in a tone that she knew well—a tone that had governed her life since their first meeting in the Limehouse canal, when she was just four years old. "But this is the last time, d'you hear? The very last. For you've passed beyond this, Birdie. I ain't yer master no more. We're on different roads now and must stick to 'em."

"Of course," Birdie answered—because Alfred was right. He *wasn't* her master. They *were* on different roads. And for this very reason she no longer had to do what he said.

She could plot out her own course, toward her own goal, in her own way. And if that meant a bit of unofficial bogling—well, then Alfred wasn't going to stop her. Certainly Miss Eames wasn't. If Birdie wanted to be a music-hall singer with a sideline in bogling, there was no reason why she should abandon that dream.

"So shall we give Jem's doll a try, while we're about it?" she suggested, bright eyed and keen voiced. "Since there's more'n one way to skin a cat, it might be the same for a bogle. Don't you think so, Mr. Bunce . . . ?"

Glossary

AREA: the basement-level entrance under the front door of many nineteenth-century terrace or row houses, often with railings around the top

BAIRN: a Scottish word for child

BALLAST HEAVER: a person who loads ballast into the holds of empty ships

BASILISK: a legendary reptile said to cause death with a single glance

BEAK: a magistrate

BEDLAMITE: an insane person

BOB: a shilling

BOGLE: a monster, goblin, bogeyman

BROLLY: an umbrella

BROUGHAM: a one-horse carriage with an open seat in front for the driver

BUGGANE: a huge ogre-like creature, native to the Isle of Man

CADGER: a beggar

CAFFLER: *see* rag-and-bone man

CHINK: money

CIUDACH: a Scottish cave-dwelling monster

COAL WHIPPER: a person who unloads coal from ships

COSH: a blunt weapon

COSTER: a street seller

COVE: a man

CRACKSMAN: a burglar, lock picker

CRIB: a house

CROW: a lookout

DEADLURK: an empty building

DIPPER: a pickpocket

DIMMICK: a counterfeit coin

DOWNY: cunning, false

DUNNAGE: clothes and possessions

EARTH CLOSET: a seat placed over a deep hole in the ground for relieving oneself

FLAM: lie

FLUX: diarrhea

FUATH: an evil Gaelic water spirit

FUSTIAN: coarse, cotton-linen cloth

GAMMONING: lying

GANGER: a supervisor

GAOL: jail

GLOCKY: half-witted

GRIDDLER: a beggar

GRIDDLING: begging

GRINDYLOW: a bogeyman from Lancashire or Yorkshire, typically found in bogs or lakes

GRUBBER: another term for mudlark

HACKNEY CAB: a two-wheeled carriage for hire

HACKNEY CARRIAGE: a four-wheeled carriage for hire

HANSOM CAB: another term for hackney cab

HOBBLER: a boat tower, someone who tows boats

HOBYAH: an English fairy-tale goblin

HOIST: to steal, shoplift

HOOK IT: move it

HURRIER: a girl aged five to eighteen who draws coal in a mine

JACK: a detective

JEMMY: a crowbar

KNUCKER: a kind of water dragon from Sussex, England

LAG: a convict, jailbird

LAGGED: jailed

LAY: method

LURK: a trick, scam

LURKER: a criminal

LUSHERY: a low public house

MERE: a lake, pond

MOOCHER: a tramp

MUCK SNIPE: a tramp

MUDLARK: a child who scavenges on riverbanks

MUMPING: begging

NAVVY: an unskilled laborer, especially one who does heavy digging

NIBBED: arrested

NOBBLE: to hurt

OMNIBUS: a very large horse-drawn vehicle for moving large numbers of people

POTTLE: a container holding half a gallon

PRIG: a thief, or to steal

PRIVY: toilet

QUID: a pound, or about two dollars in today's money

RACKET: a shady or illegal pursuit

RAG-AND-BONE MAN: a collector of rags for making paper and bones for making glue

SENNIGHT: a week

SHELLYCOAT: a Scottish goblin that haunts rivers and streams

SHIRKSTER: a layabout

SKIPPER: a person who sleeps in sheds and outbuildings

SLAVVY: a maid of all work

SLOPS: old clothes

SPIKE: a workhouse

TOFF: a well-to-do person

TOFFKEN: the dwelling of well-to-do people

TOGS: clothes

TOOLING: pickpocketing

TOSHER: a sewer scavenger

TRAP: a policeman

WHITE LADIES: ghosts of a very particular type

WIPE: a handkerchief

WORKHOUSE: an institution that houses and feeds paupers

WORRICOW: a Scottish hobgoblin

THE BOGLES ARE BACK—
AND SCARIER THAN EVER IN THE NEXT INSTALLMENT OF THE CHARMING AND CHILLING BOGLE TRILOGY.

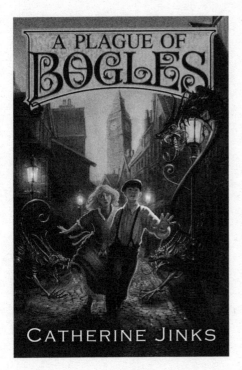

Jem Barbary spent most of his early life picking pockets for a wily old crook named Sarah Pickles—until she betrayed him. Now Jem wants revenge, but first he needs a new job. Luckily Alfred the bogler needs a new apprentice since Birdie has moved up in the world. As more and more orphans disappear under mysterious circumstances, Alfred, Jem, and Birdie find themselves waging an underground war in a city where monsters lurk in every alley. Soon they discover that there's only one thing more terrifying than facing a whole plague of bogles: facing the sinister people from Jem's past . . .

Turn the page for a sneak peek at

A PLAGUE OF BOGLES

LONDON, ENGLAND, C. 1870

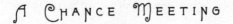
A Chance Meeting

The man stationed at the door was small and stout. He had a red face, blue eyes, and wispy gray curls. His satin-breasted coat was trimmed with silver lace. His top hat was the color of mulberries.

"Walk in! Walk in! Now exhibiting!" he boomed. "The best show in London, ladies and gentlemen! A menagerie of mythical beasts! Living, breathing monsters for only one penny!"

The narrow shop front behind him was plastered with brightly colored advertisements. One of them showed a picture of a very young girl cracking a whip at something that looked like a giant toad.

"See our griffin! See our mermaid! See our erlking!" cried the man in the purple hat, tapping at the picture with his bamboo cane. "See Birdie McAdam, the Go-Devil Girl, tame a fierce bogle and a dainty unicorn!"

Across the road, Jem stopped short. He stood goggle-eyed as the crowds surged past him. In one hand he carried a cheap broom. On his feet he wore nothing but a thick layer of mud.

For a moment he stared at the man in the purple hat. Then he darted forward, dodging a pile of horse manure and the rattling wheels of a carriage.

"See the world's greatest novelties, ladies and gentlemen! Marvel at the legendary two-headed snake of Libya! Touch a genuine dragon's egg for only one penny!" The red-faced showman raised his voice a little, drowning the chant of a nearby coster selling nuts and whelks. "Now exhibiting! Satisfaction guaranteed! The world's greatest wonders, here in Whitechapel Road!"

He was perched high on a wooden box, with a good view of all the bobbing umbrellas that filled the street. But he didn't see Jem until the boy tugged at his coat.

"Sir? Hi! Sir?"

Glancing down, the man saw only a filthy little crossing sweeper in a ragged blue shirt and striped canvas trousers, torn off at the knee. A cap like a cowpat cast the boy's gleaming brown eyes into shadow. It also concealed most of his thick, black, glossy hair—which was his best feature, though it made his head look too big for his body.

"Hook it," the man growled. "Go on."

"Please, sir, I'm a friend o' Birdie McAdam. Will you let me in? She'll want to say hello."

"Get out of it, I said!"

Jem flushed. "I ain't gammoning you, sir! Jem Barbary's the name. Why, Birdie and me—we used to knock around Bethnal Green together when she were just a bogler's girl. Ask *her* if we didn't!"

The only reply was a quick swipe with the bamboo cane, which left a red welt on Jem's knuckles. He jumped back, grimacing. Then he retreated a few steps to take stock of the exhibition venue. It was a small, two-story building wedged tightly between a pastry shop and a public house. Over the door was a faded sign, but Jem couldn't read it. Nor could he see any side alleys piercing the impenetrable wall of shop fronts breasting the street.

But the public house was on a corner, and would probably have a rear yard of some kind. Jem's gaze moved up a drainpipe, along a brick ledge, and across a roof that bristled with chimneys. He'd burgled many a house in the past, and this one was no strongbox. He thought that he could probably find another way in—without paying a penny for the privilege.

"Begging your pardon, lad, but is it true?" a soft voice suddenly asked. "Do you really know Birdie McAdam?"

Startled, Jem spun around. He found himself staring up at a pretty young woman in a velveteen mantle. She had rosy cheeks, gray eyes, and lots of rich brown hair piled up under a hat that was barely big enough to support all the feathers, flowers, veils, and ribbons sewn onto it.

She was sheltering from the rain under a pink silk parasol.

"What's it to you?" he said, wondering why a decent-looking female would approach him in the street like a common beggar. The young woman glanced around nervously before leaning down to address him.

"I'm Mabel Lillimere," she murmured. "I'm a barmaid at the Viaduct Tavern, on the corner o' Newgate Street. If you *are* a friend o' Birdie's, and can persuade her to talk to me, I'll stump up your fee so as you and I both can get in." Eyeing his grubby face with a touch of suspicion, she added fiercely, "But if you're lying—why, I'll box your ears so hard, you'll have your left ear on the right side o' your head and your right ear on the left!"

This threat didn't worry Jem. He'd suffered worse. "Why not talk to her yerself?" he wanted to know.

"Because she'll not see me! Or so *he* says." Mabel gestured at the man in the purple topper, who was now reminding all the damp pedestrians scurrying past him that Birdie McAdam was "well known to the public" owing to "newspaper reports of her bogle-baiting prowess." "Mr. Lubbock, he calls himself," Mabel continued. "Claims he's in charge. Says Birdie's not inclined to speak to the public. Says she's too shy, and needs to rest her voice."

Jem snorted. "Well, *that's* a flam," he declared. "Birdie's as forward as they come. Did you offer him extra?"

"Tuppence."

"Then he's a-humming you." His suspicions confirmed, Jem scowled at Mr. Lubbock. "I'll wager Birdie ain't here. Last time I saw her, she were living with a fine lady near Great Russell Street, eating plum cakes every day and wearing lace on her petticoats. Why would she want to come back to the East End and work in a penny gaff like this'un, when there's fine folk as think she's too good for the life?"

Mabel's face fell. Her troubled gaze slid toward Mr. Lubbock. "You think that there feller is lying, then?"

"Why not?" Jem shrugged. "He's a slang cove. Lying's what they do best." Studying the barmaid with frank curiosity, he added, "Why d'you want to speak to Birdie? You can't be kin—she ain't got a soul to call her own."

Mabel hesitated. At last she said, "I read about Birdie in the newspapers last summer, and never thought of her again till I passed this here gaff. Then I saw her name and recollected how she killed them monsters that you find in privies and coal holes and chimneys and such." Seeing Jem shake his head, Mabel frowned. "Didn't she?"

"Birdie *helped* kill 'em," Jem corrected. "She were bait for the bogles. Alfred Bunce did all the killing."

"Alfred Bunce?"

"The bogler. Didn't you read about him, too? He were in the papers, same as Birdie."

Mabel bit her lip. "I daresay," she mumbled. "But the little girl is what stuck in my head. There was a picture, as I recall. Such a pretty thing, with all them golden curls . . ."

"And Mr. Bunce ain't pretty, which is why there wasn't no pictures of *him*." By now Jem was feeling confident. He knew that he was onto something, so he fixed the barmaid with a shrewd and penetrating look. "You got a bogle problem, miss?"

The barmaid sighed. "I think so."

"Why?"

"On account o' poor Florry." Edging farther beneath the jutting first-floor window of the pastry shop, Mabel suddenly blurted out, "Florry used to be our scullery maid. She went down into the cellar last month and never did come out. And not a trace of her was left, though Mr. Watkins and me looked high and low—"

"Who's Mr. Watkins?" Jem interrupted.

"The landlord. He keeps the place. And would never have took it on, had he known."

"Known what?"

"About the *beer cellar.*" Mabel shuddered, as if someone had walked over her grave. "The tavern's fresh built, but the cellar's old. There used to be a prison on that very spot, for debtors and the like, and our cellar was where they put 'em. I never go down if I can help it. Not without Mr. Watkins. Even before Florry vanished, I misliked the air. It felt . . . ." She paused for a moment, frowning. "It felt bad," she said at last. "Unwholesome. As if someone had died there."

Jem thought back to the previous summer. He thought about Alfred and Birdie. He thought about the two bogles that still haunted his dreams; the one he'd glimpsed at a gentleman's house near Regent's Park, and the one he'd helped to kill some four months later, in a cutting on the London and North Western Railway.

"How old was Florry?" he inquired.

"That I can't tell you. Twelve, perhaps? But she was very small."

"Then it could have bin a bogle as took her." Jem tried to inject a note of authority into his voice. "You should talk to Alfred Bunce. Mr. Bunce will know what to do. He's a Go-Devil Man. He kills bogles with the same spear Finn MacCool used to kill fire-breathing dragons in times past."

"But how can I talk to Mr. Bunce if I don't know where he is?" Mabel objected. Then she narrowed her eyes at Jem, who grinned when he saw her skeptical, measuring look. "I suppose *you* do," she said wryly. "Is that your lurk? Are you touting for this cove?"

"I'll take you straight to him for tuppence ha'penny," Jem offered. And as she rolled her eyes in disgust, he argued his case. "Mr. Bunce don't care to go bogling no more. He changed lodgings a while back on account of it. Where he is now, there's no one knows what he used to do, and no one to plague him as a consequence. But he'll listen to *you*, I'll be bound."

"Why?" asked Mabel. "Why am I so different?"

"You ain't," said Jem. "You got a kid gone, same as all the others. That's why he'll listen." Seeing her confusion, he tried to explain. "Bogles eat children. Mr. Bunce don't like that. He don't like using kids as bait, neither, which is why he stopped bogling. There's a boy lodging with him now— a mudlark called Ned—who'd be a deal happier bogling than scavenging on the riverbank. Mr. Bunce won't oblige him, though. Thinks bogling's too dangerous." Jem paused, then took a deep breath. "But what if someone should come along, a-weeping and a-wailing, asking for help?" he concluded. "Mr. Bunce ain't got it in him to turn 'em down. *That's* why he changed his lodgings."

Mabel nodded slowly. She seemed to understand. "Where does he live now?"

"Near enough," Jem replied, "if we take a bus there."

Mabel's lip curled. She raised one finely plucked eyebrow. "Oh ho!" she exclaimed. "So it's the omnibus fare you're after now, is it?"

Again Jem shrugged. "Unless you want to *walk* to the Strand," he said.

"Mr. Bunce lives near the Strand?"

"Off Drury Lane. But that's all I'll tell you." Gazing up at Mabel from beneath his cap, Jem held out one dirty palm. "Tuppence ha'penny," he repeated. "You'll be needing me there to soften him up, like."

Mabel sniffed. Then she grunted. Then she glanced up at the sky, which was low and gray and as wet as a sponge.

"We'll take a bus," she remarked, before turning to Jem with a crooked smile. "By the by, how old are you?"

"Eleven."

"And already you're bargaining like a Billingsgate fishmonger!" There was a touch of admiration in Mabel's tone. "I'll give you a ha'penny up front," she said. "The rest you'll get when we reach his crib."

"Done."

"And if this here is a caper, my lad, I'll give you *such* a hiding—never mind what I tell the police when I'm done!"

She scowled at Jem, who beamed back. But then something else occurred to him, and his smile faded.

"You ain't acquainted with Sarah Pickles, by any chance?" he asked, fixing her with a quizzical look.

"Sarah Pickles?" Mabel sounded perplexed. "Who's she?"

"It don't signify." Sarah Pickles was a private matter, which Jem didn't want to discuss. Not in the street with a perfect stranger. So he flapped his hand, turned on his heel, and made for the bus stop.